Framed in Love

Clifton Wilcox

Fredericksburg, Virginia

Print ISBN: 978-1-969770-04-3

EBook ISBN: 978-1-969770-03-6

Published by Windward Publishing LLC., Fredericksburg, Virginia.

Library of Congress Cataloging in Publication Data

Wilcox, Clifton

Framed in Love

Windward Publishing, LLC

2025

Dedication

For the one you can no longer touch,
but still see every time you close your eyes.
Some loves aren't lost—they're framed.

Clifton Wilcox

Contents

Books by Clifton Wilcox

Non-Fiction

Scape Goat: Targeted for Blame

Groupthink: An Impediment to Success

Bias: The Unconscious Deceiver

Witch-hunt: The Assignment of Blame

The Fall of the Kingdom of Northumbria

Witch-hunt: The Class of Cultures

Road to War: The Quest for a New World Order

Envy: A Deeper Shade of Green

The Rise of the Nazi SS

The Horrible Void Between the Trenches

Fiction

Cool's Last Stand

Where Despair Comes to Play

The Monuments Must Bleed

Keeper of the Fallen Ages

I, Monster

Harvest of Eyes

The Case Against Jasper

Crimson Plume: The Song of Corvus

Echoes of the Forgotten

Prologue

Some tales start with a kiss.

This one begins with lightning.

Framed in Love is not a typical love story. It doesn't unfold behind the high school gym or in a city cafe, or during a summer road trip. No, it happened in silence, on the still surface of a painted world— where time holds its breath, and a boy tells a girl he will wait for her but can't. Other times, it's simply a picture on the wall.

David Cross is not your normal hero. He doesn't save the world, and he doesn't wield magic. But what he does have — that one life-altering strike — is the ability to walk into the quiet beauty of a canvas. And within that impossibility, he discovers Abby. Timeless. Trapped. Waiting in a garden that never dies. From the first time their eyes met, they could feel it.

This is a story you haven't encountered. What follows is part romance, part mystery, part slow-burn heartbreak. And as David sinks into a painted love, you'll find yourself questioning the boundaries between art and reality. Between memory and imagination. Between what we're willing to leave behind—and what we'll fight to keep alive at any cost.   This book poses the question: How do you love someone made of brushstrokes? How do you say goodbye to someone who never ages, even as you do? And perhaps most painfully— what would you sacrifice to stay in a world where you are seen, when the actual one never saw you? *Framed in Love* is for the readers who believe in that quiet magic. In stolen moments. In love that feels both impossible and inevitable. It's for anyone who's lingered too long in front of a painting and had it stare back. And if you've ever loved someone from afar, in secret, in the defiance of time itself — this story already lives inside you.

Welcome inside the frame.

Chapter 1
The Storm and the Canvas

There was tension in the air you could almost touch. The heavy, pregnant breath of summer hung over them, ripe for a storm. Sketchbook in hand, David balanced precariously on the roof of his run-down garage and felt a delicious wave of excitement. He didn't typically go in for showy weather; in fact, he somewhat preferred the pale greys of the cloud-covered day to the blinding spectacle of an August mid-afternoon summer downpour. But somehow tonight, the storm had more attitude, as if somehow charged with a surge of electrical energy to match his own frenzied emotions.

He'd been drawing the twisted oak tree in his backyard with its limbs clutching at the bruise-purple sky. The wind howled, whipping his hair across his face, blurring the lines between the tree and the approaching storm. In the chaos, there was a strange sort of relief, it seemed to him, a counterpart to the internal chaos that had plagued him for months. Breaking up with Brenda, the looming pressure of college applications, the ever-present feeling of being…incomplete.

Lightning forked across the sky, a hot white serpent of fire, then the roar shuddered through him, a sound without reason that shook the foundations of his world. David flinched, instinctively ducking his head, his sketchbook clutched protectively to his chest. He felt a strange prickling sensation, not painful, but intensely electric, coursing through him, starting from his fingertips and spreading like wildfire through his entire body. Then, as quickly as it had begun, it vanished, leaving him breathless and oddly… different.

The storm still beat down upon them, but David was oddly unruffled, a tranquil ease replacing the normal agitation that clung to him like a second skin. He closed his eyes and breathed in the musky sweet smell of the August air. When he opened his eyes the world felt …crisper. More vivid. The hue of the storm, the vibrant indigo of the canopy, the inflamed red of the clouds, vibrated with an intensity that bordered on the unbearable. Even the leaves on the oak tree shimmered with an unearthly glow in the dousing wind.

He tried to dismiss it as simply being an adrenaline rush from nearly being struck by the lightning. But something felt profoundly altered. It wasn't that his senses had been heightened; it was something more, a subtle shift in his perception of reality, a new layer of awareness that seemed to lie just beneath the surface. He felt…connected. To something. He didn't know what, but he felt it, knew it, a silent hum running through his veins.

Later, back inside the warmth of his attic room, the storm still raging outside, David found himself inexplicably drawn to a dusty, antique painting that had been gathering dust in a forgotten corner. He'd seen it countless times before, a piece his grandmother had left him, a somewhat mediocre landscape depicting a Victorian park. But tonight, it seemed to call to him, a silent, irresistible summons.

The canvas was surprisingly heavy, the wooden frame worn and cracked with age. As his fingers brushed the surface, tracing the image of a particularly gnarled tree, similar to the one he had been sketching. As he did, a strange energy pulsed beneath the painting, a faint warmth radiating from the seemingly lifeless artwork. The pigment bursting, alive with an almost unnatural intensity.

He hesitated for a moment, a flicker of apprehension crossing his mind, a funny sort of faintness had overwhelmed him. This was ridiculous, he told himself. But something – a powerful, compelling force – pulled him forward. Then there was a strange, disorienting sense of a rush, a sensation of being pulled through a narrow tunnel, a panorama of colors and changing textures. Suddenly, when he opened his eyes, it was a totally different world.

He was not in his attic anymore.

He was standing in a glorious Victorian park; the air filled with the smell of the damp earth and flowers blooming. The colors were impossibly vibrant, the greens of the grass impossibly lush, the blues of the sky some incredible color of its own. The trees themselves were taller, more glorious than anything he had ever seen, and the tree branches were intertwined in a tapestry of the slats of sunlight and darkness. A light wind ruffled the leaves, bringing with it the fragrance of honeysuckle and roses.

It was an idyllic world, a flawless imagining of nostalgia, but something was … not right. Slightly melancholic, somehow. There was a low-key sense of mourning underneath the surface appeal, a sense of something incomplete, undone.

Then as he cautiously moved forward, he caught sight of her.

A girl looking away, nestled under a weeping willow tree. Her red hair draped down her shoulders like a silken waterfall, shimmering in dazzling golden highlights. She was dressed in a long, white dress, material that seemed nearly impossibly both frail and fine. She turned, and David breath caught in his throat as he saw her face.

Her eyes were like the sea after a storm, deep and captured, and there appeared to be depths beyond depths in them. Looking thoughtful, her lips curved into a slight smile as she spoke.

"You've finally arrived," she said, her voice like the gentle chime of distant bells. "I've been waiting for you."

David felt a cold chill, mixing strangely with wonder and surprise. Somehow, in ways he could not explain, he had entered a painting. And this girl, this beautiful, magnificent creature, was trapped within it, alongside him. The painting's reality, once simply a depiction, was now his, and hers, a vibrant, dangerous, and breathtaking shared world. The weight of his newfound power, and the mystery of his arrival, settled heavily upon him, leaving him both strangely exhilarated and terrified. He had no idea what to expect, only a growing sense of unease that was eclipsed only by the stunning and captivating presence before him. The storm outside was nothing compared to the storm brewing within his heart.

The girl's words hung in the park, a frail resonance in the stillness of the air. He was captivated by her, by the way the sun caught the auburn strands of her hair, by how her eyes, the color of a stormy sea, held a depth that seemed to swallow him. He was utterly speechless, his mind struggling to reconcile the impossible reality of his situation.

To come to terms with the sheer impossibility of his situation. He'd was inside the painting, which defied all reasoning. This was not a dream; the smell of honeysuckle and moist earth was too real, the feel of the grass beneath his feet too substantial. And she, Abby — he somehow knew her name — was as real as he was.

He opened his mouth as if to speak, to ask the questions that had scratched at the periphery of his mind, but no voice emerged. The sheer incomprehensibility of it left him stunned, his head ringing with the dramatic change in reality. He had always been a creature of reason, a practical soul who took comfort in the predictability of each day. And yet here he was, lost in a world where the laws of physics appeared to yield to the command of a brushstroke, a world in which reality was fluid and pliable.

He gazed about, trying to capture into his memory an impossibly perfect scene. The weeping willow by the pond where Abby sat was a grand example of the variety, the limbs hanging like somber tears above the silent pool. The pond was a replica of the blue sky, the clouds drifting lazily across its surface like brushstrokes of cotton candy. The air teemed with birdsong, a symphony of flutes and warbles in the silent forest. A gentle wind rustled the leaves, passing on secrets he did not know.

But beneath the visual beauty, he felt an undercurrent of subtle discord, a scent of melancholy that lingered like a phantom scent. The vibrant colors seemed slightly muted, the perfect symmetry slightly altered. The park was immaculate, yet it lacked a certain... vitality. It was a beautiful scene, meticulously rendered, yet it felt frozen in time, preserved in a state of perpetual stasis. A chilling thought struck him: was this perfect world a prison? Was Abby, as beautiful as she was, trapped here just as he was?

He took a step closer, the grass soft and yielding beneath his feet. Somehow, he felt connected to this place, and that very sense of belonging was both exhilarating and terrifying. It was as if he had always been there, though he had come just a few moments earlier. He was drawn to Abby, he felt this magnetic pull to her, that no matter how he tried, he would fall back to orbiting her.

"It's... beautiful," then he was back to speechlessness as his voice sounded thin and reedy in their peaceful surroundings. And he was so painfully aware of himself, his own reality, trespassing this perfect, delicate place.

Abby smiled, a sad, knowing smile that pulled at his heartstrings. "It is," she agreed, her voice a lovely counterpoint to the birds. "But it is also... incomplete."

Her words confirmed his suspicions.

It was a not-so-perfect wonder of this world. This seemingly flawless world was anything but. There was a missing piece, a void that resonated with a deep and unsettling emptiness. He felt a surge of empathy, a deep understanding of her situation. He wasn't just an intruder; he was a potential savior. But how could he possibly help her? How could he escape this painted reality, and what would happen to her if he did?

"How... how did I get here?" he said in an almost inaudible voice. The question hung heavily in the air, a tangible manifestation of his confusion and fear.

There was such a depth of comprehension in Abby's eyes, his gaze softened. "You came over through the portal," she said, pointing to the twisted old oak, its limbs stretching up to where the sky was an unlikely shade of blue. "The lightning... it created a rift. A temporary breach."

The oak tree! The very tree he'd been sketching when the lightning hit. There was an instant, irrefutable connection. The lightning hadn't merely made him sensitive; it had given him access to the space between life and art. It was exhilarating and terrifying to consider. He had encountered a force he could not understand, a force that was both miraculous and menacing.

"A temporary breach," he repeated, the words staying in the air like fragile ornaments. He understood the implications immediately. His presence here was fleeting, a temporary intrusion in a world that was not his own. The question was, how long did he have? And more importantly, what would happen when the breach closed? Would he simply vanish? Would Abby be left alone, imprisoned in her painted cell?

The thought was chilling. He glanced at Abby, her beauty still on display in this place of sadness. Her eyes were sorrowful but sparkled with hope and anticipation. She had been waiting for him, she'd told him. But for what? What was her purpose, and what was his?

He was realizing that he could not just stand here and marvel at the wonder of this place. He needed answers. He needed to understand the nature of the portal, the limits of his power, and most importantly, the fate of Abby, the girl who had been waiting for him within the canvas. The burden of responsibility lay on him, heavy and undeniable. The storm outside might have passed, but the storm within him was just beginning to rage. He had to uncover the secrets of the painting, the mystery of its creation, and the story of the girl trapped within its confines, before the portal closed and he lost her forever. The adventure, once a simple act of curiosity, was rapidly transforming into a desperate race against time. And at its heart was Abby – a girl as captivating as she was mysterious, and a connection that surpassed the boundaries of reality itself. Their shared existence was a precarious one, balanced on the edge of a knife, and the consequences of failure were far too horrifying to contemplate.

The air was thick with honeysuckle and soaked earth, a fragrance both familiar and yet alien. He'd never encountered a scent like it before, but it was like a chord being struck inside him — dusty and old, but familiar all the same. The park stretched before him, a wondrous panorama of meticulously crafted detail. Every blade of grass had its certain place, every leaf on the aged oak trees was a tribute to the artist who designed them. Yet, beneath the surface beauty, there was an undertone of melancholy, a quiet dissonance, that spoke age and sorrow. The hues, though bold, lacked the vibrancy of life, somehow muted by time and age. It was a moment frozen in time; a picture-perfect snapshot stuck in never-ending afternoon.

Abby sat against the base of the biggest of the oaks, her auburn hair a cascade in the sun, spun gold. She was even more lovely in person, and her slate grey eyes held something wise beyond her young face. Her dress was a plain cotton gown the faded color of roses, as if it belonged to another time, a mere hush of days now gone. She looked at him with that curious absorption of wonder and weariness. The way she sat, so poised yet somehow vulnerable, stirred something deep within him, a protective instinct he hadn't known he possessed.

"You came," she said, her voice a murmuring melody, just loud enough to be recognized over the whispering of the leaves. The words were an affirmation, an acknowledgment of his unbelievable reality. He had come through the painting, into her world, a world painted onto canvas yet somehow more real than his own.

"I... I don't understand," he mumbled, his voice shaking softly. The enormity of the situation bore down on him, the sheer improbability of it all threatening to overwhelm him. He was inside a painting, conversing with a girl who claimed to have been trapped there for decades. It surpassed anything he'd ever imagined, a narrative so fantastic it could only exist in the pages of a fantastical novel. Yet, here he was, living it.

Abby smiled, a melancholy smile that made his heart ache. "It's a really long story," she replied, casting a glance toward the serene pond whose surface shimmered with the impossible blue of the sky. "A story of a girl who wished, and a wish that went terribly wrong."

He sat down beside her, the grass plush and yielding beneath him. He felt no pain, no prickling sensation of the canvas against his skin. This was real, as real as the beating of his own heart. He gazed at Abby, having a thousand questions to ask, but not one word with which to frame a single one. He felt a strange kinship with her, a bond forged in the crucible of this shared, impossible reality.

She started with her story from the very beginning, her voice painting a picture of sadness and yearning. She had once been a young artist too, obsessed with capturing the beauty of the world on canvas. One stormy evening, she had wished upon a falling star, a desperate plea for the ability to truly immerse herself in her creations, to experience the world she painted as vividly as she saw it in her mind's eye. Her wish, spoken in the heat of passion and youthful naiveté, had been somehow granted in a way she never could have anticipated.

The wish had drawn her into the painting she was working on, this very Victorian park. It had been decades, maybe more, she couldn't be sure. Time had lost its meaning within the confines of the canvas. The park, so meticulously detailed, had become her prison. She was forever trapped in an idyllic landscape, forever watching the seasons change, the clouds drift, yet unable to leave, unable to change anything.

She spoke of the loneliness, the despair, the slow, agonizing erosion of hope. She spoke of the moments of clarity, the brief bursts of awareness when she felt her own presence straining against the boundaries of the paint, the frantic silent pleas that went unanswered until now. Her story was a lament, a bittersweet melody of longing and acceptance, a testament to the unwavering resilience, even in the face of unimaginable confinement.

He listened, captivated by her words, his heart aching with empathy. He had always considered himself a realist, a grounded individual who relied on logic and reason. Yet, this fantastic story, told by a girl trapped within a painting, resonated with a truth he couldn't deny. It was a tale of yearning, of dreams and their unforeseen consequences, a narrative that spoke to the deepest parts of his being. And she, Abby, was the heart of that story, a beacon of hope shining through the darkness of her confinement.

Her story continued, and as she spoke, he began to notice a subtle shift in the atmosphere. The colors seemed even more muted now, the perfect symmetry even more strained. The flawless beauty of the park was slowly fading, a silent testament to the fragility of their reality. He realized with a sudden chill that her story wasn't just a tale of the past; it was a warning about the present, about the imminent threat to their shared existence.

Abby paused, her voice catching in her throat. "The painting… it's fading," she whispered, her gaze fixed on the pond where the reflection of the sky was becoming distorted, the colors bleeding into each other, creating an unsettling blur. "My world… it's disappearing."

He reached out to take her hand, his fingers brushing against her skin. He felt an electric shock, a surge of energy that connected them, a shared heartbeat in the face of impending doom. He knew then that he wasn't just a visitor, a passive observer. He was a part of her story, an integral piece of her fate. He was the one she had been waiting for, the one who could possibly save her. But how? And what would the cost be?

The question hung in the air between them, unspoken yet heavy with significance. The fading light cast long shadows across the park, amplifying the melancholic beauty of their surroundings. The perfect world was crumbling around them, and time, in this painted reality, was running out. His heart pounded in his chest, a drumbeat of urgency echoing the imminent threat. He had come into this world through a miraculous stroke of fate, yet the task before him was far from miraculous; it was nothing short of a desperate race against time, a fight to save not only the girl he was falling for but the world they shared, a world that was disappearing before his very eyes. The storm that had brought him here had passed, but a more violent tempest was brewing within his own soul. He had to find a way to help her, to save her, before it was too late. Before they both were lost forever.

"There are rules," Abby said, her voice barely a whisper, her gaze distant, lost in the fading hues of the painted sky. The once-vibrant blue was now a bruised purple, the clouds swirling with an unnatural, unsettling energy. The perfect symmetry of the park, the meticulously arranged foliage, now seemed fractured, broken, like a shattered mirror reflecting a distorted reality.

"Rules?" David echoed, his voice strained. He felt the chill of fear creeping into his soul, a cold dread that had nothing to do with the late afternoon chill that was settling over the painted world. He'd come here expecting wonder, a fairytale escape, but the reality was harsher, more fragile, more terrifying.

Abby nodded, her eyes locking with his. "The painting... it's a vessel, a container. It has its own limitations, its own boundaries. And we are bound by them."

She gestured to the meticulously painted landscape surrounding them. "This world... it's not truly alive. It's an imitation, a reflection of the artist's imagination, frozen in time. The trees don't grow, the flowers don't wilt, the seasons don't change in the normal way. They shift as the artist's memory of the scene changes; the slightest variation in her mind alters the scene ever so slightly, making this place seem a little less real each time I notice it."

David stared at her, trying to grasp the implications of her words. It wasn't just a painting; it was a self-contained ecosystem, governed by the whims of its creator, bound by the very strokes of paint that formed its reality. He looked at the pond again; the water was now a murky green, the reflection of the sky utterly distorted.

"And what about us?" David asked, his voice a mere breath. "Are we bound by the same rules?"

Abby hesitated. "We are…different. We're anomalies, exceptions to the rules. My wish…it shattered the boundaries, allowed me to exist within this world, to become a part of it. Yet I also became a prisoner of this illusion, forever a reflection of the artist's past. My ability to

13

interact with this space is limited. I can influence the flow of time within the painting only in the smallest ways, a minute change here, an imperceptible shift there. I cannot create anything new, only respond to what was painted."

"And you?" David asked, his heart pounding. He felt a tremor run through the painted ground beneath his feet.

Abby's eyes flickered; a shadow crossed her face that had nothing to do with the fading light. "My presence here is...unnatural. It's a strain on the painting, a disruption to its equilibrium. The more I interact with this world, the more fragile it becomes. That's why it's fading."

She pointed to a nearby oak tree, its branches now bare, the leaves having vanished, leaving behind only skeletal limbs of stark, lifeless wood. It was the first sign of the complete disintegration of the reality surrounding them. "See? The essence, the life, is draining away."

David felt a cold wave of fear wash over him. He'd come here for an adventure, a refuge from his mundane life, but this wasn't the escapism he'd expected. It was a desperate fight for survival, a struggle against the very fabric of reality. He suddenly felt the desperate urgency of this situation, understanding that this world was decaying.

"So what happens if the painting fades completely?" David asked, his voice trembling.

Abby closed her eyes, her face etched with a profound sadness. "Then... I disappear. I cease to exist. My essence would be lost within the fading of the painting, and there's no coming back. Even if I had the power to leave, the world would reject me, and I would simply cease to be."

The fear in her voice was palpable, a raw, visceral emotion that resonated deep within him. He looked around at the deteriorating landscape, the fading colors, the vanishing details, and felt a wave of panic wash over him. He had to find a way to save her, to somehow fix this fractured reality, but he had no idea where to begin.

Abby opened her eyes again, her gaze steady, unwavering. "There's another rule," she said, her voice low. "A rule about outsiders. People from the outside world, like you. Your presence here is also a

14

drain on the painting, but your impact is greater than mine. The longer you stay, the faster it fades."

David's blood ran cold. He was not just a visitor; he was a catalyst for destruction, unknowingly hastening the demise of this fragile world and the woman he was falling for. The weight of this realization pressed down on him, crushing him under its immense burden. He was torn; he wanted to stay with her, to explore this magical world, but his very presence was killing it.

"What can we do?" he asked, his voice barely a whisper. The wind rustled through the skeletal branches of the oak tree, a mournful sigh echoing his despair.

Abby looked at him, a flicker of hope in her eyes. "There might be a way," she said, her voice filled with uncertainty. "A way to stabilize the painting, to restore its balance. But it's risky, and I don't know if it will work."

She paused, gathering her thoughts. "The painting is a reflection of the artist's memories, her emotions. If we can somehow tap into those memories, understand what caused this imbalance, perhaps we can find a way to restore it. It's a gamble, a desperate attempt, but it's our only chance."

David looked at the decaying beauty around him, the fading colors, the disappearing details, and knew that he had to try. He knew that his life outside of this reality was no longer the only reality to worry about. This painted world had become as real to him as his own, and losing it, losing Abby, would be a fate far more unbearable than any imaginable reality.

He took her hand, his fingers intertwining with hers, feeling the faint pulse of her life, her connection to this fading world. "Tell me," he said, his voice firm despite his fear, "Tell me everything. About the artist, about the painting, about the rules. We have to find a way."

Abby took a deep breath, her eyes shining with a fragile hope. She began to tell him the story of the artist, a woman consumed by grief and loss, a woman whose emotions had somehow bled into her art, creating this fragile, melancholic world. As she spoke, David listened intently, piecing together the fragments of the story, searching for a clue, a way to save both Abby and the world they shared, a world that was fading away before his eyes, a world that he felt an impossible bond with. He knew the path ahead would be treacherous, fraught with danger, but he was ready. He was ready to fight for their survival, to unravel the mysteries of this painted world, and to face whatever lay ahead in their desperate race against time. He had to, for her, for them, for the beautiful, fragile reality that was slowly vanishing around them. The fate of both their worlds now rested in his hands. The storm had passed, but the tempest of their shared fate was only just beginning.

Abby's narrative unfolded like a slow unraveling of a tightly wound tapestry, each thread revealing a new layer of complexity, a new facet of the artist's tormented soul. The artist, a woman named Stephanie Moreau, had been a renowned landscape painter in the late 19th century, her works capturing the ethereal beauty of the English countryside with breathtaking precision. But beneath the serene surfaces of her canvases lurked a deep well of sorrow, a profound grief that had shadowed her life after a tragic loss. Stephanie had painted this particular park – the very park that now housed Abby and David – shortly after the death of her beloved daughter, a young girl named Connie who possessed an uncanny resemblance to Abby.

The painting, Abby explained, was more than just a representation of a place; it was an imprint of Stephanie's memories, her emotions, her unresolved grief. Each brushstroke, each meticulously rendered detail, was infused with her sorrow, her longing, her desperate attempt to hold onto a lost love. The fading of the painting, therefore, was not merely a deterioration of the artwork; it was a reflection of Stephanie's own fading memory, her inability to reconcile with her loss. The melancholic essence of the painting, Abby explained, was subtly but undeniably changing the very rules of the painted space, warping the landscape, making the space inherently unstable.

"The painting is a vessel of her grief," Abby said, her voice barely audible above the rustling leaves of the few remaining trees that hadn't been completely consumed by the encroaching decay. "And her grief is consuming it." She traced a finger across a patch of withered flowers; the vibrant colors reduced to muted shades of brown and grey. "The flowers are wilting because her memory of Connie, once vivid and bright, is fading. It's like a mirror reflecting a dying star, its light slowly extinguishing itself."

David felt a chill. He'd never thought of a painting in such a way, never considered the emotional weight it could carry, the hidden stories it could hold. He looked at Abby, her face illuminated by the fading light, her eyes reflecting the sorrow of the artist, the fear of her own impending disappearance. He reached out and took her hand, feeling the fragility of her existence, the tenuousness of their shared reality.

"So, what about the escape?" David asked, his voice a low murmur. He felt a desperate hope, a flicker of defiance against the encroaching darkness. He needed to believe there was a way out, a way for them to survive.

Abby hesitated, her gaze drifting to the increasingly distorted sky. "There might be a way," she said slowly, her voice laced with caution. "But it's extremely risky. It involves tampering with the very essence of the painting, re-igniting Stephanie's memories, forcefully shaping her past in a way it may not want to be changed. It could lead to a complete collapse. It could even destroy the painting altogether. The consequences could be far worse than the fading itself."

She explained that the painting's stability was intricately linked to Stephanie's emotional state, her ability to accept her loss, and let go of her grief. The painting's decay wasn't simply decay; it was a physical manifestation of Stephanie's unresolved trauma. The key to saving the painting, and therefore Abby, lay in finding a way to mend Stephanie's emotional wounds, to help her find peace and acceptance.

"The painting is a reflection of her mind," Abby continued, her eyes fixed on a distant, fading willow tree, its branches now almost entirely gone, leaving only a suggestion of a graceful form. "If we can somehow access her memories, perhaps we can find a way to stabilize the painting, to restore its balance, to help her accept her loss."

David felt his heart sink. The task seemed insurmountable, an impossible feat of emotional engineering, a desperate gamble with reality itself. He looked at the decaying beauty around them, the fading colors, the vanishing details, and felt the weight of responsibility crushing him. He was responsible for Abby's survival, and his presence here was speeding up the process of her demise.

"How do we access her memories?" David asked, his voice strained. He felt the urgency of the situation pressing down on him, the ticking clock of their dwindling time.

Abby's brow furrowed. "I'm not sure," she admitted. "There are clues hidden within the painting itself. Symbols, hidden within the details, subtle shifts in the perspective that hint at her emotional state. These clues may hold the key to unlocking her memories, but it will require meticulous observation, patience, and a keen eye for detail. We must decipher her intentions. This may not work, but it's our only chance."

She pointed to a seemingly insignificant detail in the distance – a small, almost imperceptible variation in the pattern of the cobblestones in the pathway. "See that?" she said. "That's not a mistake. It's a clue. A subtle alteration, a hint of her shifting memories, her changing emotional state. It's like a breadcrumb trail, leading us towards the heart of her grief."

The task ahead seemed daunting, a needle-in-a-haystack search for emotional clues within a world that was itself crumbling before their eyes. David felt a wave of despair, the weight of the situation pressing down on him. But looking at Abby, her unwavering gaze, her quiet determination, he found a renewed sense of purpose. He had to try. He had to save her. He owed it to her.

"Let's start," he said, his voice firm, despite the tremor of fear that still ran through him. He took her hand again, feeling the comforting warmth of her skin against his, a lifeline in the face of their looming doom. Together, they would navigate this dangerous, fragile world, searching for a way to access Stephanie's memories, hoping that within those memories lay the key to their salvation. The path ahead was fraught with uncertainty, but they had each other, and that was enough to fuel their desperate attempt at escape. They had to succeed. Their very existence depended on it.

Days bled into weeks as David and Abby painstakingly searched the decaying landscape for clues. They examined every detail, every brushstroke, every subtly shifting element of the painted world. Each day, the painting deteriorated further, the colors fading, the details dissolving, the overall sense of reality in the painting weakening. The painted park felt less real each day. The vibrant greens of the foliage turned to sickly yellows, then to muted browns, mirroring the artist's slow descent into despair.

They discovered that hidden within the seemingly random arrangements of trees and flowers were intricate patterns, geometric sequences that subtly shifted as Abby manipulated small details within the painting. They found cryptic symbols embedded within the architecture of the painted buildings, their significance still eluding them. They noticed small changes in the landscape that did not align with how it was initially painted, such as the shifting alignment of the stars and the unnatural curving of some of the painted pathways. Abby, drawing on her inherent connection to the painting, was able to slow down this decay through small acts of preservation, but such efforts were merely delaying the inevitable.

David found himself drawn into the world of Stephanie, poring over her life, her letters, her other paintings. He visited libraries and archives, collecting information on her life, her inspirations, and the circumstances surrounding her daughter's death. The more he learned about Stephanie, the more he understood the emotional weight hidden within the painting. He understood the emotional turmoil and the unresolved loss at the heart of its decay.

Slowly, painstakingly, they began to decipher the symbols, the patterns, the hidden messages within the painting. It was a race against time, a desperate struggle against the fading of the canvas, the crumbling of their world, a terrifying race against the decay of reality itself. The emotional toll on both David and Abby was immense.

The closer they got to understanding Stephanie's grief, the more intense the changes in the painting became. The decay accelerated, and new cracks appeared in the painted reality, threatening to tear their world apart. David realized that tampering with Stephanie's memories was an incredibly dangerous gamble. They were playing with forces beyond their comprehension. The risk was immense, but the alternative, the complete annihilation of their reality, was far worse.

One evening, as the painted sun began to set, casting long, distorted shadows across the landscape, they stumbled upon a hidden passage within the painting, a secret garden tucked away behind a seemingly solid stone wall. This hidden garden, a place never before seen or observed by David and Abby, represented a part of Stephanie's memory that had been suppressed, a memory that held the key to unlocking the secrets of the painting's existence.

They discovered that Stephanie had intentionally hidden this garden, burying it beneath layers of pain and denial. The garden, lush and vibrant, untouched by the decay of the rest of the painting, represented a flicker of hope, a memory of joy and happiness that Stephanie had subconsciously preserved. This hidden memory proved to be the key to restoring balance to the painting. This newfound area represented a place of solace, a reflection of a time when Stephanie was not overcome by her grief, a time before the loss that had consumed her life and manifested itself through her art.

The hidden garden held a subtle, hidden key: a way to not just stabilize the painting, but to create a pathway of escape for Abby. It offered a way for Abby to transcend the boundaries of the canvas, to step outside the confines of Stephanie's fading memories and enter a new, independent existence.

The path to escape, however, was not simply a matter of walking out of the garden. It was a treacherous journey through Stephanie's subconscious, a journey into the depths of her grief, a confrontation with the raw, unyielding pain of loss. This represented both a path of hope and a journey into the dark corners of the artist's soul. The possibility of escape was now within their grasp, but the price of freedom remained uncertain and potentially catastrophic.

Chapter 2
A Shared Reality

The days that followed were a blur of shared sunlight and whispered secrets. The decaying park, though a constant reminder of their precarious existence, became their shared sanctuary. They explored its hidden corners, discovering forgotten pathways, rediscovering the beauty within the slowly fading landscape. Each discovery, each shared moment, strengthened the bond between them, weaving a tapestry of intimacy that defied the limitations of their unusual circumstance.

David, accustomed to the structured routine of his life, found himself captivated by the spontaneity of the painted world. He learned to read Abby's subtle cues, her silent gestures, her shifting gaze – a language born of shared vulnerability and a desperate need for connection. He watched as she carefully tended to the few remaining flowers, her touch gentle, her movements deliberate, as if each gesture held the weight of her fragile existence. He marveled at her resilience, her unwavering spirit in the face of their impending doom.

Abby, in turn, was drawn to David's unwavering support, his quiet determination to help her escape. She found comfort in his presence, a reassuring anchor in a world that was slowly disappearing. His unwavering belief in their ability to overcome the challenges before them was a powerful antidote to her own creeping despair. She discovered within him a strength she hadn't known she needed, a strength that mirrored her own tenacity, and their shared experiences created a resilient love that fortified their hope.

Their days were spent not just in the desperate search for clues, but also in building a life together within the confines of their decaying world. They shared stories, dreams, and fears. David recounted his life outside the painting, the mundane details of school, friends, and family, all of which felt distant and unreal in this shared landscape. Abby, in turn, revealed the intricacies of her existence within the canvas, her memories of Stephanie, the artist who had inadvertently created her.

Evenings were spent nestled amongst the few remaining trees, the setting sun casting a warm, ethereal glow on their faces. They would share simple meals – berries gathered from the dwindling bushes, nuts found hidden amongst the fading leaves. These shared meals were more than just sustenance; they were acts of defiance against the decay around them, precious moments of shared humanity amidst the encroaching darkness. They held hands, their fingers intertwining, a silent pact of mutual support and enduring affection. The simple act of touching felt profound, a connection that transcended the boundaries of time and reality.

David learned to appreciate the subtleties of Abby's world, the way the light filtered through the leaves, the subtle shift in the wind, the changing colors of the sky. He learned to listen to the silence, to hear the whispers of the fading world, to sense the subtle emotional shifts that echoed Stephanie's turmoil. He became attuned to the fragility of their existence, understanding that each moment spent together was a precious gift.

Their bond deepened not just through shared hardship, but through shared joy. They laughed together, watching mischievous squirrels scamper amongst the decaying branches. They found solace in the few moments of peace, cherishing the quiet beauty that remained within the fading landscape. They discovered a profound appreciation for the simple things in life, things they had previously taken for granted: the warmth of the sun, the sound of the wind, the shared silence between them, the comfort in each other's arms.

They created rituals that cemented their connection: tracing patterns in the dust, mimicking the shifting stars in the fading sky. They recited poetry they had read aloud, sometimes in hushed tones to themselves, sometimes aloud to each other, their voices echoing in the almost vacant landscape, a testament to their resilience, a celebration of their shared reality. They would watch the sun rise and set together, sharing a quiet moment of contemplation and appreciation, a mutual acknowledgment of the fleeting nature of their existence.

One day, they stumbled upon a hidden meadow, untouched by the decay that surrounded them. It was a vibrant patch of color, a testament to a time before the painting began to fade. Wildflowers bloomed in profusion, their colors vivid and intense, a stark contrast to the muted tones of the rest of the park. They spent hours in this hidden sanctuary, surrounded by the beauty of life resisting decay, a beacon of hope against the backdrop of the failing landscape. It became their secret place, a sanctuary where they could escape the creeping despair of their situation.

In this meadow, amidst the vibrant blooms, they shared their deepest fears and hopes. David confessed his anxieties about leaving Abby, the knowledge that their time together was limited. Abby admitted to her fear of fading away, of being lost forever in the artist's forgotten memories. These vulnerable confessions deepened their connection, solidifying their bond through shared pain and mutual understanding.

The meadow wasn't just a beautiful anomaly; it became a symbol of their love. It was a testament to their resilience, a representation of their unwavering determination to find a way out of their predicament. It served as a refuge from the growing instability, a place where the love they shared could flower amidst the decay. The meadow was a testament to their shared existence, a poignant reminder of the beauty that could exist even in the face of inevitable loss.

As the weeks turned into months within the painted world, the painting continued to fade, but their love grew stronger. The fading landscape served as a constant reminder of their precarious situation, but it also became a backdrop for their blossoming relationship. They faced their fear, their struggles, and their mutual impending loss not as individuals, but as a united couple, their love an indestructible shield against the encroaching darkness. The emotional intimacy they forged in this decaying world proved to be a powerful force, binding them together even as their world was crumbling around them. Their love story unfolded amidst the fading colors, a testament to their enduring connection in a world defined by loss and uncertainty. The strength of their bond served as the light that guided them on the treacherous path ahead. They held on to that light, clinging to each other, defying the very forces that threatened to destroy them, and finding solace in the love they had created together. Their bond was the single most powerful force in this ephemeral world, a testament to the resilience of the human spirit in the face of overwhelming odds.

The first crack appeared subtly, a hairline fracture near the base of an ancient oak, barely noticeable against the already weathered texture of the canvas. David, preoccupied with showing Abby a particularly vibrant patch of wildflowers, almost missed it. Abby, however, her senses sharpened by the ever-present awareness of their precarious existence, pointed it out with a hushed gasp. It was a small thing, insignificant perhaps, but it cast a long shadow over their idyllic meadow.

The discovery sent a ripple of unease through their shared reality. The quiet joy they had found in the hidden meadow was replaced with a tense vigilance. They examined the painting more closely, their hands tracing the edges of the cracks that now seemed to be multiplying like insidious vines, creeping across the canvas. The cracks weren't just confined to the meadow; they were spreading, snaking their way through the park, marring the once-vibrant landscape. The once-clear sky was now streaked with unnatural distortions, the colors shifting and swirling in ways that defied the laws of nature, or at least, the laws of nature within a painted world.

The subtle changes were unnerving, a constant reminder of the fragility of their world, a palpable sense of impending doom that clung to them like a shroud. Their shared meals, once joyous occasions, were now tinged with a bittersweet melancholy. Their laughter, once spontaneous and carefree, was now punctuated by silent moments of apprehension. The whispers of the fading world, once almost comforting in their quietude, now carried a sense of foreboding, like the rustling of approaching shadows.

The distortions weren't limited to the physical landscape. Abby's memories, once vivid and clear, began to flicker and fade, like a candle flame in a sudden gust of wind. She would recount incidents from her life within the painting, only to have the details slip away mid-sentence, replaced by a vacant stare and a chilling silence. The faces of people she remembered were becoming increasingly blurred, the scenes she vividly recalled dissolved into hazy, indistinguishable forms. It was as if the painting, in its decay, was actively erasing her past, consuming her memories one by one.

David, witnessing these changes, felt a wave of despair wash over him. His own memories of his life outside the painting began to feel less real, more like distant dreams. The vibrant colors of his own world, the faces of his family and friends, began to fade in his memory, overshadowed by the haunting beauty and impending doom of Abby's world. He feared he was becoming as ephemeral as she was, his existence becoming as fragile as the paint itself.

The changes in the painting also affected their interactions. The shared sunlight, once a symbol of their connection, now felt cold and distant, casting long, distorted shadows that seemed to mirror their growing fears. The simple act of holding hands, once a profound expression of their love, now carried a chilling awareness of their fleeting time together. The shared silence, once a testament to their deep understanding, was now filled with an unspoken anxiety, a mutual recognition of their approaching end.

They tried desperately to find a way to stop the decay, searching every corner of the painting for a clue, a hidden mechanism, a way to reverse the damage. But their efforts proved futile. The cracks continued to spread, the distortions intensified, and Abby's memories faded further. Their shared reality was unraveling before their eyes, a testament to their precarious existence.

One evening, as they sat in the fading light of the meadow, surrounded by the spreading cracks, Abby confided in David her deepest fear – the fear of being completely forgotten, of ceasing to exist not only within the painting, but within the memories of the artist herself. Her voice trembled with the weight of her despair, echoing the growing instability of the world around them. The flowers in the meadow, once vibrant and full of life, now began to wilt, their colors losing their intensity, mirroring Abby's fading memories.

David, in turn, confessed his own fear – the fear of losing her, of losing the connection they had forged within this dying world. He acknowledged his own fading memories of his own life, the gradual blurring of his own reality as he spent more time in the decaying world of the painting. The lines between their two realities were becoming increasingly blurred, and David wondered if he, too, was in danger of being lost forever.

Their fears, once separate and individual, now intertwined, forming a painful knot of mutual despair. But amidst the despair, their love grew even stronger, a defiant flame in the face of encroaching darkness. They clung to each other, their bodies pressed close, finding solace in the warmth of their shared humanity, their enduring connection a testament to their resilience.

The final weeks were marked by a gradual fading of the landscape. The trees withered and crumbled, their branches breaking and falling, leaving behind barren and cracked earth. The vibrant colors of the meadow turned to muted shades of grey and brown, the flowers wilting and decaying. The sun, once a beacon of warmth and hope, now seemed cold and distant, its light weak and diffused. The sky, once clear and blue, was now filled with swirling clouds of distortion and decay, reflecting the impending collapse of their shared reality.

Even amidst the devastation, they clung to the remaining moments, cherishing each shared breath, each shared touch, each shared glance. Their love became a refuge, a sanctuary against the encroaching darkness. They held each other close, finding strength in their shared vulnerability, their bond as strong as ever despite the fading world around them. The final sunset was a masterpiece of pain and beauty, a poignant reminder of the ephemeral nature of their shared reality.

As darkness fell for the last time, Abby faded, leaving behind an empty canvas and a heartbroken David. But the cracks in the canvas, the distortions in the background, the fading colors, they all bore witness to their extraordinary love. The painting itself, a testament to a love that transcended time and space, held the lingering essence of their shared reality, a silent echo of a love that defied the boundaries of art and life. The memory of their love, like the faintest trace of paint, endured long after the painting itself had completely vanished.

The transition back to his own world was jarring. The vibrant, albeit decaying, colors of Abby's world were replaced by the muted tones of his own room. The scent of wildflowers and damp earth gave way to the sterile smell of his neglected textbooks. The weight of his absence settled heavily upon him, a stark contrast to the shared lightness he'd experienced with Abby. He found himself staring blankly at his books, the words swimming before his eyes, unable to focus on anything but the memory of Abby's fading smile, the chill of the last shared sunset. His studies, once a source of ambition and satisfaction, felt meaningless, a pale imitation of the vibrant reality he'd found within the canvas.

Days blurred into weeks. The neatly stacked textbooks on his desk became a chaotic pile, a testament to his neglect. Assignments remained unfinished, tests unstudied. His once-organized room became a reflection of his inner turmoil; clothes lay scattered, dishes piled in the sink, a testament to his disinterest in the mundane tasks of everyday life. The world outside the painting felt distant, unreal, a mere shadow of the compelling reality he'd found within the artwork.

His friends, initially intrigued by his newfound eccentricities, began to express concern. Todd, his closest friend, noticed the change immediately. Todd, a pragmatic and level-headed individual, noticed David's withdrawal. He'd always been a reliable presence in Todd's life, a constant source of support and companionship. Now, Todd found David distant, preoccupied, even secretive. His cheerful demeanor was replaced by a quiet melancholy, a withdrawn stillness that disturbed Todd deeply. He'd try to engage David in conversations, invite him to their usual hangouts, but David's responses were short, distracted, his mind seemingly elsewhere.

"Dude, are you okay?" Todd asked one evening, finding David staring blankly at a half-finished pizza. The usual banter and laughter between them were absent. The concern in Todd's voice was palpable; his expression etched with worry.

David mumbled a response, something vague and unconvincing. He knew Todd was worried, he felt guilty for neglecting their friendship, but explaining his obsession with a painting seemed impossible. How could he explain the girl trapped within a canvas, the shared reality they'd constructed, the heartbreaking reality of its demise? The words felt inadequate, a pale representation of the depth of his emotional turmoil.

Angie, another close friend, also voiced her concerns. Angie, known for her insightful and empathetic nature, sensed that something profound was troubling David. She noticed his disheveled appearance, the dark circles under his eyes, the haunting emptiness in his gaze. She tried a gentler approach, less direct than Todd's confrontation, offering support rather than demanding answers. She invited him for a coffee, attempting to coax him out of his shell, to break through the wall he'd erected around himself. But even Angie's warmth couldn't penetrate David's emotional fortress. He pushed her away, unconsciously, hurting her with his silence, his inability to articulate the depth of his pain.

Their concern only fueled David's guilt, a heavy weight adding to the burden of his grief. He found himself avoiding their calls, their texts, the very presence that had once brought him joy. He retreated further into himself, spending hours staring at the painting, lost in the haunting beauty of Abby's world, even though all that remained was a blank, empty canvas. The silence of his room mirrored the emptiness he felt inside, an echoing void left by Abby's absence. The vibrant colors of his own world seemed dull, lifeless in comparison to the fading masterpiece he had come to cherish. Even the familiar faces of his family felt distant, their voices muted compared to the whispers of Abby's forgotten world.

His parents, too, noticed the alarming shift in his behavior. His mother, a perceptive and caring woman, tried to engage him in conversation, expressing concern for his declining grades and his apparent withdrawal from family activities. His father, typically reserved, expressed concern through practical means; fixing David's broken headphones, cleaning his room without comment, offering him meals without prompting. Their efforts, though well-intentioned, only intensified David's feeling of guilt and inadequacy. He couldn't explain his emotional turmoil, the inexplicably profound loss he experienced. The words seemed inadequate, the reality too bizarre to comprehend.

His neglect extended beyond his studies and relationships. Simple acts of self-care were neglected. He stopped showering regularly, neglecting his hygiene. His once-sharp clothes were replaced with rumpled attire, a reflection of his inward decay. He lost his appetite, surviving on instant noodles and energy drinks, fueled by his obsessive need to connect with Abby's world, even though the connection was shattered, the world itself nonexistent. Sleep became a distant memory, replaced by restless nights spent reliving his shared reality with Abby, haunted by the fading colors, the decaying landscape, and the ultimate fading of Abby's presence. He was trapped in a cycle of grief, a prisoner of his own memories.

The weight of his guilt grew heavier each day. He knew he was hurting the people who cared about him, yet the pull of his obsession with the painting, the desperate need to somehow reconnect with Abby, was overwhelming. He was teetering on the brink, his world unraveling, much like Abby's painted world had done. He was drowning in the sea of his grief and neglect, trapped between the memories of a vibrant reality and the bleakness of his own, his very existence feeling as fragile as the faded paint on the canvas. The silence of his room screamed louder than any word could express his pain, a silent testament to his self-imposed isolation and the devastating consequences of his obsession. His once vibrant life had become a canvas of muted tones, a reflection of the empty space Abby had left behind. His neglect was a testament to the depth of his loss and the inability to reconcile with the loss of his extraordinary love. His world was fading, just as Abby's had, slowly, painfully, leaving behind a blank canvas of his own existence.

The first sign was subtle, almost imperceptible. A blush of faded rose where the vibrant crimson of a rose bush once bloomed. Then, a patch of greyish-green where the emerald lawn had sprawled. It was as if the very essence of the Victorian park was slowly leaching away, the colors draining like water from a cracked vase. The change was gradual, insidious, mirroring the creeping dread in David's heart. He'd noticed it during one of his visits, a fleeting moment of unease before dismissing it as a trick of the light, a momentary lapse in the painting's illusion. But the next time he entered, the fading was undeniable. More than just a shift in hue, it was a tangible decay, a slow erosion of the world he'd come to cherish.

The once crisp lines of the buildings softened, blurring into indistinct shapes, their details melting away like melting wax. The intricate patterns on Abby's dress, once a breathtaking display of artistry, now appeared smudged and faded, the vibrant colors dulled to a melancholic pastel. The vibrant blue of the sky transformed into a washed-out, almost sickly, pale blue. The very air seemed to thin, the crispness of the Victorian atmosphere replaced by a hazy, indistinct quality. The once bright sunlight dimmed, casting long, skeletal shadows that stretched across the decaying landscape like grasping claws.

Abby noticed it too. Her eyes, usually bright and full of life, held a flicker of fear, a reflection of the unraveling world around her. Her smile, once a beacon of warmth and joy, now carried a fragile quality, the edges tinged with apprehension. Their shared picnics, once filled with laughter and carefree abandon, were now overshadowed by a pervasive sense of impending doom. The carefree games they played, the whispered secrets exchanged under the shade of ancient trees, were now punctuated by moments of silence, heavy with unspoken fears. The very air crackled with a tense energy, a palpable sense of unease that hung over them like a shroud.

The fountain, once a sparkling centerpiece of the park, now sputtered and wheezed, its water a sluggish, muddy stream rather than the clear, cascading water of their earlier days. The vibrant flowers around it drooped, their once vibrant petals now dull and lifeless. The leaves of the trees, previously lush and vibrant, now browned and withered, falling to the ground in a steady, unsettling pattern. Even the birdsong, once a melodic symphony, was replaced by a discordant chorus of unsettling sounds. The world was not just fading; it was actively dying.

Their conversations shifted, subtly at first, then with increasing urgency. They spoke less of their shared dreams and hopes, and more of the growing instability of their reality. The playful banter was replaced by hushed whispers, their discussions focused on their dwindling time together, the imminent collapse of their fragile world. Their shared laughter was replaced by tearful embraces, the weight of their imminent separation becoming almost unbearable.

Abby became withdrawn, her once boundless energy replaced by a quiet sadness. She spent hours sitting by the fading fountain, staring into the muddy water, her reflection a ghostly apparition in the murky depths. She spoke less, her words carefully chosen, each one a precious jewel in a diminishing treasure trove. Her eyes held a depth of sorrow that mirrored the decaying landscape around her. She was losing more than just her vibrant world; she was losing her very essence, her life force fading along with the colors of the painting.

David's heart ached with every passing day. He watched helplessly as the world they'd built together crumbled before his eyes, its beauty slowly succumbing to an inexorable decay. He tried to fix things, to reverse the fading process, but his efforts were futile. He spent hours within the painting, desperately trying to revitalize the wilting flowers, to mend the crumbling buildings, to somehow restore the vibrant colors to the landscape. But his efforts only served to exacerbate the damage, accelerating the decay and hastening the inevitable.

The fading was not just a visual phenomenon; it affected their senses too. The sweet scent of wildflowers was replaced by a musty, earthy odor, the sharp tang of the air replaced by a thick, suffocating stillness. The sounds of the world grew fainter, the bustling energy of the Victorian park replaced by an eerie silence, broken only by the mournful creak of dying branches. Even the taste of their shared picnics seemed altered, their once delicious treats now lacking their vibrant flavors. It was as if the very essence of their shared reality was dissolving, transforming into a pale, lifeless imitation of its former glory.

The fear gnawed at them both, a constant, oppressive weight that hung over their every interaction. The fear was not of death, but of oblivion, of complete erasure, of being swallowed whole by the encroaching nothingness. The realization that their shared existence was ephemeral, a fleeting moment in time, a fragile bubble of reality trapped within a decaying canvas, intensified their desperation and amplified their love.

The nights were even worse. The once star-studded sky was now a murky, inky blackness, devoid of celestial brilliance. The moon, once a source of romantic illumination, was shrouded in a hazy obscurity, a muted reflection of the decaying world below. The darkness seemed to seep into their very bones, amplifying the pervasive sense of loss and despair. Sleep offered no respite, only nightmares filled with dissolving landscapes, fading colors, and the chilling realization of their impending separation.

David's visits became shorter, more infrequent. The guilt he felt towards his friends and family was overwhelming, but the thought of abandoning Abby to a certain oblivion was even more unbearable.

31

Each visit became a painful farewell, their embraces longer, their kisses more profound, each moment etched in their memory like precious stones. The reality of his choices—staying and hastening the collapse of both their realities or leaving and sacrificing his love for Abby's continued existence—weighed heavily upon him. The vibrant colors of his own world seemed to grow more muted with each visit, a reflection of his internal struggle and his growing despair.

The painting itself, once a source of wonder and joy, now seemed to reflect David's internal turmoil. It had become a mirror of their fading love, its deteriorating condition a tangible representation of their precarious situation. The once vibrant artwork was now a hauntingly beautiful testament to a love story that was nearing its tragic end.

The canvas seemed to weep; the fading colors a silent lament for their doomed relationship. The silent decay of the painting was a chilling foreshadowing of the inevitable end. The once-vibrant colors now served as a painful reminder of the beauty that was slowly slipping away, leaving behind an empty, desolate landscape. His obsession, once a source of joy, had become a relentless torment, its burden nearly unbearable. The fading colors of the painting were a stark reflection of the fading hope in David's own heart, a poignant reminder of the heartbreaking choices that lay ahead. The silence within the painting was a chilling reflection of his own internal struggle, his own impending loss, a haunting premonition of the agonizing farewell that awaited him.

The once-vivid reality of the Victorian park was fading, mirroring the fading hope in David's own heart, the slow, inevitable demise of their shared reality, a poignant reminder of the devastating choices he must make. The decaying landscape seemed to mirror the slow erosion of his own happiness, a constant, painful reminder of the love he was soon to lose.

The air hung heavy, thick with a silence that pressed down on David like a physical weight. It wasn't the quietude of a peaceful afternoon, but a suffocating stillness, pregnant with unspoken fears. He'd noticed the subtle changes before, the fading colors, the decaying landscape, but this... this was different. This was a palpable sense of impending doom, a chilling premonition of what was to come.

Abby stood by the fountain, her usually vibrant dress now a muted shade of grey, her reflection a ghostly shimmer in the murky water. The once-bright sparkle in her eyes was dulled, replaced by a haunting sadness that mirrored the decaying world around her. She turned, her gaze meeting David's, and a wave of profound sadness washed over him. It wasn't the playful, mischievous glint he had grown to cherish, but a deep, unsettling sorrow, a sorrow that spoke of losses yet to come. The fountain, once a sparkling centerpiece, now coughed and sputtered, its water a sluggish stream, mirroring the slow, painful decline of their shared reality.

"David," she began, her voice barely a whisper, each word a fragile fragment of a fading dream. "The painting... it's weakening. Because of me... because of you."

The words hung in the air, heavy with unspoken implications. The realization struck David with the force of a physical blow. His visits, his presence within the painting, were not just a source of joy and connection, but a catalyst for destruction, a slow, agonizing erosion of the very fabric of Abby's world. He had been so lost in their idyllic romance, so consumed by the magic of their shared reality, that he hadn't seen the warning signs, hadn't understood the price of their impossible love. The guilt that washed over him was a tidal wave, threatening to drown him in self-recrimination.

"It's my fault," he whispered, his voice barely audible above the mournful creak of dying branches. "I've been coming too often. I haven't thought... I haven't considered the consequences."

Abby nodded, her eyes brimming with tears. "It's not your fault, David. It's just... the boundaries are fragile. The connection... it's too strong. My world can't sustain it." She reached out, her hand brushing against his, a silent acknowledgment of the shared burden of their impossible love. The touch sent a jolt of electricity through him, a stark reminder of the profound connection that bound them together, a connection that was simultaneously their greatest joy and their greatest curse.

The weight of their predicament pressed down on them, a suffocating blanket of despair. The vibrant colors of their shared world continued to fade, the once-crisp lines blurring into indistinct shapes, the intricate details dissolving like melting snow. The once-lush gardens wilted, the flowers drooping, their petals losing their vibrant hues, transforming into lifeless, brown husks. The ancient trees groaned, their branches brittle and bare, their leaves falling in a steady, unsettling rain. The very air seemed to thin, its crispness replaced by a thick, suffocating stillness.

Abby took a deep breath, steeling herself for what she had to say. "The longer you stay, the faster it fades. The more you are here, the less I become. Soon... soon there will be nothing left." Her voice cracked, the words barely a whisper against the backdrop of their dying world. The reality of her words hit David like a punch to the gut. He was not only losing his escape, his sanctuary; he was losing Abby.

The silence that followed was deafening, broken only by the mournful sigh of the wind rustling through the dying trees. The weight of their predicament pressed down on them, an oppressive blanket of despair that threatened to suffocate them both. The reality of their situation was undeniable; their love, while profound and magical, was also destructive, a force that was slowly erasing the very world that held them together. The beautiful world they shared was withering, decaying, and dying before their eyes, and there was nothing they could do to stop it.

David looked around at the decaying landscape, at the wilting flowers, the crumbling buildings, the fading sky. It was a mirror of his own soul, a reflection of the pain and anguish tearing him apart. The vibrant colors, once a source of joy, were now a painful reminder of what he was about to lose. The laughter and joy that had once filled their days were replaced by a heavy silence, broken only by the occasional sigh or tear. Their shared picnics, once moments of carefree abandon, were now somber affairs, overshadowed by the imminent threat of oblivion. The sweet scent of wildflowers had been replaced by a musty odor, the crispness of the air by a suffocating stillness. The sounds of the world faded, the once-melodious birdsong now replaced by a chilling silence, broken only by the unsettling creak of dying branches.

He thought of his life outside the painting, his family, his friends, his studies. He'd neglected them all, lost in his obsession with Abby and their shared world. He felt the pang of guilt, the weight of his neglect, but even that was overshadowed by the impending loss of his beloved. The thought of leaving Abby, of sacrificing their love for her continued existence, was almost unbearable. It was a cruel choice, a heart-wrenching decision that tore at the very fabric of his being.

Days bled into nights, each visit a shorter, more agonizing farewell. Their embraces grew longer, their kisses more profound, each moment etched into their memories like precious gems. The vibrant colors of his own world seemed to grow even more muted, a reflection of his internal struggle and his despair. He knew he had to make a choice, a devastating choice, one that would shape the rest of his life, and the life of the girl he loved more than anything.

He found himself spending less time in her world, each visit shorter, filled with a poignant sorrow. The realization that their time together was finite hung over them, a heavy, suffocating cloud. The silence that once felt peaceful now echoed with the unspoken understanding of their impending separation, a silent testament to the tragic reality of their situation. The joy they once shared felt like a distant memory, replaced by the crushing weight of their imminent parting.

Abby's strength began to wane. Her laughter became rarer, her smiles less frequent, replaced by a quiet acceptance of their fate. The vibrant spark in her eyes dimmed, mirroring the fading colors of the world around them. The once-boundless energy that had defined her was replaced by a weary quietude, a subtle acceptance of their inevitable separation. The once-vibrant park that they shared felt more like a tomb, a stark reminder of the fleeting nature of their relationship and its impending end.

The weight of their impending farewell was palpable. Every shared moment felt precious, every touch, every word, every stolen glance, a treasure to be cherished and remembered. The beauty of their shared reality became intertwined with the sadness of their imminent separation, their love story playing out in a landscape that mirrored its inevitable end. They clung to each other, their love a beacon of hope in the face of despair, a testament to a connection that transcended the boundaries of time and space, a connection that would endure even after the painting faded. But the knowledge of their impending parting loomed over them, a shadow that couldn't be ignored, a heartbreaking truth they couldn't escape. The once-vibrant colors continued to fade, but their love, despite its precarious circumstances, remained as a powerful force, a lasting testament to a love that defied reality itself.

Chapter 3
The Price of Love

The setting sun cast long shadows across the wilting meadow, painting the scene in hues of orange and purple that seemed to mock their fading world. David sat beside Abby, their hands intertwined, the familiar warmth a small comfort against the chilling premonition of loss. The silence between them wasn't uncomfortable; it was a shared understanding, a silent acknowledgment of the inevitable. It was the quiet before the storm, the calm before the final curtain fell.

Abby leaned against him, her head resting on his shoulder. He felt the delicate tremor in her body, a silent testament to the toll their predicament was taking. He traced the lines of her face, memorizing every curve, every freckle, every imperfection that made her uniquely, exquisitely her. He wanted to etch her image into his very soul, to preserve her memory even when the painting itself ceased to exist.

"Remember the first time we met?" She whispered, her voice barely audible above the mournful rustling of the dying leaves.

David smiled, a bittersweet expression that mirrored the complexities of their situation. "The chaos, the swirling colors, the way you looked at me, as if you had been waiting for me your entire life." He remembered the startled look on her face, the hesitant curiosity in her eyes, the way her hand had reached out to him, bridging the gap between worlds. It seemed like a lifetime ago, a different lifetime, one filled with vibrant colors and the carefree joy of discovery.

They spent the next hours recounting their shared memories, revisiting the moments that had woven the tapestry of their unlikely love story. They laughed, remembering their clumsy first dance, the way they discovered hidden pathways in the park, the countless picnics beneath the ancient oak tree that now stood skeletal and bare. Each memory was a precious gem, a shard of a reality that was rapidly fading, but whose brilliance burned ever brighter in the face of its impending demise.

As night fell, the world around them grew darker, the once-vibrant colors fading into a monochrome landscape of greys and blacks. The air grew colder, a tangible manifestation of their impending separation. They huddled closer together, their bodies seeking warmth, their souls seeking solace in each other's presence. The dwindling light illuminated the depths of their eyes, reflecting the turmoil and the sorrow that lay heavy within their hearts.

"I wish I could stay here forever," Abby whispered, her voice thick with unshed tears.

"Forever isn't something we get to choose," David responded, his own heart aching.   He looked at her, at the love shining in her eyes, at the strength that despite everything, still held her together. He knew he had to make a choice, a devastating choice. He had to find a way to save her, even if it meant losing her. He had to accept the heartbreaking truth that their love, for all its intensity, for all its magic, was a destructive force in this reality. He had to accept that their impossible love had a price, and that price was his own presence in her world.

He held her close, burying his face in her hair. He inhaled the scent of wildflowers, a lingering fragrance that soon would vanish along with everything else. The scent was a poignant reminder of their fleeting reality, of the precious moments they shared, and of the painful truth of their inevitable goodbye.

They spent the remaining hours exploring the limits of their connection. David attempted to paint her, seeking to capture her essence on canvas, transferring a piece of her from the fading painting into a new, permanent reality. He knew it was a futile attempt, a desperate grasp for a permanence that might not be possible, but the act itself was an act of love, a desperate attempt to preserve her existence, even in a small, imperfect way.

As he worked, Abby sat beside him, watching the strokes of the brush capture the essence of her features, her soul. Every brushstroke felt like a tender caress, a poignant farewell, a preservation of moments that were quickly slipping through their fingers. The act of painting became a sacred ritual, a loving farewell, a solemn goodbye.

The paintings became imperfect renderings of perfect moments, imperfect reflections of an enduring love.

But the act also brought to light the constraints and limitations of their bond. David discovered he couldn't replicate the vibrancy of her reality; the colors remained muted, the details blurred, a pale imitation of the luminous reality she inhabited. It was a tangible representation of the limitations of their connection, a painful reminder that their love story couldn't exist outside the confines of the painting itself.

They discussed the implications of their bond. Abby spoke of the subtle shifts she'd sensed in her world; the gradual fading of the colors, the weakening of the boundaries between the painting and the outside world. She'd felt the canvas thinning, the edges dissolving, the reality of her existence dissolving into a faint echo. Her own vitality was waning, mirrored by the withering vegetation and the crumbling structures surrounding them. The vibrant beauty of her world was dissolving into a shadowy twilight, mirroring the fading light of her life and reflecting the approaching end of their love story.

The realization hung heavy between them, a cloud of unspoken words, a chilling premonition of the end. Yet, even as their world crumbled around them, they shared a kiss that transcended the boundaries of time and space, a kiss that resonated with an enduring love. Every touch, every gaze held the profound weight of their imminent separation, creating memories as bright and vivid as the fading colors of their shared world. Every shared moment held a poignant sweetness, each instant forever etched in their memory, a bittersweet reminder of their impossible love.

David, realizing the gravity of the situation, proposed a compromise; a heart-wrenching decision that demanded a sacrifice of epic proportions. He would relinquish his entry into the painting, permanently severing their direct connection, accepting the profound loss of their daily intimacy, their shared reality. The thought was a crucl sword, twisting and turning in his gut, each rotation a wave of despair. But he understood that his presence, his connection, was the very catalyst that was destroying Abby's world. To save her, he had to leave her.

The final day arrived; a day etched in their memories as both the beginning of an unimaginable grief and a testament to the strength of their love. They spent the final hours together, clinging to each other, savoring the last vestiges of their shared reality. As the colors of their world bled into shades of grey, their love burned even brighter, a defiant flame against the encroaching darkness. As the last rays of the setting sun painted the sky in farewell hues, their love remained, an unwavering testament to a bond that transcended time, space, and the very boundaries of reality. Their goodbye was not a termination but a transition, a poignant farewell to a shared existence while forever binding their souls through the immeasurable strength of their love. The price of their love was immense, a sacrifice beyond measure, a parting of hearts that would echo through eternity.

Their love, though born in a painted world, would live on, transcending its limits and etching itself into the very fabric of their souls, proving that some loves, like the strokes of a master painter, are forever.

The weight of their impending separation pressed down on David like a physical burden. He knew he had to act, to find a solution, a way to preserve Abby's existence even if it meant sacrificing their connection. He had spent countless nights staring at the painting, tracing the lines of the canvas, searching for a clue, a hidden message, anything that might offer a lifeline. Their love story, so vibrant and full of life, was fading like the colors in Abby's world, and he refused to accept this fate.

His desperation fueled a frantic search for answers. He abandoned his studies, neglecting his friends and family, consumed by the urgent need to find a solution. He scoured the internet, delving into forums and online communities dedicated to art history and unusual phenomena. He contacted art conservators and experts, pleading for any information that might help him understand the painting and perhaps reverse its decay. He even sought out fringe theorists in an effort clinging to any possibility, no matter how improbable.

His efforts yielded little but frustration and disappointment. Most dismissed his claims as fantasy, a figment of an overactive imagination. Others were intrigued, but ultimately unable to offer any practical solutions. The feeling of helplessness gnawed at him, intensifying the pain of his impending separation from Abby. He knew he couldn't continue like this, endlessly chasing shadows, while

Abby's world continued to dissolve around her. He needed a more focused, a more methodical approach.

One rainy afternoon, huddled in the quiet solitude of his room, amidst stacks of research papers and half-empty coffee cups, his gaze fell upon an old, leather-bound book his grandfather had left him. It was a weighty tome, filled with yellowed pages and intricate illustrations, a comprehensive history of Victorian art. He'd almost forgotten about it, buried amongst his other belongings. Now, the book seemed to call to him, a beacon in his growing despair. With trembling hands, he opened the book, the musty scent of aged paper filling his senses. He began to scan the pages, his eyes darting across the text, searching for any mention of similar paintings, similar phenomena. He read about renowned artists and their masterpieces, about artistic movements and techniques. But nothing seemed relevant. His hope began to wane, the weight of his impending failure settling heavily on his shoulders. He was about to give up, to surrender to the inevitable loss, when a particular illustration caught his eye.

It depicted a painting remarkably similar to the one Abby inhabited. The style was almost identical, the composition strikingly familiar. Underneath the image, a small paragraph described the painting's mysterious origin. It spoke of a rumor, a local legend, about a painting that held a secret, a hidden world accessible only to those with a special gift. The artist, it claimed, had imbued the painting with a fragment of his own soul, creating a pocket of reality within the canvas.

A surge of excitement coursed through David. He read the paragraph again and again, absorbing every detail. This was it, he thought, a potential key to understanding Abby's predicament and saving her. The text mentioned a hidden symbol, a barely discernible mark on the painting's frame, a symbol said to hold the key to unlocking the painting's secrets. Could this be the answer?

The next few days were a whirlwind of activity. David painstakingly examined the painting, scrutinizing every detail, every brushstroke, every crack in the varnish. He used magnifying glasses and even specialized UV light, searching for the hidden symbol mentioned in the book. He felt a surge of hope, a renewed sense of purpose, a determination that bordered on obsession.

Finally, after hours of meticulous searching, he found it. A tiny, almost invisible mark etched into the ornate frame of the painting. It was a complex symbol, a swirling vortex of lines and shapes, reminiscent of ancient Celtic knotwork. He carefully sketched the symbol, capturing every minute detail, preserving it for further study. He knew he was getting closer, that he was on the verge of unlocking the painting's secrets, of finding a way to save Abby.

His research extended far beyond the initial art history book. He delved into the world of symbology, studying ancient cultures and their belief systems. He learned about the power of symbols, their ability to encode information, to act as portals between worlds. He discovered that the symbol he had found was linked to an ancient Celtic myth about a gateway between the earthly realm and the otherworld. Could this be the key?   Driven by renewed hope, David painstakingly deciphered the symbol, piecing together its meaning, interpreting its hidden message. He discovered that the symbol wasn't just a decorative element; it was a complex code, a map to a hidden dimension within the painting. It provided a blueprint for navigating the boundaries between reality and the painted world, a guide to manipulating the fabric of space and time. He understood that the painting wasn't just a static image; it was a dynamic entity, a living testament to the artist's imagination.

With a mix of trepidation and excitement, he carefully recreated the symbol on a new canvas, using materials specified in ancient texts he had discovered during his research. He infused the symbol with his own energy, his own intent, his own desperate plea to save Abby. He hoped his actions wouldn't irrevocably damage the existing artwork or the world Abby inhabited. He understood that manipulating such power came with potential consequences.

The process was arduous, demanding, and exhausting. He spent sleepless nights, fueled by caffeine and adrenaline, working tirelessly to complete the symbol. He questioned if he possessed the necessary skill or power to achieve his goal. But the thought of Abby, of her fading world, of their imminent separation fueled his determination. He had to try, no matter the risk. He had to find a way to rescue her from the confines of the painting, without shattering the fragile boundaries between their worlds.

Finally, after weeks of tireless work, the symbol was complete. He stood before his new canvas, feeling both exhilaration and apprehension. He held his breath, and with a deep breath, focused his mind, he activated the symbol, pouring his hopes and intentions into the vibrant image before him.

The air crackled with energy; the room filled with an almost palpable tension. A faint light emanated from the canvas, growing brighter, stronger, until it blazed with an almost unbearable intensity. David braced himself for whatever might happen next, ready to face the consequences of his actions, ready to accept the price of his love.

The painting pulsed with light and color, the symbol radiating an almost mystical aura. David closed his eyes, his heart pounding in his chest. He could feel the pull, the subtle shift in reality, the convergence of two worlds. He was about to discover if his desperate attempt had succeeded or failed. He could only hope, pray, and wait to see if he could save the woman he loved, the woman whose existence depended on his success. The fate of their impossible love hung precariously in the balance.

The symbol pulsed with a soft, inner light, a gentle luminescence that seemed to breathe in time with David's own heartbeat. He leaned closer, his breath misting on the cool surface of the canvas. He traced the intricate lines of the vortex with a trembling finger, feeling a strange connection, a resonance that vibrated deep within his bones. It wasn't just a symbol; it was a key, a doorway, a conduit to another reality.

But as he studied it more closely, a chilling detail emerged. Within the swirling lines of the Celtic knotwork, he noticed a series of smaller, almost imperceptible glyphs. They weren't part of the main symbol; they were superimposed, almost like an afterthought, a hidden message within the message. His heart sank. This wasn't just a solution; it was a warning.

Using his knowledge of symbology and ancient languages, David painstakingly deciphered the secondary glyphs. It was a cryptic message, written in an archaic dialect of Gaelic, describing a tragic tale of lost love and artistic obsession. The message spoke of the painter, a tormented soul named Paul Gillette, who had poured his very essence into the painting, creating not just a landscape, but a reflection of his own fractured heart. He had fallen deeply in love with a woman who had tragically died, and in his grief, he had created this world within the canvas, a world where she lived on, immortalized in paint.

But the message revealed something even more disturbing. Paul had not merely painted a world; he had trapped a part of himself, his soul, within the painting, intertwining his existence with that of his beloved. The act had cost him dearly, draining his life force, slowly consuming him until he eventually succumbed to his despair, his final breath mirroring the fading colors of his masterpiece. The secondary glyphs detailed the ritual, the sacrifices made, and the terrible price of such artistic hubris.

David felt a shiver. This was no mere painting; it was a prison, a testament to the devastating power of grief and obsession. Abby's existence wasn't just threatened by the decay of the canvas; it was intrinsically linked to the artist's tragic fate. The painting was dying, and with it, Abby was fading. The hidden message wasn't just a solution; it was a warning. To save Abby, he would have to understand the depth of Paul Gillette's sacrifice, the terrible bargain he had struck with the forces that governed reality and art.

The weight of this knowledge pressed upon David. He had to find a way to unravel Paul's tragic tale, to understand the mechanics of his creation, and perhaps, to find a way to reverse the process, to free Abby without sacrificing her world, or perhaps, without sacrificing himself. He spent weeks immersed in his research, poring over historical records, searching for any trace of Paul Gillette, studying the painter's life and the circumstances surrounding his death.

He unearthed accounts of Gillette's life, a chronicle of intense creativity and profound loss. He found letters, sketches, and journals filled with passionate devotions of love, followed by harrowing expressions of despair and regret. He discovered that Gillette had become increasingly isolated, consumed by his art, neglecting his friends and family, mirroring David's own actions in his desperate attempt to save Abby. The parallel was unsettling, a chilling premonition of David's own potential fate.

He learned that Gillette had been fascinated by Celtic mythology, specifically the legends of fae realms and hidden dimensions. He had meticulously studied ancient symbols, seeking to unlock the secrets of otherworldly travel, a gateway to realms beyond human comprehension. His obsession, fueled by his grief, had led him to create the painting, a desperate attempt to bridge the gap between life and death, to reunite with his beloved.

David discovered that Gillette's technique was unique, a complex layering of pigments and mediums, imbued with a subtle but powerful magical resonance. The painting wasn't just paint on canvas; it was a living entity, a tapestry woven from emotions, dreams, and despair. Gillette had harnessed a subtle form of energy, a life force, to create the illusion of a world within the frame.

But the process was unsustainable. The artist's life force was the fuel, the energy that sustained the painted world. As Paul Gillette faded, so did his creation. This realization hit David like a blow. To save Abby, he needed to understand how to replenish the painting's energy, to somehow feed the life force that sustained it. This knowledge wasn't contained within the cryptic glyphs or historical accounts, it was something Paul Gillette had intuitively understood, and something David needed to learn.

David spent countless nights staring at the painting, contemplating the artist's technique, his struggles, his triumphs, his ultimate failure. He realized that Paul Gillette's tragic story wasn't just a cautionary tale; it was a roadmap. The hidden message wasn't just a warning; it was a guide. He had to find a way to replicate the artist's technique, to create a new source of energy, a counterbalance to the fading life force of the painting.   Days blurred into weeks, weeks into months. David's obsession grew, consuming him completely. He neglected his studies, his friendships, his family, his very life, mirroring the tragic fate of Paul Gillette. He lived and breathed the painting, immersed in its mysteries, its beauty, its sorrow. The line between obsession and salvation blurred, the boundaries of his own reality fading as the painting itself disintegrated.

Finally, after countless hours of experimentation and research, David arrived at a breakthrough. He understood the process, the delicate balance of artistic skill and arcane knowledge required to sustain the painted world. He realized that he couldn't simply replenish the energy; he had to create a new, sustainable source, a symbiotic relationship between the painting and reality. He needed to find a way to channel a different kind of energy, one that wouldn't drain his life force or lead to the same tragic fate as Paul Gillette.

He began to work tirelessly, constructing a new symbol, a counterpart to the one he had found within the frame. This new symbol, however, wasn't a copy; it was an evolution, a refined version that would create a stable and sustainable flow of energy. He poured his heart, his soul, his very being into the creation, imbuing it with his love for Abby, his determination to save her, his understanding of the artist's tragic mistake.

This was his final chance, his last desperate gamble. He understood the risks; he was walking a tightrope, balancing on the precipice of success and utter devastation. But he was determined to defy the tragic fate of Paul Gillette, to rewrite the ending of their story, to secure a future for himself and the woman he loved, even if it meant facing the price of their impossible love. The fate of their love story, the fate of Abby, rested upon this final, desperate act. The final piece of the puzzle was in his hands, and the time for decision had come.

The air in David's room felt heavy, thick with the scent of linseed oil and despair. The painting, once a vibrant window into another world, was now a crumbling ruin. The once-lush Victorian park was marred by fissures that snaked across the canvas like angry veins, bleeding into the surrounding landscape. The colors, once rich and saturated, were dulling, fading into muted shades of grey and brown. Abby, her form once sharp and defined, was becoming indistinct, her features blurring as if melting into the decaying canvas.

Panic clawed at David's throat. He watched, helpless, as the world he had come to love, the world that held his beloved Abby was slowly dissolving before his eyes. The gentle, rolling hills were now jagged, fractured lines; the meticulously painted flowers were mere smudges of color. The very fabric of Abby's existence was unraveling, threatening to erase her from reality entirely.

He touched the canvas, his fingers tracing the edges of a particularly deep crack, feeling the brittle texture beneath. It was as if the painting itself was crying out in pain, its silent screams echoing in the quiet of his room. The vibrant green of the grass was now a sickly yellow-brown, the trees were skeletal, their leaves reduced to ghostly whispers of their former selves. Even the sky, once a brilliant cerulean, was clouded over, a dull, oppressive grey mirroring the despair that choked David.

He remembered the cryptic glyphs, the hidden message from Paul Gillette, the warning of a tragic price. He had understood the mechanics, the delicate balance of artistic skill and arcane knowledge required to sustain the painted world, but he hadn't fully grasped the fragility of it all. The weight of his responsibility pressed down on him, heavy and suffocating. He was not merely an observer; he was the keeper of this fragile world, the custodian of Abby's existence.

His new symbol, the counterpoint to Gillette's creation, lay unfinished on his desk, a testament to his frantic efforts, a desperate gamble in the face of impending doom. He'd poured every ounce of his being into its creation, his love for Abby, a tangible force woven into its intricate lines. He'd spent sleepless nights refining it, agonizing over each detail, his hand trembling as he meticulously crafted the glyphs, imbuing them with his hope and his fear. But would it be enough? Was it even possible to reverse the process, to mend a world that was falling apart at the seams?

Days bled into nights as David continued his desperate struggle. He studied the deteriorating painting with a magnifying glass, meticulously documenting the progression of the decay. He noted the patterns, the way the cracks spread, the sequence in which the colors faded. He tried to discern a pattern, a rhythm to the disintegration, hoping to find a clue, a hint of a solution in the chaos.

He delved deeper into Paul Gillette's life, searching for any undiscovered element, any piece of the puzzle that could provide a solution. He discovered Gillette's personal journals, hidden away in a dusty attic of a forgotten museum archive. They detailed not only his artistic process but also his emotional turmoil, his descent into despair, his struggle to come to terms with his beloved's death.

The journals revealed a meticulous artist consumed by grief, driven by the desperate need to recapture a lost love. Gillette's writings spoke of a deeper magic, a form of energy he had harnessed through painstaking ritual, imbuing his art with a piece of his very soul. He had sought not merely to depict a world, but to create one, a refuge from the pain of his loss.

But the journals also exposed the limitations of his technique, the unsustainable nature of the process. He had literally poured his life into his work, sacrificing his health, his sanity, his very being to keep his created world alive. The fading of the painting wasn't just a decay of pigments; it was the manifestation of his own dwindling life force.

David felt a cold dread creeping into his heart. He was walking the same path as Gillette, mirroring his descent into obsessive creation, sacrificing his own life for the sake of his love. He had neglected his studies, his friends, his family, consumed entirely by his desperate attempts to save Abby. His own world was blurring, reality fading into the surreal landscape of the painting. The parallels were too stark, too disturbing.

He was staring into a mirror reflecting his own potential fate, a chilling premonition of his own demise. He needed to find a solution, and fast, or he too would be consumed by the painting, his love turning into a deadly trap. He spent weeks creating variations of his symbol, altering the angles, tweaking the glyphs, tirelessly experimenting until his hands were raw.

He was searching for a delicate balance, a counterpoint to Gillette's tragic mistake, a way to infuse the painting with a sustainable life force without draining his own vitality. He knew he needed to channel a different kind of energy, an external source that would feed the painted world without consuming him. But where would he find such a thing?

The answer came to him unexpectedly, in a forgotten passage in one of Gillette's journals, a cryptic reference to a forgotten ley line, a powerful source of earthly energy that pulsed beneath the very ground where the artist had created his masterpiece. The ley line, Gillette wrote, was a conduit of raw, untamed energy, capable of sustaining a painted world indefinitely. But it was also volatile, dangerous, capable of destroying both the painting and the one who attempted to harness its power.

David knew the risk. He understood that he was playing a dangerous game, risking not only Abby's life but his own. Yet, he felt a surge of resolve, a desperate hope rising in his chest. He had to try. He had to find a way. He had to save Abby. The fate of their love, the fate of their impossible world, hung precariously in the balance, a gamble only he could take. He packed his bag, a mixture of apprehension and determination fueling his steps as he prepared to venture into the unknown, to confront the forces that governed reality and art, and to face the price of his impossible love. The imminent collapse of the painting wasn't just a threat; it was an ultimatum, a final test of his devotion.

The journey to the ley line was arduous. It led him far from the familiar streets of his hometown, deep into the heart of a sprawling, ancient forest, where the air hung thick with the scent of damp earth and decaying leaves. The path was barely discernible, overgrown with tangled vines and thorny bushes that clawed at his clothes. He followed Gillette's cryptic directions, his heart pounding a frantic rhythm against his ribs. Each step was a gamble, a leap of faith into the unknown. Doubt gnawed at him, whispering insidious lies, painting images of failure and loss. He pushed onward, fueled by a desperate hope that was as fragile as the painting itself.

The forest seemed to breathe around him, the rustling leaves whispering secrets he couldn't understand. Twisted branches reached out like skeletal fingers, their gnarled forms seeming to watch his every move. The deeper he ventured, the more oppressive the atmosphere became, the shadows lengthening, the sunlight fading into a perpetual twilight. He felt a sense of unease, a prickling sensation on his skin, as if he were being watched, observed by unseen eyes in the dense undergrowth.

Finally, after what felt like an eternity, he reached the clearing described in Gillette's journal. In the center stood an ancient oak, its branches reaching towards the heavens like supplicating arms. The air here vibrated with an almost palpable energy, a hum that resonated deep within his bones. This was it – the ley line.

He approached the tree cautiously, his senses heightened, his heart thrumming in his chest. He felt the surge of energy, a raw, untamed power that both exhilarated and terrified him. It felt like a living thing, pulsing with a life force that was both ancient and primordial.

Following Gillette's instructions, David carefully positioned himself, preparing to channel the ley line's energy into the painting. He had devised a complex ritual, a delicate dance between his own magical ability and the raw power of the earth. It was a perilous undertaking, a delicate balancing act between life and death. One wrong move, one miscalculation, and the ley line's untamed energy could obliterate both him and the painted world he sought to save.

He closed his eyes, focusing his mind, his will, his entire being on the task at hand. He visualized the painting, Abby's face, the vibrant colors of the Victorian park. He felt the energy of the ley line coursing through his veins, a surge of power that threatened to overwhelm him. He fought to maintain control, to harness this raw force, to channel it into the intricate glyphs he had painstakingly created.

The process was agonizing. The energy surged through him, a torrent of power that pushed him to his limits. His body ached, his muscles strained, his mind reeling under the intense pressure. Sweat beaded on his forehead, and his breath came in ragged gasps. Yet, he held on, his determination unwavering, his love for Abby fueling his resolve.

Slowly, painstakingly, he began to weave the energy into the painting. He could feel the decaying canvas responding, the cracks slowly mending, the colors returning, the features of Abby regaining their sharpness and definition. It was a slow, arduous process, but he could feel the painting stabilizing, its life force gradually being restored. He saw the fissures disappear, the vibrant hues return, the world within the canvas gradually rejuvenating. The oppressive grey of the sky cleared, replaced by a cerulean blue, mirroring his own growing hope.

As the painting healed, a profound sadness settled over him. He knew that this restoration came at a cost. The ley line's energy, while powerful, was inherently unstable. His prolonged presence continued to destabilize the painting. He was the catalyst for its decay. His love for Abby was the fuel for the painting's decay and the reason for its precarious existence.

A heartbreaking realization dawned upon him. He couldn't stay. His presence was a poison, slowly killing the very world he was trying to save. He had to leave Abby, to sacrifice their love for her survival. The thought tore at him, a jagged wound that refused to heal. The tears welled in his eyes, blurring his vision, but he couldn't afford to hesitate. He had to act.

With a heavy heart, he severed the connection, drawing back the energy he'd channeled into the painting. He felt a wrenching pain, a severing of a bond that was as real and tangible as any physical connection. The world within the canvas shimmered, stabilized, and finally settled. The vibrant colors remained, Abby's smile fixed in time, unaware of the sacrifice made for her existence.

He stood there, watching the painting, his heart breaking into a million pieces. Abby was safe, her world secure, but he was left with an emptiness that echoed the silence of the ancient forest. He had made the heartbreaking choice, sacrificing his own happiness for her continued existence. He had saved her world but lost his own. He turned and walked away, leaving behind the painting, leaving behind his love, leaving behind a part of himself that would forever remain trapped within the vibrant colors of the canvas.

The walk back was long and arduous, each step heavy with grief. The forest seemed darker, the silence more profound. He carried the weight of his sacrifice, a burden that would forever remain a part of him. He returned to his room, the painting now a poignant reminder of his impossible love, a testament to a choice made out of profound love and immense sacrifice. He knew he would never forget Abby, the girl trapped in a painting, whose existence he had saved at the cost of his own happiness. Their story, a tale of impossible love and heartbreaking sacrifice, would forever remain etched in his memory. The vibrant colors of the painting were a constant, yet bittersweet, reminder of his choice.

The following weeks were a blur of numbness and grief. He tried to resume his studies, but the words on the page swam before his eyes, devoid of meaning. His friends reached out, concerned by his sudden withdrawal, but their attempts to comfort him felt hollow and insincere. He couldn't explain the depth of his loss, the weight of his sacrifice. How could he convey the agony of losing someone who existed in a world beyond comprehension, a love that transcended time and space?

He revisited the painting often, his gaze lingering on Abby's face, searching for some sign, some acknowledgment of his sacrifice. But the painting remained silent, a vibrant tableau frozen in time, a world untouched by the emotional turmoil that raged within him. He knew, intellectually, that she was safe, that her world was secure, but that knowledge provided little solace. The absence of her presence in his life left a gaping hole, a profound emptiness that threatened to consume him.

He found solace only in his art, pouring his grief onto canvas, attempting to capture the intangible, the ephemeral, the essence of a love that defied the boundaries of reality. His paintings reflected his emotional turmoil, his struggle to come to terms with his loss, the haunting beauty of a love that existed beyond the tangible. Through his art, he sought to immortalize Abby, to keep her memory alive, to preserve the essence of their connection, even though their worlds were now irrevocably separated.

He knew he would always carry the weight of his decision, the sacrifice he made for the woman he loved. But he also knew that his love for Abby would endure, a testament to a connection that transcended the limitations of time and space, a bond that would forever remain, a vibrant and haunting echo in the chambers of his heart. The painting, once a gateway to another world, now stood as a monument to their impossible love, a symbol of a heartbreaking choice made out of selfless devotion and eternal love. The painting, once a vibrant window, was now a treasured memento, a poignant reminder of a love that would endure, a love he had sacrificed for the sake of her eternal existence.

Chapter 4
Sacrifice and Acceptance

The final moments stretched out, each second an eternity. He knelt before the painting, his reflection shimmering in the vibrant colors of the Victorian park. Abby stood before him, her hand outstretched, her eyes mirroring the boundless love and sorrow that filled his own heart. The air crackled with the residual energy of the ley line, a subtle hum resonating in the quiet stillness of his room. He could still feel the faint thrumming of that incredible power, a phantom sensation lingering after the intense exertion of the ritual. It was a bittersweet reminder of the power he wielded, the sacrifices he made.

He reached out, his fingers brushing against the smooth surface of the canvas, a silent farewell across the chasm of reality. The warmth of her hand felt strangely real against the painted surface, a ghostly contact that lingered even after he drew back. He traced the delicate lines of her face, each stroke a poignant reminder of the time they spent together, the laughter, the whispered secrets, the burgeoning romance that had bloomed in such an improbable setting. Her smile, so bright and hopeful, was a stark contrast to the aching sadness filling his heart.

"I have to go, my love," he whispered, his voice thick with unshed tears. The words hung heavily in the air, a final, agonizing farewell. He felt the pang of separation, a profound and visceral loss that tore at his very soul. The silence that followed was deafening, broken only by the soft rhythm of his own heart, a drumbeat of grief echoing the emptiness in his soul. He braced himself for the pain of letting go, the agonizing severance of a bond that had defied all reason, all logic, all boundaries of space and time.

Abby's eyes, usually sparkling with mirth, were now clouded with a confusion that mirrored his own inner turmoil. He saw a flicker of understanding, a fleeting recognition of his unspoken sacrifice. The connection was too profound for her to be entirely unaware of the changing energies, the subtle shifts in their reality. She knew, on some level, that their time together was ending. He saw the beginning of understanding in the subtle shifts of her eyes. A tear traced a path down her painted cheek, as if the painting itself was weeping alongside him.

He forced a smile; a painful imitation of the joy he'd shared with her within that world and wished her a reality free from the looming threat of dissolution. He promised to remember, to cherish the memories they had created together. He promised to keep her alive in his thoughts, in his art, in the silent chambers of his heart where their love would forever reside. He hoped that she would be at peace, a peace that he himself couldn't achieve. Their love wasn't a physical thing, not in this sense, he knew, but it was real, intense and true.

The finality of his decision settled upon him like a shroud. He could feel the ley line energy waning, the connection dissolving, the bridge between their worlds crumbling. He knew that this was his ultimate sacrifice; his very being resonating with the immense love and grief that would forever remain with him. He would always cherish this memory, this extraordinary love that transcended the boundaries of the real and the unreal. The last of the connection faded, leaving behind a profound sense of loss that was as real and tangible as the lingering scent of paint and canvas.

He stepped back, watching as the painting seemed to breathe, to settle into its newfound stability. The colors, vibrant and sharp, seemed to gleam with a renewed life force. He could see Abby, her beautiful face forever fixed in a peaceful smile, forever young, forever vibrant. The painting, once a fading canvas, now shimmered with a renewed vitality, an emblem of the extraordinary connection they had shared. He watched the painting until the details became almost too sharp for him to look at any longer.   He didn't know if he would ever paint again. He had poured so much of his heart and soul into portraying their extraordinary love that it now felt sacrilegious to use that same medium for anything else. Every stroke felt like a betrayal of the emotions he poured into saving Abby's world. Would his art ever again capture the depths of emotion he had experienced? He could only hope to find some semblance of peace. He had saved her, and for that he could forgive himself. The pain that gnawed at his insides was a testament to that love, he supposed.

He turned away, leaving the painting behind, leaving Abby in her timeless world. The room fell silent, the only sound the heavy thud of his heart against his ribs, a mournful rhythm echoing the profound loss he felt. He went for a walk, the familiar streets of his town seeming strangely alien, the world around him a muted echo of what it once was. He felt like a ghost himself, walking the streets with a heart ripped open, leaving a trail of emotional fragments in his wake.

Days bled into weeks, and the grief slowly began to take hold. The vibrant colors of the painting, once a source of joy, were now a constant reminder of his loss, a sharp, stabbing pain in his chest. Sleep offered little respite, his dreams filled with fleeting images of Abby, her face a mixture of joy and understanding, her eyes reflecting both their happiness and their sorrow. He woke with a start each morning, the weight of his sacrifice pressing down on him, making even the most simple tasks feel monumental.

His friends' concerns seemed hollow, their words of comfort offering little solace. He couldn't explain the depth of his loss, the complexity of his sacrifice. How could he possibly convey the agony of losing someone who existed in a world beyond comprehension, a love that transcended time and space? Their attempts felt clumsy and inadequate, leaving him feeling more isolated and alone than ever before. It was a love that no one could understand.

He tried to return to his studies, but the words on the page swam before his eyes, devoid of meaning. His art lay untouched, the canvas mocking his inability to express the turmoil within him. He couldn't bring himself to use his brushes again, the very act feeling like a violation of the memory of his extraordinary love. The pain in his heart was so profound he couldn't even pick up his brushes without weeping.

He found a strange solace in revisiting the painting, his gaze lingering on Abby's face, searching for some sign of recognition, some acknowledgment of his sacrifice. But the painting remained silent, a vibrant tableau frozen in time, its world untouched by the emotional tempest that raged within him. He longed to see some sign, some way for her to know his feelings.

Slowly, painstakingly, he began to paint again, but this time, his canvas was filled not with vibrant colors and joyous scenes, but with the muted tones of grief, the somber hues of loss. He poured his pain onto the canvas, his brushstrokes reflecting the turmoil within him, the haunting beauty of a love that defied the boundaries of reality. Through his art, he sought to immortalize Abby, to keep her memory alive, to preserve the essence of their extraordinary connection, even though their worlds were now irrevocably separated.

The years passed, and the pain gradually began to soften, the sharp edges of grief becoming rounded and less painful. He still visited the painting, his gaze lingering on Abby's face, but the sadness was tempered with a sense of peace, a profound acceptance of the sacrifice he made. He knew that their love story was unique, impossible, a vibrant testament to a connection that transcended time and space. The painting remained a cherished memento, a silent monument to a love that would endure forever, a poignant reminder of a heartbreaking choice made out of selfless devotion and eternal love. The painting stood as a testament to their impossible love, a love that he would always cherish, a love that transcended the boundaries of reality.

The world rushed back at him, a cacophony of noise and movement after the serene stillness of Abby's Victorian park. The mundane hum of traffic replaced the subtle hum of the ley line; the sharp scent of exhaust fumes clashed with the lingering aroma of oil paint and wildflowers. His own room, once a sanctuary, now felt cold and empty, a stark contrast to the vibrant warmth of the painted landscape he had left behind. The familiar comfort of his belongings felt alien, strangely detached, as if he was looking at them through a thick, distorting lens. It was as though he'd been living a double life, and now he was thrust back into the less satisfying, less magical half.

The silence in his room was deafening, a stark contrast to the vibrant energy he'd left behind. He found himself straining his ears, listening for echoes of Abby's laughter, the rustle of her skirts against the painted grass, the soft murmur of her voice. It was a futile search, a desperate attempt to cling to the remnants of a reality that had abruptly vanished. The world felt muted, drained of color, every sound, every sight, a pale imitation of the vivid reality he had inhabited for what felt like a lifetime, but was ultimately only a stolen moment in time.

His friends' attempts at normalcy were jarring. Their casual conversations about school, parties, and trivial concerns felt insignificant, almost offensive in the face of the profound loss he carried within him. He tried to engage, to participate, to force a semblance of his old self back into existence, but the words felt hollow, his laughter forced and unconvincing. He felt like an actor in a play, desperately trying to follow a script he no longer understood.

His studies became an impossible burden. The intricate equations, the complex theorems, the dense prose of literary texts, all seemed meaningless, irrelevant. His mind, once sharp and focused, was now clouded with a persistent grief, his concentration fractured, his thoughts drifting back to the painted world, to Abby's face, to the shared laughter and whispered secrets. He couldn't focus on the task at hand, or on any task for that matter. He found himself staring out of the window, lost in the melancholic beauty of the mundane, trying to find some connection to the breathtaking beauty he had known within the painting. He could still feel the warmth of her hand, the ghost of her touch lingering on his fingertips.

His room, once his haven, now felt like a cage. The walls seemed to close in on him, each object a painful reminder of the life he had temporarily abandoned. He would wander aimlessly through his house, touching his possessions as though trying to reconnect with himself, trying to feel grounded again in the reality he so carelessly let slip through his fingers.

The act of eating was a difficult task. Food held no appeal, its flavors bland and uninspiring, offering no comfort, no solace, just another reminder of the emptiness within him. Sleep offered little escape; his dreams were filled with fragmented images of Abby, their fleeting moments of joy and sorrow, their impossible romance, a constant reminder of the gaping hole that her absence had created in his life.

Even his relationship with his parents seemed strained. Their well-meaning words of concern fell flat, unable to reach the depths of his emotional turmoil. He found himself withdrawing, isolating himself from their attempts at comfort and understanding. How could he explain the immeasurable loss, the impossible love, the extraordinary sacrifice he had made? Their concern felt like an intrusion, a crude and clumsy attempt to mend a wound that was beyond repair.

He tried to paint, hoping to capture the essence of his loss, to give form to the intangible pain that consumed him. But his hand trembled, the brushstrokes hesitant and uncertain, the colors muted and lifeless. The vibrant colors of his previous works felt like a betrayal of the somber beauty of his current emotional landscape. The vivid memories of Abby's world seemed to mock him from the canvas, a painful reminder of his loss. He tried different styles, different techniques, different mediums – watercolors, charcoal, oils – but nothing seemed to capture the depth of his grief, the haunting beauty of his lost love. Each attempt felt like a futile endeavor, a desperate attempt to claw back something he could never recover. He felt like his talent, his passion, was fading along with the vibrant colors and landscapes that once flooded his canvases.

Days bled into weeks, weeks into months. The initial sharp pain began to dull, replaced by a persistent ache, a constant reminder of his sacrifice. He found a strange comfort in revisiting the painting, his gaze lingering on Abby's serene face, finding a sense of peace in her eternal youth, her unwavering beauty, knowing she was safe and whole, despite their separation.

He discovered a new form of expression, a way to honor Abby's memory, to reconcile his grief. He began to write, pouring his emotions onto the page, creating stories that explored themes of loss, sacrifice, and impossible love. His words flowed freely, capturing the emotional turmoil, the extraordinary connection he had shared, the impossible romance that transcended the boundaries of time and space. His stories became his outlet, a way to give shape and form to his grief, to immortalize Abby's memory, and to find solace and peace in the recounting of their bittersweet tale.

He shared his stories with his friends, his family, and eventually, with the world. His words resonated with others, who found comfort and understanding in his experiences. His writing became a testament to his loss, a celebration of his extraordinary love, a poignant reminder of a sacrifice made out of pure devotion. He began to heal, to accept the reality of his loss, while still cherishing the memories of the impossible love he shared with Abby within the painted world.

He learned that love, even in its most unconventional forms, could leave an indelible mark on the soul, a lasting legacy that transcended time and space. And though his heart would forever bear the scar of his sacrifice, it was a scar that bore testament to a love that was unique, impossible, and eternally beautiful. He found peace in the knowledge that their love story, though tragically short, would live on in his heart, his art, and his words. The painting itself remained a silent, vibrant testament to a love that defied all odds, a monument to a love that even the boundaries of reality couldn't erase.

The initial awkwardness with his friends was palpable. Todd, his best friend since kindergarten, greeted him with a hesitant hug, a mixture of concern and uncertainty in his eyes. Todd's usual boisterous energy was muted, replaced by a cautiousness that mirrored David's own internal turmoil. Their conversations, once filled with effortless banter about video games and upcoming football games, now felt stilted and forced. The silence between their words felt heavier than the words themselves. David tried to fill the gaps, recounting mundane details of his day, but the words felt hollow, a clumsy attempt to bridge the gap that had opened between them.

Angie, with her bright smile and infectious laughter, was equally hesitant. She approached him tentatively, her usual playful teasing replaced by a gentle concern. She listened patiently as David stumbled through explanations, his attempts to articulate his experience falling short. Her empathy, however, was genuine, her unwavering support a quiet balm to his wounded soul. She didn't press him for details, understanding the limitations of language in expressing the inexpressible. Instead, she offered a listening ear and the comforting presence of friendship, a simple act of kindness that meant more than any grand gesture. Their shared history, the memories of countless sleepovers, whispered secrets, and inside jokes, acted as a bridge, strengthening their bond despite the emotional distance that had grown between them.

Their attempts at rebuilding their friendship started small – a casual coffee date, a shared movie night, a walk through the park. These ordinary activities, once taken for granted, now felt precious, a carefully constructed bridge across the abyss of their separation. Each shared laugh, each fleeting moment of connection, served as a reminder of the strength of their friendship and the enduring power of human connection.

The process of reconciliation was gradual, a slow and painstaking rebuilding of trust and understanding. David had to actively participate, actively listening to his friends, sharing what he could manage to articulate about his experiences, and accepting their concerns, questions, and sometimes, their skepticism. There were moments of frustration, of unspoken words hanging heavy in the air, moments when the gulf between their realities seemed unbridgeable. But through persistence, patience, and a willingness to forgive his own shortcomings, he gradually began to reclaim the connections he had allowed to slip away.

He found himself opening up more, not just about the painting, but about the feelings of isolation and loss that had consumed him. Todd, initially reserved, became a surprising source of strength, offering a practical perspective, devoid of the romanticism David had initially projected onto the experience. He helped ground David in the reality of his situation, gently nudging him back towards his studies and his daily life. Their conversations, while still different from before, now included a genuine exchange of thoughts and feelings, a deeper understanding of each other's struggles and vulnerabilities.

Angie provided a different kind of support. She understood the depth of David's emotional turmoil, his struggle to reconcile his extraordinary experiences with the mundane reality of his life. Her creative nature allowed her to appreciate the artistic beauty of his experience, seeing past the inexplicable nature of it all. She listened patiently to his stories, drawing parallels to her own artistic pursuits, finding common ground in their shared passion for self-expression. Her empathy helped him to see the beauty in his experience, even in its sorrow.

Their acceptance wasn't immediate or unconditional. There were moments of disbelief, of awkward silences, of hesitant glances. But their underlying friendship, the years of shared history and mutual respect, proved strong enough to withstand the strain. They understood that David's experience had been profound, life-altering, and that his struggle to integrate it into his life was a process that would take time, patience, and mutual understanding.

Rebuilding his relationship with his parents proved to be a more difficult challenge. The initial coldness remained, a heavy blanket of unspoken words and unspoken fears. His father, a practical man of science, found it hard to accept David's story, dismissing it as a figment of an overactive imagination, a byproduct of stress and academic pressure. His mother, though more empathetic, still struggled to comprehend the depth of his emotional turmoil. She worried about his well-being, his declining grades, his withdrawal from their family life, but couldn't fully understand the reason behind his changes.

David attempted to explain, but his words often fell short of conveying the emotional depth and complexity of his experience. The language of science, the framework of his father's worldview, failed to capture the essence of his impossible love, the ethereal beauty of Abby's world, the poignant sacrifice he had made. The shared moments of connection with his parents were precious, but they were peppered with misunderstandings and emotional chasms. He realized he couldn't force them to accept something they couldn't comprehend.

He found solace in writing, in crafting narratives that explored themes of sacrifice, loss, and impossible love. He wrote about Abby, about their shared moments of joy and sorrow, about the wrenching decision he had made. He wrote not just for himself, but for his parents, hoping that through the medium of storytelling, he could bridge the gap in understanding. His words were an attempt to share the essence of his experience, to convey the emotional reality that eluded simple explanation.

His parents' reactions to his writing were tentative at first, but slowly, cautiously, their understanding grew. His father, surprised by the emotional depth of David's work, began to see the sincerity of his experience, recognizing the depth of his son's emotional turmoil in the vulnerability of his storytelling. His mother, always more receptive to his artistic endeavors, found a new level of appreciation for his writing, recognizing the strength and resilience hidden beneath the surface of his grief.

The process wasn't easy, but it was a starting point. The shared act of reading his stories, of discussing his characters and their struggles, became a new form of communication, a bridge to understanding and empathy. The act of sharing his experience, not directly but indirectly through his stories, helped to heal some of the wounds and mend the fractured bonds within his family.

It wasn't a complete reconciliation, but it was a significant step forward, a promise of future understanding and healing. Through his writing, David found a way to share his experience, to make sense of his loss, and to gradually rebuild the shattered fragments of his relationships. The process was slow, painful at times, but ultimately, it was rewarding, leading him towards a more profound understanding of himself, his friends, and his family. The painting, though a source of profound loss, also served as a catalyst for growth, helping David to rebuild his relationships on a deeper level of understanding and empathy.

The days that followed were a strange blend of relief and melancholia. The painting, hanging quietly in David's room, no longer pulsed with the vibrant energy of his connection. The frantic, almost feverish brushstrokes of the Victorian park scene had calmed, the colors less saturated, the edges less defined. It was as if the painting had exhaled, letting go of the strain of his constant presence. Yet, in its stillness, a new kind of sadness had settled.

The once bright, almost incandescent greens of the grass had muted to a softer, more subdued hue. The vibrant reds of the flowers seemed to have lost some of their intensity, their petals appearing slightly wilted, delicate. Even the sky, previously a brilliant, almost otherworldly blue, had shifted to a paler, more pensive shade. The change was subtle, almost imperceptible at first glance, but David, intimately familiar with every detail of Abby's world, noticed the shift immediately. It was a visual representation of the emotional toll their impossible love had taken.

He found himself staring at the painting for hours, searching for any trace of Abby, a flicker of movement, a glint of her eyes. Of course, there was nothing. The painting remained static, a silent testament to their shared history. He could almost feel the weight of their separation, the lingering echo of her laughter, the ghostly scent of her perfume, the phantom touch of her hand.

The changes in the painting were more than just aesthetic. The overall atmosphere had shifted. The once joyous vitality of the park was replaced by a quiet melancholy, a sense of peaceful resignation. The birds no longer sang with the same carefree abandon, their melodies now carrying a hint of wistful longing. The fountain, once a symbol of exuberance, now trickled with a subdued gentleness, its spray less vigorous, its rhythm more measured. Even the shadows seemed to have deepened, stretching long and thin across the path, as if embracing the painting in a somber embrace.

It was a poignant reminder of their shared experience, a visual echo of the emotional turmoil he had endured. The painting, once a gateway to a world of boundless joy and impossible love, now served as a poignant memorial, a bittersweet reminder of what he had lost. But within that sadness, David found a different kind of peace, a quiet acceptance of the sacrifice he had made. He had saved Abby, ensuring her continued existence within the canvas, and in doing so, had also preserved the memory of their extraordinary connection.

He returned to his studies, slowly reintegrating into his former life. His grades, though still not perfect, were improving. The weight of his secret, the burden of his impossible love, had lessened, replaced by a gentler sorrow, a quiet ache in his heart. His relationships with his friends and family were healing, albeit slowly.

Todd helped David refocus his energy on his future, urging him to apply to colleges, encouraging him to pursue his passion for writing. Angie, with her artist's eye, continued to offer her support, her understanding extending beyond words, expressed in shared silences, understanding glances, and a gentle touch on his arm. His parents, while still grappling with the unexplainable nature of his experience, had found a new level of appreciation for his writing, recognizing the depth of his emotions through his stories. David continued to write, pouring his heart and soul into his stories. He wrote about Abby, not as a fantasy, but as a tribute to their love, a testament to their bond that transcended the boundaries of time and reality. He explored themes of sacrifice, acceptance, and the enduring power of love. He wrote about the bittersweet joy of their connection, the wrenching pain of their separation, and the quiet peace he had found in letting go. His writing became a form of therapy, a way to process his emotions, to make sense of his experience, and to share his story with the world.

The painting remained a constant presence in his life, a silent observer of his journey. He would often find himself gazing at it, lost in memories, reliving their shared moments, cherishing the echoes of their love. The subtle changes in the painting reflected the stages of his own healing process, the muted colors mirroring the softening of his grief, the quiet atmosphere reflecting the growing peace in his heart.

One day, while examining the painting closely, he noticed a minuscule change – a single wildflower, a delicate violet, had bloomed in a corner of the park where there had previously been nothing. It was small, almost insignificant, easily overlooked, but David recognized it as a sign, a tiny whisper of Abby's continued presence within the canvas. It was a subtle affirmation that their love, though altered, hadn't entirely faded. It was a reminder that despite the heartbreak of their separation, the memory of their connection would endure, a precious treasure within the confines of his heart.

The subtle shift in the painting mirrored David's own emotional transformation. He learned to live with the ache of loss, carrying the memory of Abby not as a burden, but as a precious keepsake, a reminder of the beauty and intensity of their impossible love. He continued to write, his stories infused with the magic of their connection, a way to keep her memory alive, to share the story of a love that defied all boundaries.

His life had returned to a semblance of normalcy, but it was a normalcy enriched by the extraordinary experience of his impossible love, an experience that changed him profoundly, forever shaping his understanding of love, loss, and the enduring power of the human spirit. The painting, a silent witness to their extraordinary love story, served as a lasting reminder of the profound impact Abby had on his life, and the beautiful, albeit painful, sacrifice he made for her. His life, once defined by his connection to the canvas, was now a tapestry woven with threads of memory, hope, and the quiet, enduring love he carried in his heart. The painting, no longer a gateway, but a poignant reminder, held a place of honor in his life, a silent testament to a love that would forever transcend the boundaries of reality.

The scent of linseed oil, faint but persistent, clung to the air around the painting, a subtle reminder of Abby's world. David often found himself inhaling deeply, trying to recapture the fragrance of the Victorian park, a perfume of damp earth, blooming roses, and the slightly metallic tang of the fountain's water. It was a futile attempt, of course, a ghost of a sensation, yet the act itself offered a small comfort, a fleeting connection to a reality that was forever beyond his reach.

He'd started keeping a journal, a small, leather-bound book that mirrored the aged texture of the painting's frame. In its pages, he documented not just the changes in the artwork – the subtle shifts in color, the gradual softening of the lines – but also the subtle alterations in his own emotional landscape. The journal became a repository of his grief, his acceptance, and the slow, painstaking process of healing. He wrote about the phantom pains, the moments when he felt Abby's presence so acutely, it felt as if she were still brushing against him. He documented the recurring dreams, vivid and surreal, where he walked with her once again through the sun-dappled paths of the Victorian park, the air thick with laughter and whispered secrets.

He wrote about the guilt that consumed him, the persistent undercurrent of regret that accompanied the quiet contentment he was slowly finding. Had he made the right decision? Was there another way? The questions swirled in his mind, a persistent hum beneath the surface of his daily life. He'd tried to rationalize it, to convince himself that he'd done what was necessary, that he'd saved her from complete oblivion, but the truth was, a part of him would always mourn the loss.

His art mirrored his internal struggle. His sketches, once filled with vibrant, almost chaotic energy, reflecting his frenzied attempts to understand his experience, now showed a new level of depth and maturity. His lines were bolder, more deliberate, his color palettes more subdued. He painted landscapes, mostly, serene scenes of quiet solitude, mirroring the inner peace he was painstakingly cultivating. There were recurring motifs – a solitary tree silhouetted against a twilight sky, a single wildflower pushing its way through cracked pavement, a gentle stream flowing towards a distant horizon. Each painting was a quiet meditation on loss, acceptance, and resilience.

His friends noticed the change. Todd noticed the quiet confidence that had settled over David, replacing the earlier uncertainty and anguish. He saw the way David carried himself, his shoulders straighter, his eyes holding a new depth of understanding. Angie was aware of the subtle shifts in his emotions. She didn't pry, didn't demand explanations, but simply offered her unwavering support, a silent presence that spoke volumes. His parents, too, sensed the difference. They still didn't fully understand his experiences, but they saw the transformation in his personality, the newfound clarity in his eyes, the quiet intensity in his work.

One evening, while lost in his journal, David noticed a passage he'd written months earlier, a passage filled with raw grief and self-recrimination. He reread it, and a wave of sadness washed over him. But this time, it wasn't the same agonizing pain. It was a different kind of sorrow, a mellowed ache, seasoned by time and tempered by acceptance. He realized he wasn't just surviving; he was thriving, albeit in a way he could never have imagined. He'd learned to live with the absence of Abby, to find joy and meaning in the ordinary moments of his life. He'd woven her memory into the fabric of his being, not as a burden, but as a precious thread, strengthening the tapestry of his existence.

He continued to visit the painting, not with the frantic desperation of his earlier visits, but with a quiet reverence. He would sit for hours, studying the nuances of the light and shadow, marveling at the delicate details he had almost missed before. He noticed a new detail – a tiny bird's nest hidden amidst the branches of an oak tree, subtly painted but overlooked in his earlier, frenzied observations. It was a new addition, a minuscule detail, almost imperceptible, yet it served as a silent testament to Abby's enduring presence.

He started to understand that the painting wasn't just a container holding Abby; it was a living entity, constantly evolving, changing in response to both his emotional state and her own subtle shifts within the canvas. It was a shared space, a testament to the extraordinary bond they'd shared, forever altered but never truly broken. The painting, in its own way, was healing too. The muted colors were gradually regaining their vibrancy, the lines regaining their sharpness. The process was slow, almost imperceptible, but it was happening, a tangible sign that their connection, albeit transformed, still resonated.

His writing became his catharsis. He wrote not just about Abby, but about the complex interplay of reality and imagination, the boundaries between the tangible and the intangible. He wrote about the transformative power of love, the pain of loss, and the quiet strength found in acceptance. His stories drew from his own experience, weaving elements of magic and realism, exploring themes of sacrifice, resilience, and the enduring power of memory.

One day, he received an email from a publisher. They'd read his manuscript, a collection of short stories inspired by his experiences, and wanted to offer him a contract. It was a moment of overwhelming joy, a validation of his journey, a sign that his pain, his struggles, his love for Abby had been transformed into something beautiful and lasting. The acceptance of his manuscript felt almost like a blessing, a sign that Abby was still with him, guiding him, supporting him, even from beyond the confines of the painting. He thought of the wildflower, the tiny violet blooming in the corner of the canvas and smiled. It was a sign, a silent acknowledgment, that their extraordinary love story was not over, but had simply transformed, finding a new kind of immortality within the pages of his book and the enduring memory in his heart. The painting remained, a constant companion, a quiet witness to his journey, and the enduring legacy of his impossible love. It was no longer a gateway to another world, but a window to the heart, forever preserving the memory of their extraordinary connection. The sacrifice he had made was bittersweet, but it was a sacrifice he had made with love, ensuring Abby's safety and the preservation of their unique bond – a love that transcended time and defied the boundaries of reality.

Chapter 5
Echoes of the Past

The publisher's acceptance wasn't just a professional breakthrough; it felt like a validation of his entire experience, a whispered confirmation that his impossible love with Abby had left an indelible mark on the world, even if that world existed primarily within the confines of a single painting. He found himself drawn to research the original artist, a woman named Stephanie Moreau, whose life, as he soon discovered, mirrored his own in unexpected ways.

His initial search online yielded little. Stephanie Moreau was a ghost, a whisper in the annals of art history. A few sparse mentions in obscure auction catalogs, a single black-and-white photograph showing a woman with eyes that held the same haunted beauty he remembered in Abby's, a woman whose smile hinted at a sadness that went deeper than mere melancholy. He learned she'd been a recluse, working primarily in oils, her creations imbued with a strange, ethereal quality that was impossible to replicate. Her life was a mystery, shrouded in an almost deliberate obscurity.

Determined to uncover more, David delved into archives, spending weeks poring over dusty documents, yellowed newspaper clippings, and faded letters. He discovered that Stephanie had lived a solitary life, her only known companion an elderly housekeeper who died before David began his research. There was no mention of family, no record of lovers, only her art, a series of enigmatic landscapes and portraits that hinted at a hidden life, a world of secrets whispered between the brushstrokes.

The more David learned about Stephanie, the more he felt a peculiar resonance, a sense of uncanny familiarity. He learned that she had created the painting in a fit of grief, a testament to a lost love. Her journals, eventually found in a private collection in a forgotten corner of the National Gallery, revealed a story of heartbreak that mirrored his own. Besides painting her pain about Connie; she, too, had fallen in love with someone beyond her reach, a man who existed in her imagination, a man she could only visit in the spaces between reality and fantasy.

Her journals were a labyrinth of cryptic entries, vivid descriptions of a world she'd built on canvas, a world inhabited by the man she loved. She wrote of the process of creating the painting, how she'd poured her grief, her hopes, her desperation into each brushstroke. She'd poured her soul onto the canvas, making the painting a conduit, a bridge to the man who haunted her dreams, and her existence. She spoke of the painting's gradual transformation, how it mirrored her own emotional state, how its vibrancy waxed and waned with her moods. She described the sacrifices she made to preserve the beauty and permanence of the world she'd created for him. The sacrifices that she endured to ensure that he would remain safe and unchanged within the painting.

It was through these journals that David finally understood the true nature of the painting. It wasn't just a static image; it was a living, breathing entity, a reflection of the artist's soul, constantly changing and evolving. The fading he had witnessed wasn't a sign of decay, but a reflection of Stephanie's own fading hope, her own struggle with loss. Her vibrant colors dulled as her heart broke, and they seemed to gradually recover their vibrancy and life as she started to heal her own broken heart.

Stephanie's journals also held a clue to the small, almost imperceptible changes David had noticed in the painting over time. She wrote of her belief that the painting, once imbued with a sufficient degree of emotional energy, could become sentient, aware of those who interacted with it. She talked about her hope that he would someday reach out to her through the art, and the hope that she would someday find him and connect with him.

David discovered that Stephanie's lost love was not a fictional construct, but a real person, a man who died tragically young. She had painted him into the canvas, creating an alternate reality where he could live forever. She'd placed him in a world that was both a refuge and a prison, a world born of love and heartbreak. And she hoped to create a painting that she could someday inhabit with her love.

He realized that he, too, had become a part of the painting's narrative, a figure etched into its history, connected to Stephanie's tragedy by a strange, cyclical pattern of love and loss. He saw his own reflections in her words, in her struggles. He saw his reflection in the characters from her painting. The reflection of love, the reflection of loss, and the reflection of his own healing. He was no longer just an observer; he was a participant in a centuries-old narrative, a continuation of a story that transcended time and space.

The discovery deepened his understanding of his own experience, transforming his sorrow into something more profound, something akin to awe. He realized he wasn't alone in his impossible love, in his struggle with the boundaries of reality and imagination. He understood that his connection with Abby wasn't unique; it was a part of a larger, ongoing narrative of human longing, a tale that had been retold and reimagined through the ages.

David continued to write, his stories growing richer, more nuanced, infused with a deeper understanding of love, loss, and the enduring power of the human spirit. His work now held a resonance that went beyond mere storytelling; it was a testament to the shared experience of humanity, to the enduring power of art to transcend the limitations of time and space. He continued to visit the painting, not as a conduit to Abby, but as a pilgrimage to the memory of their love, a reminder of the extraordinary connection that had transcended the boundaries of the canvas and the boundaries of reality. He felt a closeness to the artist, a connection that went beyond mere admiration. He recognized the pain, the loss, the beauty, and the resilience within the painting, and within her life.

He often found himself lingering before the painting, imagining Stephanie standing in the same spot, her brush poised above the canvas, her heart filled with a mixture of hope and despair. He felt a deep connection to her, a bond forged through shared experience, a testament to the enduring power of art to bridge the gap between different time periods and to unite those bound by the commonality of experience.

He saw in Stephanie's work not just art, but a mirror reflecting the deepest emotions of the human heart. He saw her reflection of loss and heartbreak, but also of acceptance and understanding. His own healing journey echoed hers, a testament to the resilient spirit of both the artist and their creation. He had brought his own love, loss and healing to the painting. He had healed his own life and healed the painting's life with his own experiences. The painting remained a living entity, a reflection of the artist's soul, and a testament to the endurance of love and art. He realized the painting was also a reflection of the life that she desired and the life that she lived.

The publisher's acceptance letter, crisp and official, lay on his desk, a stark contrast to the swirling emotions within him. It wasn't just the validation of his talent; it was a strange echo of his impossible love for Abby, a testament to a connection that transcended the limitations of reality. The manuscript, filled with his experiences and emotions, now held a weight beyond mere words – it held the remnants of a love lost, a love that had shaped him, changed him, and ultimately, defined him.

He started to incorporate his experiences into his writing, weaving his journey with Abby into his stories, turning the fantastical into something both tangible and believable. He found himself drawn to narratives of impossible loves, of connections that defied the boundaries of time and space. His characters were no longer just figments of his imagination; they were infused with the very essence of his own experience, each brushstroke of his writing reflecting the emotional landscape of his impossible love. He painted portraits of yearning and hope, and the heartbreaking acceptance of loss.

His writing style evolved. Initially, his work had been infused with a naive wonder, an almost childlike fascination with the magical realism of his experience. Now, his prose was deeper, richer, imbued with a maturity born from sorrow and acceptance. He wrote of the bittersweet joy of fleeting moments, of the agonizing ache of separation, and of the quiet strength of memories. His words, once vibrant and filled with the exuberance of youth, now carried a weight, a maturity that resonated with his readers on a more profound level. He had learned to use his pain, to embrace it, to let it inform his writing. He realized that the pain was an integral part of his journey. That his experiences made his art more authentic and more deeply engaging. He wrote about the pain, and the joy, and the complexity of love.

His newfound perspective also affected his relationship with the painting. He continued to visit it, not to see Abby, but to connect with the legacy of their love, to commune with the echoes of their shared experiences. He sat before the canvas, allowing the colors and textures to wash over him, remembering the laughter, the whispered secrets, the profound sense of belonging he'd found within that impossible world. The painting was no longer a portal, but a sacred space, a shrine to a memory he cherished, and a testament to a love that had transcended time and mortality. His sorrow was not a burden; it became a source of inspiration and creativity.

The visits were no longer fueled by desperation or longing, but by a quiet appreciation. He understood now that letting go was not the end, but a crucial part of the process of healing. He had found peace within the acceptance of their inevitable separation. He had reached a stage of acceptance, where he had moved from pain to a quiet recognition of their love's legacy. He understood that Abby would remain a part of his life, even if she lived only within the confines of a single painting.

The painting itself seemed to reflect this shift. The fading, which had once been a cause of intense anxiety, now seemed less ominous, more akin to a natural process of change and evolution. It was as if the canvas was mirroring his own journey of healing, gradually regaining its vibrancy as his own heart found its peace. He continued to find solace in his visits, understanding the painting's transformation as a metaphor for the ongoing process of healing that he himself was experiencing.

He started experimenting with different artistic styles, exploring new techniques, and incorporating different mediums into his work. He found himself drawn to mixed media, combining painting, drawing, and even digital art to create pieces that reflected the multi-layered nature of his own experiences. He worked on installations, creating immersive environments that sought to transport the viewer into the very heart of his storytelling. He blended his experiences with the surreal, weaving in elements of the Victorian era with science fiction.

The critical acclaim continued to grow, each new piece garnering more attention and accolades. Yet, David remained grounded. The recognition was gratifying, but it did not compare to the emotional fulfillment he found in creating. His art was not just a profession; it was a way to process his experiences, to make sense of the impossible, and to communicate the nuances of human connection. The art became his reflection, his catharsis, and his method to preserve the memory of Abby.

His personal life also began to heal. The rift with his family, initially caused by his obsession with the painting, began to mend. They started to understand the depth of his experience, the power of his love for Abby, and the profound transformation it had wrought within him. He realized that it was his inability to communicate, rather than his relationship with the painting itself, that had initially caused the strain in his relationships. He began to share his story, not as a means of seeking sympathy, but as a way of creating a deeper connection with those closest to him. His ability to communicate had not only improved his relationships but also had enabled him to better handle his emotions and to cope with his grief.

He found solace in friendships, forging bonds with other artists who understood the unique challenges and rewards of a life devoted to creativity. He learned from their experiences, shared his own struggles, and found comfort in their shared passion. He discovered a community of artists that supported him and encouraged him to explore his creative potential. The group served as a strong support network for him. The conversations about art served as a conduit for discussions about his experiences with Abby.

David's journey became a testament to the transformative power of art, a proof that even the most intense heartbreak can be channeled into something beautiful and meaningful. He transformed his grief into something new, something vibrant, something inspiring. His art was no longer merely a reflection of his experiences; it was a celebration of life, love, and the enduring human capacity for resilience and hope. He became an icon of resilience and strength, someone who had transformed their pain into something beautiful and inspirational. His transformation became a source of inspiration and encouragement for others.

His legacy extended beyond his personal healing. His work, filled with the echoes of his impossible love, touched the lives of countless readers. His stories resonated with those who had experienced their own impossible loves, their own heartbreaks, their own struggles with loss. He was able to convey the emotional impact of his experiences, communicating the pain of loss and the hope for healing and love. His art gave a voice to the emotions and experiences that were once unspoken and unheard. He became a champion for those experiencing the pain of loss, inspiring others to heal and find hope in difficult situations.

He had found a renewed purpose, not merely as an artist, but as a storyteller, a chronicler of human emotion, a beacon of hope in a world that often felt dark and hopeless. He had transformed his grief into art, and his art into a legacy of empathy and understanding. His personal tragedy had been transformed into a beacon of hope. He had not only healed himself but he had also healed the hearts of countless others. His work became an important part of the community that inspired and strengthened others to endure through difficult times. His art became a source of hope, healing, and resilience.

The first tentative step towards reconciliation came unexpectedly, in the form of a phone call. It wasn't a grand gesture, no tearful reunion or dramatic confession. It was simply his mother's voice, hesitant at first, then softening as she mentioned his father's growing concern over his withdrawn state. The unspoken guilt, the weight of his self-imposed isolation, pressed down on him. He'd been so consumed by his own grief, so lost in the echoes of Abby, that he'd failed to see the worry etched on their faces, the quiet disappointment in their eyes.

He agreed to dinner, a simple family meal in their small, familiar kitchen. The silence was thick at first, a heavy blanket woven from unspoken accusations and unspoken fears. He started slowly, sharing small details of his life, carefully avoiding the specifics of Abby and the painting, choosing instead to focus on the mundane aspects of his days. He talked about his writing, his new artistic techniques, his burgeoning career, carefully crafting a narrative that wouldn't overwhelm them. He spoke of his newfound appreciation for the simple things – the taste of his mother's cooking, the comforting familiarity of their old home, the quiet companionship of his father's presence.

His parents listened, their initial apprehension gradually melting away, replaced by a cautious optimism. They didn't pry, didn't demand explanations, but their eyes held a newfound understanding, a silent acknowledgement of the profound transformation he had undergone. It wasn't a complete healing, not in a single evening, but it was a beginning, a fragile bridge built across the chasm of misunderstanding that had separated them.

The conversation flowed more easily as the evening progressed, and David found himself sharing more than he had initially intended. He talked about the challenges of his work, the emotional toll of creating art from his grief. He spoke about the importance of sharing his experiences to inspire hope in others. He described the therapeutic process of transforming his pain into something beautiful and meaningful, something that could touch the lives of others.

The next few weeks were a slow, deliberate process of rebuilding. He visited his parents more frequently, participating in family dinners, helping with yard work, and sharing in their daily routines. He reconnected with old friends, those who had patiently waited, who had understood his silence, and who were welcoming him back without judgment.

Some relationships were irreparable; the damage had been too severe, the rift too wide to bridge. But the majority were receptive, eager to forgive, eager to reestablish the bonds that had been frayed by his preoccupation with the painting. He reached out, apologized for his absence, and admitted his mistakes. He confessed to his withdrawal and his inability to communicate, explaining the emotional turmoil he had experienced. He expressed gratitude for their patience and their understanding. He let them know that he was working on becoming a better friend and family member.

The healing wasn't linear. There were setbacks, moments of regression, where the pain threatened to overwhelm him again. But each time, he found the strength to persevere, drawing on the lessons he had learned from his experience with Abby. He discovered that true healing wasn't about erasing the past, but about integrating it, about finding a way to live with the scars, to transform them into something beautiful and meaningful. He learned to use his memories not as a source of pain, but as a source of inspiration and resilience. He used his past experiences to shape his future, enabling him to build stronger, healthier relationships with the people in his life. He channeled his emotions into his art, finding solace and purpose in his creativity.

His newfound emotional maturity extended beyond his personal relationships. It infused his work with a depth and complexity that resonated with his audience. He continued to explore themes of love, loss, and healing, but now his narratives were imbued with a sense of hope. He found new ways to express the pain of loss, and he used his artistic talents to help others cope with similar experiences. He became a source of support for those who were struggling, offering guidance and compassion based on his own hard-won lessons.

His artistic style evolved further, becoming more introspective, more nuanced. He moved beyond the purely fantastical, incorporating elements of realism, allowing his characters to grapple with the complexities of human emotions. He no longer shied away from depicting pain, sorrow, and loss, but instead, he used these themes as a backdrop for stories of redemption, resilience, and the enduring power of hope. His artwork became a powerful medium for healing and communication, bridging the gap between his personal experiences and the broader human experience.

The success of his new work confirmed his healing process. The critical acclaim was no longer just a personal validation, but an indicator that he was effectively conveying his message, connecting with his audience on a deeper level. He understood that his art was a way to not only share his story, but to create a sense of community, to help others find meaning in their own struggles. He realized that his experiences could resonate with people from all walks of life, and this realization allowed him to broaden his message, focusing on the power of healing, the importance of community, and the enduring strength of his character.

The painting remained a constant presence in his life, but its significance had shifted. It was no longer a portal to a lost love, but a symbol of his journey, a testament to his personal growth and transformation. He visited it occasionally, not with longing, but with a quiet sense of gratitude and acceptance. The painting served as a reminder of his past, a catalyst for his personal transformation, and a source of inspiration for his ongoing artistic journey.

David's life, once dominated by the impossible love for Abby, had transformed. The echoes of the past remained, woven into the fabric of his being, shaping his art, informing his relationships, and giving his life a depth and meaning that he could never have imagined. The pain had been intense, but it had ultimately forged him into someone stronger, more resilient, and more compassionate. He had rebuilt his relationships, not just with his family and friends, but with himself, discovering the strength he possessed, the ability to transform pain into purpose, and the importance of embracing his past to create a future filled with love, hope, and healing. His story was a powerful reminder that even in the deepest darkness, healing and transformation are possible.

The acceptance didn't arrive in a single, dramatic epiphany. It wasn't a sudden burst of clarity, banishing the pain and replacing it with serene tranquility. Instead, it was a slow, gradual process, a subtle shift in perspective, like the slow turning of a tide. It began with small, almost imperceptible changes. He found himself looking at the painting less frequently, the once-consuming obsession fading into a quiet, contemplative appreciation. The vibrant colors, once a source of both joy and anguish, now held a gentler, more melancholic beauty. He started to see it not as a portal to a lost paradise, but as a cherished memory, a testament to a love that, though impossible, had profoundly shaped his life.

He began to incorporate the memory of Abby, not into his art directly, but into the very fabric of his being. The whimsicality and vibrant energy she embodied infused his personality, adding a layer of depth and complexity to his interactions with others. He found himself embracing spontaneity, a stark contrast to the rigid routine that had defined his life before. He became more open to new experiences, more willing to take risks, to let go of the fear of vulnerability that had once held him captive. He approached his work with renewed vigor, the emotional turmoil he'd experienced fueling his creative drive. His art became more profound, more emotionally resonant, infused with a quiet poignancy that resonated deeply with his audience.

His relationships with his friends and family flourished. He didn't attempt to erase the past or pretend it hadn't happened; he simply integrated it into his present, accepting that his experiences had shaped who he was, and that those scars, though painful, had added depth and resilience to his character. He learned to appreciate the quiet moments, the simple joys of everyday life, things he'd previously overlooked in his obsession with the painting. He reveled in the warmth of his mother's hugs, the shared laughter with his friends, the quiet companionship of his father. He discovered that true happiness wasn't about escaping pain, but about embracing it, learning from it, and transforming it into something beautiful and meaningful.

One day, while browsing through an antique bookstore, he stumbled upon a worn, leather-bound journal. Its pages were filled with delicate watercolors, depicting scenes of a bygone era – a bustling Victorian market, a quaint cobblestone street, a sprawling garden overflowing with vibrant flowers. The style was reminiscent of the painting, though less fantastical, more grounded in reality. He was inexplicably drawn to it, a sense of familiarity washing over him. He purchased the journal, its pages a silent echo of Abby's world, a subtle reminder of their shared journey. He found himself captivated by the artistry, the delicate strokes of the brush, the intricate details. It wasn't the same as seeing Abby herself within the painting, but it was a connection, a tangible link to the world they had shared. He began to understand that the echoes of Abby weren't limited to the painting itself; they were woven into the very fabric of his life, a persistent, subtle presence that shaped his thoughts, his feelings, and his actions.

He started incorporating similar stylistic elements into his own artwork, finding inspiration in the journal's delicate watercolors, drawing parallels between the Victorian era depicted in the journal and the emotional landscape he navigated within himself. His artistic expression transformed, incorporating a more refined realism, a gentler touch. The fantastical elements remained, but they were now tempered by a deeper understanding of human emotion, a capacity for empathy that had blossomed through his experience with Abby. The vibrancy of his art remained, but it was now infused with a sense of quiet contemplation, a melancholic beauty that reflected the bittersweet nature of his love for Abby.

He continued to write and paint, exploring themes of loss, love, and acceptance. He channeled his emotions into his art, transforming his personal struggles into narratives that resonated with a wide audience. His work explored the complexities of grief, the challenges of moving on, and the enduring power of love. He found solace in the creative process, using his art as a medium for self-expression, healing, and ultimately, creating a lasting tribute to the extraordinary love he had shared with Abby.

He began to give lectures and workshops in small regional venues, sharing his experiences and encouraging others to embrace their own journeys of healing and self-discovery. He spoke openly about his relationship with Abby, not as a tragic tale of impossible love, but as a testament to the transformative power of human connection. He encouraged his audience to embrace the beauty of their own experiences, to find meaning even in the midst of suffering, and to learn from their past struggles to build a stronger, more resilient future. His stories of resilience and self-acceptance resonated with people from all walks of life, offering comfort and hope to those who had experienced similar losses.

He realized that the power of his art wasn't merely in its aesthetic beauty but in its capacity to connect with the human experience on a deeper level. He was no longer just an artist; he had become a storyteller, a guide, a beacon of hope for those who felt lost and alone. His art became a powerful tool for communication, allowing him to share his emotions, his struggles, and his ultimate triumph over adversity. He used his platform to promote empathy, compassion, and understanding, fostering a sense of community among those who had experienced profound loss.

Years passed. The painting remained in his possession, a silent testament to a love that transcended the boundaries of reality and time. He visited it less frequently, but when he did, it wasn't with the same agonizing longing. It was now a source of quiet reflection, a reminder of the journey he had embarked on, and the significant growth he had experienced. He saw the fading canvas not as a symbol of loss, but as a testament to the impermanence of life itself, and the enduring power of love.

David's life was no longer defined by the loss of Abby, but by his ability to transform that loss into something beautiful and meaningful. The echoes of the past remained, but they were no longer a source of pain. They had become a part of him, shaping his character, informing his art, and enriching his relationships with others. He had found peace, not by forgetting Abby, but by accepting her into the tapestry of his life, weaving her memory into the fabric of his being, forever grateful for the love they had shared, and for the lessons it had taught him about the resilience of the heart and the enduring power of hope. His life had become a story of transformation, a testament to the healing power of acceptance and the profound beauty of embracing the echoes of the past. The painting, once a symbol of impossible love, now served as a powerful reminder of his own incredible journey of healing and the capacity for love to endure, even beyond the boundaries of the physical world.

The years that followed were a tapestry woven with threads of quiet remembrance and unexpected joy. The vibrant colors of Abby's world, once a source of intense longing, now resided within the gentler hues of his everyday life. He didn't see her face in every passing cloud, nor did he hear her laughter in every rustling leaf. The intensity of his obsession had faded, replaced by a deep, abiding affection, a quiet understanding that resonated in the stillness of his heart. It was a connection that defied the constraints of time and space, a silent communion that transcended the physical separation.

He found solace in his art, his canvases becoming mirrors reflecting not just the fading image of Abby within the painting, but the evolving landscape of his own soul. His brushstrokes were no longer frantic, desperate attempts to recapture a lost paradise. They became deliberate, precise, imbued with a quiet melancholy that spoke of a love both profound and poignant. He painted landscapes reminiscent of Abby's world – sun-dappled meadows, whispering trees, and starlit skies – but they were infused with a personal touch, a subtle undercurrent of longing that added depth and complexity to his artwork.

His relationship with his family deepened. The guilt and self-absorption that had once consumed him gave way to a newfound appreciation for the simple joys of connection. He spent hours with his father, sharing stories, building a bond stronger than the walls that had previously separated them. His mother's love, once taken for granted, now felt like a precious gift, a constant source of comfort and support. He realized that true connection wasn't about escaping reality, but about fully engaging with it, finding beauty and meaning in the everyday moments shared with those closest to him.

He started to understand that his experience with Abby hadn't merely confined itself to their shared moments within the painting's world; it had seeped into his very being, changing him in ways he couldn't have ever imagined. His once-rigid routine had given way to a newfound appreciation for spontaneity, an understanding that life's greatest joys often came unexpectedly.

He sought out new experiences, embracing the unknown with a courage born out of the profound vulnerability he had encountered with Abby. His confidence soared not by silencing the echoes of his loss, but by weaving them into his present existence, accepting them as an integral part of his story.

His friendships, once strained by his absorption into the painting's world, blossomed anew. He shared his story, not with the expectation of sympathy, but with a quiet honesty that allowed others to see beyond the romanticized version of his experience. His friends listened, offering not empty platitudes, but genuine support, empathy, and unconditional acceptance. Their understanding helped him process his grief, validating his feelings and reinforcing the idea that his pain was a shared experience and not something to be isolated or ashamed of.

He found a quiet rhythm to his life, a balance between remembering and moving forward. He continued to visit the painting, but the intensity of his emotions had softened. He spent these visits not frantically searching for Abby, but observing the subtle changes in the fading colors, the slow deterioration of the canvas. The painting, once a portal to another world, became a contemplative space, a silent witness to his journey of healing and acceptance.

He didn't erase Abby from his memory, nor did he attempt to forget their extraordinary connection. Instead, he integrated her into the tapestry of his life, making her a part of his narrative, not as a source of pain, but as a source of strength and inspiration. He discovered that even in loss, there could be profound growth, a deepening of understanding and empathy for himself and the world around him.

His art evolved, reflecting this newfound equilibrium. His canvases were no longer filled with frantic brushstrokes conveying despair and longing. Instead, they were characterized by a balanced use of light and shadow, reflecting both the darkness of his loss and the resilience of his spirit. The vibrant colors, once emblematic of his all-consuming obsession, were now tempered by a deeper understanding of human emotion, a quiet contemplation that transcended the simplistic division between joy and sorrow.

He found himself drawn to stories of otherworldly romance, tales of love that defied the conventional boundaries of reality. He started writing novels that explored similar themes, blending fantastical elements with emotionally resonant characters whose journeys mirrored his own. He channeled his experience into his fiction, creating characters who found strength in their losses, who embraced the bittersweet nature of love, and who discovered the capacity for connection even in the face of heartbreak. His writing resonated deeply with readers who saw a reflection of their own lives within his tales, finding solace and hope in his portrayals of love, loss, and acceptance.

His success as an author solidified his sense of purpose, proving to him that his journey of healing could inspire and empower others. He used his platform to spreading a message of hope and resilience. He shared his story openly, challenging the stigma surrounding grief and encouraging others to embrace their own emotions without judgment.

The connection to Abby remained, not as an aching void, but as a quiet understanding, a persistent echo that resonated in the stillness of his heart. It was a connection that transcended the boundaries of reality, a love that had shaped his life in profound and unexpected ways. He carried her memory within him, not as a burden, but as a source of strength, a constant reminder of the transformative power of love, even in the face of heartbreak. The painting, once a symbol of impossible love, became a testament to his journey of healing and acceptance, a reminder that even in the darkest of times, where the human spirit could endure and find beauty in the echoes of the past. The faint scent of her favorite lavender, a lingering memory tucked away in his subconscious, served as a subtle, persistent reminder, a gentle whisper reminding him of the extraordinary love they had shared. His life was proof that even beyond the realms of physical reality, love could leave an enduring legacy.

Chapter 6
A New Beginning

The scent of rain on dry earth, a scent he'd always associated with Abby's world, drifted in through his open window. It wasn't the vibrant, almost overwhelming perfume of her world, but a softer, more muted version, a memory filtered through time and distance. He smiled, a small, knowing smile that spoke of acceptance and peace. The years hadn't erased the memory of Abby; they had simply reshaped it, molded it into a cornerstone of his being, a testament to a love that transcended the confines of reality. He no longer felt the gnawing emptiness that had once consumed him. The void had been filled, not with a replacement, but with a deeper understanding of himself, a more profound appreciation for the connections he had in his own world.

His family, once distant figures in the background of his obsession, were now central to his life, their love a constant source of strength and comfort. He cherished the ordinary moments—a shared meal with his father, a quiet evening spent reading with his mother—moments that were once overlooked, overshadowed by the intensity of his feelings for Abby.

His friendships had deepened too. He'd cautiously shared his story, not seeking pity, but offering a glimpse into the extraordinary journey he had undertaken. His friends listened, not with disbelief or judgment, but with understanding. They helped him navigate the complexities of his grief, validating his feelings, and reminding him that he wasn't alone in his experience. Their acceptance was a balm to his soul, a reminder that even the most fantastical experiences could be understood and shared.

His art had transformed. His canvases no longer screamed with the frantic energy of his obsession. Instead, they resonated with a quiet confidence, a newfound serenity that reflected his inner peace. The colors, once vibrant and intense, were now more nuanced, reflecting the complexities of his emotional landscape. He painted not just landscapes reminiscent of Abby's world, but scenes from his own life, infused with a gentle melancholy, a sense of quiet contemplation. His brushstrokes were deliberate, precise, each stroke carrying the weight of his experiences, the echoes of his journey.He continued to visit the painting, but his visits were different now. He no longer sought a reunion with Abby; he went to observe, to witness the slow, inexorable fading of the colors, the gentle disintegration of the canvas. The painting was no longer a portal to another world; it was a monument to a love that had irrevocably changed his life. It was a reminder of the ephemeral nature of time, the bittersweet beauty of a love that defied the constraints of reality.

He began to write again, not out of a desperate need to recapture Abby, but out of a desire to explore the themes that had shaped his own life. He penned stories that blended fantasy and realism, creating characters who grappled with loss, longing, and the enduring power of love. His writing resonated deeply with his readers, who found solace and understanding in his exploration of complex emotions. He discovered that his own journey of healing could provide comfort and inspiration to others, a testament to the universal nature of love, loss, and the transformative power of acceptance.

He found a new love, a love that was grounded in the reality of his present life. This love was not a replacement for Abby, but a testament to his capacity for connection and his ability to move forward while honoring the past. This new relationship was built on a foundation of shared experiences, mutual respect, and a deep understanding of the complexities of life and love. It was a love that enriched his life, adding another layer to the tapestry of his experiences, without diminishing the significance of his bond with Abby.

His life wasn't defined solely by his experience with Abby. It was a rich and complex tapestry woven from the threads of his relationships, his art, and his newfound understanding of himself and the world around him. He embraced the challenges and joys of his life with a newfound courage, his heart open to the possibilities of connection and growth. He realized that true happiness wasn't about escaping reality or denying his past, but about integrating his experiences, both joyful and painful, into the fabric of his present life.

86

He started mentoring young artists, sharing his experiences and offering guidance to those struggling with their own creative journeys. He found immense satisfaction in helping others find their voice, in nurturing their talents, and in reminding them that their art was a reflection of their own unique experiences and perspectives. He encouraged them to embrace their vulnerability, to draw strength from their experiences, and to create art that resonated with authenticity and emotion.

He began traveling extensively, seeking inspiration in new cultures and landscapes. He found beauty in the mundane, marveling at the intricate details of the natural world, finding inspiration in the unexpected encounters and the simple joys of everyday life. His travels expanded his perspective, enriching his understanding and deepening his appreciation for the diversity of experiences.

He continued to evolve as an artist, his style becoming more sophisticated, more nuanced, his brushstrokes more confident and deliberate. He explored new techniques, experimenting with different mediums and styles, constantly pushing the boundaries of his creativity. His art became a reflection of his journey, a testament to his resilience and his capacity for growth and transformation.

He understood that the painting wasn't just a portal to another world; it was a mirror reflecting his own journey of self-discovery. The fading colors weren't a symbol of loss but a reminder of the transient nature of all things, a reminder to cherish the present moment. Abby's world remained within the painting, but her essence, her spirit, resided within him, woven into the fabric of his being. It was a constant reminder of the transformative power of love, even in the face of loss.

He remained connected to the memory of Abby, not with a sense of grief or regret, but with a deep sense that mirrors gratitude. He cherished the memories, the lessons learned, the growth experienced. He had loved, had lost, and had emerged stronger, wiser, and more compassionate. He understood that loss wasn't an ending but a transformative process, a catalyst for growth and self-discovery. And in embracing the changes that Abby's presence had initiated, he discovered a deeper appreciation for the beauty and fragility of life, and the profound capacity for love, resilience, and connection. The world, once seen through the lens of his obsession, was now a vibrant canvas teeming with opportunities for connection, growth, and the quiet, enduring joy of a life lived fully and authentically. The faint scent of lavender, a lingering whisper of his extraordinary love, remained a gentle reminder of the transformative power of a love that defied the boundaries of reality.

The canvas stretched before him, a pristine expanse of white, mockingly blank yet brimming with untold possibilities. He hadn't touched a brush in months, the vibrant colors of Abby's world having faded, not just in the painting, but within his own soul. The emptiness he'd felt after their farewell had been a stark, echoing void, but now, a different kind of quiet had settled within him, a quiet that held the promise of creation.

It wasn't a rush to fill the void, to replace Abby with another image, another world. It was a gentle stirring, a reawakening of the creative spirit that had lain dormant, stifled by the all-consuming nature of his obsession. He picked up a brush, hesitant at first, the weight of it unfamiliar in his hand. The brush, a familiar tool, suddenly felt alien, as if a lifetime had passed since he last held it. He dipped it into the cobalt blue, a color he'd always associated with the depth of Abby's eyes, and with a trembling hand, made the first tentative stroke.

The initial strokes were hesitant, unsure, reflecting the uncertainty he still felt within himself. But as he continued, a rhythm emerged, a flow, a connection to something deeper than just paint and canvas. He wasn't trying to recreate Abby's world; he was expressing the emotions that had shaped him, the memories that remained etched in his soul. He painted the scent of rain on dry earth, the feeling of sun-warmed stone, the haunting melody of Abby's laughter, not as literal representations, but as emotional evocations, capturing the essence of what he had experienced.

He delved into a palette of muted tones, reflecting the subdued emotions he felt, the acceptance and peace that had settled over his life. The colors were rich and layered, reflecting the depth of his experiences and the complexity of his emotional journey. The vibrancy of his earlier work was gone, replaced by a more mature, thoughtful palette. He painted not with the desperate energy of obsession, but with the quiet confidence of someone who had wrestled with his demons and emerged victorious.

His landscapes were no longer idealized versions of Abby's world. They were subtly altered versions of the places he'd encountered in his life, the familiar streets of his childhood, the quiet parks of his youth, infusing them with a magical quality, a hint of the extraordinary woven into the mundane. He found beauty in the unexpected, in the unnoticed details, in the quiet moments that had once eluded his attention, consumed as he was by his obsession. He painted his family, their faces illuminated not by bright light, but by an inner glow of love and connection, a love he had only fully appreciated after his ordeal.

The paintings he created weren't mere reproductions of his memories; they were powerful expressions of his inner world, reflecting his journey of transformation and healing. Each brushstroke told a story, conveying the bittersweetness of loss, the enduring strength of love, and the transformative power of accepting what is. His art became a conduit for his emotions, a testament to his capacity for resilience, growth, and self-discovery.

He started showing his work, cautiously at first, then with growing confidence. His art resonated deeply with others, striking a chord within their own hearts. People saw in his paintings not just skillful technique, but a profound emotional depth, a reflection of their own experiences with love, loss, and healing. He received positive feedback, encouraging words that affirmed the value of his work, but more importantly, affirmed the value of his journey. The validation he received wasn't about external praise; it was about sharing his story and connecting with others.

His newfound success allowed him to focus entirely on his craft, and he began experimenting with new techniques and mediums. He pushed the boundaries of his artistic expression, exploring new ways to express the complex emotions that he had processed and transmuted into a more nuanced understanding of himself and the world around him. He tried sculpture, carving figures from stone that captured the essence of the characters from his past, and the spirits that had walked through his life, both real and imagined. He took up photography, capturing the transient beauty of light and shadow, translating the ephemeral nature of his past love into tangible, evocative images.

He found that his art had become his therapy, his escape, and his affirmation, a constant reminder of the transformative power of love, loss, and the indomitable spirit of the human heart. The vibrant colors of Abby's world now found their way into his palette, not as a frantic explosion of color, but as a subtle reminder, woven into the fabric of his work. The colors were used purposefully, carefully selected to convey not only emotion but also a quiet intensity, a strength that came from overcoming adversity.

His art became his legacy, a testament to his journey from obsession to acceptance, from despair to hope, from loss to love. He had transformed his pain into beauty, his grief into art, and in doing so, he had not only healed himself but had also offered a balm to the hearts of others. He understood now that his experience with Abby had not been a detour but a crucible, forging him into a stronger, more compassionate, and more profound artist. His canvas, once a battlefield of his emotions, was now a sanctuary.

He began teaching art to others, sharing his experiences and his knowledge, guiding young artists on their own journeys. He found immense satisfaction in nurturing talent, in helping others find their voices, in sharing the transformative power of art. He emphasized the importance of vulnerability, the necessity of expressing one's inner world, and the strength that comes from embracing the full spectrum of human emotions. He told them his story, not to shock or awe, but to offer a beacon of hope, to remind them that even the most extraordinary experiences could be transformed into something beautiful and lasting.

The faint scent of lavender, once a constant reminder of his loss, now held a different meaning. It was a fragrant whisper of a love that had profoundly shaped him, a love that had taught him the meaning of resilience and the power of artistic expression to heal and transcend. His past love had not been a tragedy, but a pivotal chapter in a life that was rich, complex, and full of purpose. His journey with Abby was a testament to the enduring power of love, a love that had transcended the boundaries of reality and time, leaving an indelible mark on his soul and shaping him into the artist he was destined to become. He had found his passion again, not in the pursuit of a lost love, but in the embrace of a new beginning, a beginning painted in the vibrant colors of his transformed soul. And in the quiet moments, when the world fell silent, he could still hear the faint whisper of Abby's laughter, a reminder of a love that continued to inspire him, to guide him, and to fuel the fire of his artistic expression.

The gallery opening buzzed with a low hum of conversation, a stark contrast to the quiet solitude of his studio. David stood near his latest collection, a series of landscapes imbued with a subtle, ethereal quality. He'd chosen to showcase pieces that weren't overtly fantastical, eschewing the direct depiction of Abby's world. Instead, he'd channeled the experience—the emotions, the lingering magic— into landscapes that felt both familiar and otherworldly. He watched as people paused before his paintings, their faces etched with contemplation, sometimes a quiet understanding that mirrored his own journey.

He saw his mother approach, a hesitant smile playing on her lips. Months of strained silences and unspoken anxieties had finally begun to thaw. Their reconciliation hadn't been a sudden burst of affection, but a slow, deliberate process of rebuilding trust. He'd begun to truly appreciate the quiet strength of her love, a love he'd almost taken for granted in his obsession with Abby.

"They're... beautiful, David," she said softly, her voice thick with emotion. She touched the frame of a painting depicting a sun-drenched field, the colors muted yet vibrant, radiating a sense of calm strength. "You've... changed."

He smiled, a genuine smile that reached his eyes. "I have," he admitted. "I think I've finally learned to see the beauty in the ordinary." The words felt true, a testament to his growth. He'd learned to appreciate the simple things: the warmth of his mother's embrace, the laughter of his friends, the comforting weight of his cousin's hand on his shoulder.

His cousin, George, joined them, his usual boisterous energy tempered by a quiet respect for the solemnity of the occasion. George, too, had witnessed his descent into obsession, his withdrawal from their lives. Now, he saw a different David, one who was more present, more engaged, more grounded. Their bond, once fractured, was slowly being mended. He was starting to rediscover his relationship with George, their bond stronger than ever. He found it easier to laugh with him, to share stories without the weight of his secret weighing them down. George teased him about his newfound artistic talents, which helped to loosen the tightness in his chest. They played video games, the familiar sounds of the game acting as a bridge that transported them back to the days before Abby's existence had come to dominate his world. They found peace in the simplicity of these shared moments, in their mutual understanding of love, loss, and the process of healing.

Later that evening, he found himself talking to Denise, a fellow artist he'd met at a workshop. Their conversations had started with a shared appreciation for a particular technique, but they'd quickly moved beyond the technical aspects of art to delve into deeper, more personal territory. They shared stories of their artistic journeys, their struggles, their triumphs, and their anxieties, finding a connection that went beyond their shared profession. They spoke of loss and grief, of the healing power of creativity, and of the importance of vulnerability in artistic expression. Their bond, he realized, was built on mutual understanding, on a shared empathy that had grown stronger with each conversation. They met for coffee, their time together slowly transforming into friendship, a deep connection that felt almost as magical as the connection he once felt with Abby. He valued this new friendship, cherished it and nurtured it, allowing himself to be vulnerable and open in a way he hadn't before.

He attended local art classes, reconnecting with his passion for art outside the confines of his own self-imposed isolation. There, he met a group of diverse and talented individuals, each with their own unique stories and perspectives. The collective energy of the group was inspirational and filled David with a sense of belonging he hadn't felt before. He discovered a community that offered him support, encouragement, and a renewed sense of purpose. He was no longer alone, lost in his memories, but was immersed in a community that shared his passions and values. His journey into healing was not only a solitary one, but a collaborative process that involved supportive individuals from his family, his community, and his chosen profession.

His renewed engagement with life wasn't merely about rebuilding his broken relationships; it was about forging new ones, ones rooted in mutual respect, understanding, and a shared appreciation for the complexities of human experience. He found himself drawn to people who, like him, had faced adversity and emerged stronger, their resilience etched onto their faces. He saw reflected in them not just his past experiences, but his present strength and his future hopes. He was learning to accept his experience with Abby not as something to be avoided or erased, but as a significant life experience that had brought him to this place of healing and renewal. His new friendships enriched his life, bringing a new layer of depth and connection, and reminded him of the power of connection to overcome loss and cultivate hope.

He took his healing even further by volunteering at the local community center, teaching art to underprivileged children. The joy on their faces as they discovered the magic of creating, the pride in their eyes when they completed a project, filled him with a deep sense of satisfaction. He found a profound sense of purpose in sharing his gift, in nurturing the creative spark in others. The experience brought a renewed sense of gratitude into his life, allowing him to focus his energies outward, rather than dwelling on his own personal loss. He learned to love again, not in the sense of romantic love, but in the sense of brotherly love, parental love, and familial love, and most importantly, self-love.

The past months had been a transformative period. He was no longer haunted by the fading image of Abby. Her memory remained, a poignant reminder of a love that transcended boundaries, but it no longer cast a shadow over his life. He had learned to carry that memory with grace, integrating it into the rich tapestry of his experiences. He accepted that this was part of his life experience, and not something to be ignored or pushed away. He learned to see his journey not as a tragedy, but as a testament to his strength and resilience. The pain and anguish he had endured had served as a crucible that shaped him, refined him, and ultimately, made him a stronger, more compassionate individual.

He'd learned that life wasn't about avoiding pain, but about navigating it with courage, grace, and a willingness to embrace the uncertainties of the future. He had rediscovered the joy of creation, not only in the realm of art but in all aspects of his life. He had cultivated meaningful relationships and found solace in a supportive community. He was building a life richer and more fulfilling than he could have ever imagined, a life infused with the resilience and compassion that had blossomed from the ashes of his past. And although the memory of Abby would always hold a special place in his heart, he knew he was finally ready to embrace his new beginning, a beginning painted in the vibrant hues of hope, healing, and enduring love. The faint scent of lavender still lingered, but it was now a whisper of a memory, softly woven into the rich and vibrant fabric of his life's new masterpiece.

The quiet hum of the city outside his window was a soothing counterpoint to the turmoil within. He'd spent the last few weeks meticulously organizing his studio, a process that felt oddly therapeutic. Each painting, each brushstroke, each discarded sketch held a piece of his past, a fragment of his journey with Abby. He hadn't thrown anything away; instead, he'd carefully cataloged everything, creating a visual record of his evolution. It wasn't about forgetting, he realized, but about understanding. Understanding the depth of his loss, the intensity of his love, and the inevitability of change.

He picked up a small, unassuming sketch – a quick study of Abby's face, captured in a fleeting moment of laughter. The lines were rough, the shading imperfect, yet it held a vibrancy that no finished masterpiece could replicate. He traced the lines with a fingertip, a wave of bittersweet nostalgia washing over him. It wasn't just a drawing; it was a memory, a tangible representation of a feeling so profound it still held the power to both exhilarate and break his heart. He wasn't trying to erase her from his memories; he was learning to integrate her into the narrative of his life, accepting her presence as an integral part of who he had become.

This wasn't about forgetting; it was about remembering differently. It was about shifting the focus from the loss itself to the lessons he'd learned, the growth he'd experienced. It was about celebrating the joy, the magic, the extraordinary love that had bloomed amidst the impossible. The memory of her laughter, her kindness, her fierce spirit, these were the things he wanted to hold onto. He would treasure those images, but not as anchors, not as burdens, but as precious stones of experience, each one adding to the sparkle of his life's ongoing journey.

He spent hours pouring over old photographs, letters, and journals, meticulously documenting his experiences in a way that felt both cathartic and strangely empowering. The process of revisiting his past wasn't a painful excavation, but a gentle unfolding. He found himself not dwelling on the sorrow of their separation, but rather on the beauty and uniqueness of their bond. The time he had spent with her was a precious gift, a memory that had shaped him fundamentally. It was a part of his life story, and it was a story he would always tell.

He realized that grief wasn't a linear process; it wasn't a neat progression from sadness to acceptance. It was a complex, multifaceted emotion, a tapestry woven with threads of sorrow, anger, regret, and ultimately, peace. There were days when the pain was sharp, intense, a physical ache in his chest. And there were days when a gentle wave of serenity washed over him, when the memory of Abby brought a smile to his lips rather than tears to his eyes. It was about accepting the ebb and flow of grief, acknowledging its presence without letting it consume him. It was learning to live alongside his memories, to find peace in the presence of his loss.

He began to understand that his experience with Abby wasn't an ending, but a transition. It was a chapter in his life, a significant one, but not the final chapter. He had reached a point where he could acknowledge the beauty and magic of their connection without feeling the crippling pain of separation. The intensity of his emotions hadn't lessened; they had simply been recontextualized. They had become a source of strength, resilience, and profound understanding.

He found solace in the simple pleasures of life, appreciating the warmth of the sun on his face, the laughter of children at play, the comforting silence of a quiet evening. He allowed himself to experience joy again, not as a betrayal of his past, but as a testament to his resilience. He was learning to live fully, to embrace the present moment, to find beauty in the ordinary.

He sought out support from friends and family, allowing himself to be vulnerable and accepting of their comfort. The support system he cultivated was not simply a collection of individuals, but a vital network of relationships that offered him guidance and reassurance. He discovered the importance of being open and honest about his feelings, allowing himself to be supported rather than attempting to navigate his grief in isolation.

He learned that grief wasn't something to be overcome, but something to be lived with, something to be integrated into the fabric of one's life. It was a testament to the depth of his love for Abby, a reminder of the intense and transformative experiences that had shaped him. He accepted that his memories of Abby would always hold a special place in his heart, shaping his perspective and influencing his choices, but they wouldn't define him. His life extended beyond that experience. He was building a new life, a life filled with love, joy, and a profound appreciation for the beauty and fragility of existence. The vibrant hues of his new beginnings were not meant to replace his past, but rather to complement it, adding to the richness and complexity of his life's masterpiece. He was no longer defined by his loss, but by his ability to carry its memory with grace, integrating it into the extraordinary tapestry of his life.

The scent of linseed oil and turpentine, familiar and comforting, hung in the air of his studio. Sunlight streamed through the large north-facing window, illuminating dust that danced in the golden beams. David ran a hand over the smooth surface of a new canvas, the pristine white a stark contrast to the emotional landscape he carried within him. He'd spent months wrestling with his grief, navigating the turbulent waters of loss, but a new current was beginning to pull him forward. It wasn't a forgetting, not truly. It was an acceptance, a quiet understanding that the extraordinary love he'd shared with Abby wasn't lost but transformed. It existed in the memories he cherished, in the paintings he created, in the subtle shift in his perspective on life itself.

He picked up a paintbrush, its bristles soft against his fingertips. He hadn't touched his paints with the same intensity since…since he'd said goodbye to Abby. The act of painting had always been a conduit for his emotions, a way to translate the invisible into the visible. But after their parting, the canvas had felt like a mirror reflecting only emptiness. Now, though, a different kind of emptiness existed – one pregnant with possibility. This wasn't the bleak emptiness of loss, but the expectant emptiness of a new beginning.

He started with a gentle wash of cerulean, a color that reminded him of Abby's eyes – the same clear, vibrant blue that had held a universe of emotions. But this wasn't a portrait; this was a landscape. He layered in strokes of emerald green, evoking the lush Victorian park she'd called home within the painting. He added touches of gold, the shimmering light filtering through the leaves, reminiscent of the golden sunlight that often bathed the park in Abby's world. Slowly, carefully, he built his scene, imbuing the canvas with the essence of their love, not as a literal representation, but as an emotional echo.

This painting was different. It wasn't a desperate attempt to recapture the past, but a celebration of the present, a testament to the enduring power of their connection. He painted the trees, their branches reaching towards a sky that was both bright and subtly melancholic – reflecting the bittersweet beauty of his memories. He painted the paths, winding their way through the greenery, symbolizing the meandering journey of his own life, a journey forever touched by his time with Abby. He didn't paint Abby herself; instead, he painted her absence, her lingering presence in the air, felt in the gentle rustling of the leaves, in the soft glow of the light.

He spent weeks on the painting, pouring his heart and soul onto the canvas. It wasn't easy. There were moments when the pain threatened to overwhelm him, when the memory of their parting threatened to engulf him. But he persevered, fueled by a desire to honor their love, to give it a form that transcended the limitations of reality. As he painted, he felt Abby's presence, not as a physical entity, but as a whisper, a gentle nudge reminding him of the strength and resilience she'd instilled in him.

When the painting was finished, it was more than just a picture; it was a portal. It held the essence of their extraordinary connection, a visual representation of a love that had transcended the boundaries of time and space. It was a reminder of the magic they had shared, of the beauty they had created, of the lasting impact their bond had had on his life. It was a piece of his soul, laid bare on the canvas.

He started to paint more. Each canvas was a new chapter in the story of his healing, a testament to his growing acceptance of his loss and his increasing embrace of his new life. He experimented with different styles, different colors, different approaches, but each painting carried a thread of Abby's essence – a subtle reminder of the transformative power of their love. His art became a reflection of his inner world, his thoughts, his feelings, his healing process. It was a journey of self-discovery, a testament to his ability to move forward while carrying the precious memories of his past.

One day, a gallery owner, captivated by his unique style and the profound emotions embedded in his work, invited David to showcase his collection. Hesitantly, he agreed. It was a step outside his comfort zone, a way of sharing his experiences with the world. The exhibition was a success. Critics praised his unique perspective, his ability to capture the essence of emotion through color and texture. A few strangers wrote to him, sharing their own stories of loss and healing, finding solace and inspiration in his art.

The success of his exhibition wasn't just about recognition or validation; it was about connecting. It was about reaching out, sharing his vulnerability, and realizing that his journey, his love, his loss, were not unique but universal experiences. Through his art, he built bridges, fostering connections with others who had walked similar paths. He discovered a new purpose, a new meaning in his life: using his art to help others navigate the turbulent waters of grief and find their own path towards healing.

Through his painting, he found not only a way to express his grief but also to honor his love for Abby. He realized that true love didn't end with physical separation; it lived on in memory, in the impact it had on one's life, in the changes it inspired. His love for Abby became the foundation of his resilience, the wellspring of his creative energy, and the guiding light in his journey towards a new beginning. It was a love that transcended the boundaries of reality, a legacy etched not just in his heart but also in the vibrant hues and emotive strokes on his canvases.

His story, the extraordinary journey of love and loss, became a testament to the human capacity for resilience, a narrative woven into the fabric of his life. It wasn't a tragic tale of unrequited love, but a saga of profound connection, transformative experiences, and the enduring power of human spirit. It became a story that resonated with others, offering hope and comfort, proving that even in the face of heartbreaking loss, life continues, love endures, and healing is always possible. The legacy of his love for Abby wasn't a burden, but a gift – a gift that enriched his life, fueled his creativity, and shaped him into the person he was meant to be.

He found a new love, a love that complemented the extraordinary love he'd shared with Abby, a love that embraced his past, but didn't define his future. This new love understood the depth of his past, the richness of his memories, and the strength he'd cultivated through his loss. It was a love that didn't seek to replace Abby, but to stand alongside her in the tapestry of his life. It was a love that recognized the unique marks left by his past but that also celebrated the vibrant potential of his future. It was a love that added depth and dimension to his life, a testament to his capacity to love and to live fully.

David's life became a testament to the enduring power of love, a story of transformation, and a celebration of his resilience. His art served as a bridge connecting his past and his present, a beacon of hope for others navigating their own journeys of grief and healing. His story is not only a tale of extraordinary love but also a compelling illustration of the transformative power of resilience, a story that emphasizes that while life inevitably presents challenges, it is our ability to embrace, learn from, and integrate them that ultimately defines our journey. The legacy of his love for Abby remained, woven into the fabric of his being, a reminder of the extraordinary beauty of a love that transcended the boundaries of reality. And it was a legacy that continued to inspire and uplift him, and through his art, many others. His life, a masterpiece in progress, continued to evolve, a vibrant testament to the enduring power of love and the remarkable capacity of the human heart to heal.

Chapter 7
The Art of Letting Go

The weight of his decision settled upon him like a cloak of lead, heavy yet strangely comforting. He hadn't anticipated the quietude that followed the storm of his emotions, the almost serene acceptance that had bloomed in the wake of his farewell to Abby. He hadn't anticipated the profound sense of peace that permeated his being, a counterpoint to the echoing emptiness of his studio after he'd ceased his daily pilgrimages to her world within the painting. He'd sacrificed a love beyond measure, a love that had defied the very fabric of reality, a love that had painted his world in vibrant, breathtaking hues. Yet, in relinquishing that extraordinary connection, he'd paradoxically discovered a new kind of freedom.

It wasn't a simple exchange, this letting go. It wasn't a mere extinguishing of a flame, but a careful, conscious transformation of its energy. He'd channeled the intensity of his love, the fiery passion that had consumed him, and transmuted it into something new, something more enduring. His art became the vessel for this metamorphosis, the canvas a testament to the enduring power of his sacrifice. Each stroke of the brush was a prayer, each color a memory, each composition a chapter in the ongoing narrative of his heart.

He found solace in the repetitive rhythm of his work, the methodical layering of colors, the delicate balance of light and shadow. It was a meditation, a slow, deliberate process of healing. He painted not just landscapes, but emotions – the bittersweet longing, the quiet acceptance, the burgeoning hope that had begun to take root within him. He didn't shy away from the sadness; he embraced it, incorporated it into the very fabric of his art, transforming it from a debilitating force into a source of strength, resilience, and profound understanding.

The act of creation became a ritual, a sacred space where he could confront his grief without being consumed by it. He found that the canvas was not a mere surface but a portal, a conduit connecting his past, present, and future. It allowed him to revisit their shared moments, to relive the incandescent beauty of their love, without being trapped in the pain of its loss. The paintings became a form of self-therapy, a way of processing his emotions, of making sense of the inexplicable, of finding order amidst the chaos.

The sacrifice had been necessary, he understood. He'd learned that true love sometimes demanded a letting go, a willingness to surrender in order to preserve what was most precious. His presence, he'd realized, was slowly eroding Abby's world, fading the vibrant colors of her existence, threatening to extinguish the very light of her being. To remain would have been a selfish act, a clinging to his own desires at the expense of her well-being. His choice had been agonizing, but it had been borne of a deep and profound love. It was an act of selflessness, a testament to the transformative power of sacrifice.

He often revisited the painting, the one that held Abby's world. It was fading, yes, but not in a way that reflected a complete loss. The edges were softening, the colors less intense, but there was still a subtle glow, a faint luminosity that suggested a lingering presence, a quiet vitality. It was a testament to the enduring nature of their connection, a reminder that some loves transcend the limitations of time and space. The painting became a sacred object, a tangible symbol of his love, a precious relic of an extraordinary period in his life.

He started to see his sacrifice not as an ending but as a transformation. It was the shedding of a skin, the transition from one stage of his life to another. It was a letting go that allowed for a new beginning, a new chapter in the ongoing story of his existence. He learned that loss doesn't erase memories; it simply rearranges them, reshapes them, imbuing them with a deeper, more profound significance.

His grief became the source of his creativity, a constant companion that inspired his art, giving it depth, complexity, and an undeniable emotional resonance. He found himself creating works of such emotional intensity that they transcended the boundaries of mere artistry, touching the hearts of those who viewed them. His art became

102

a conduit for empathy, a language that spoke to the universal human experience of love, loss, and the enduring capacity for healing.

His journey towards healing wasn't a linear path; it was a winding road, full of ups and downs, setbacks and breakthroughs. There were times when the pain threatened to overwhelm him, when the memories were too sharp, too raw. But he persevered, drawing strength from his love for Abby, from his acceptance of his sacrifice, and from the profound satisfaction he derived from his art.

He began to understand that letting go doesn't equate to forgetting. It is a conscious decision to release something that is no longer serving you, to make space for new growth and new beginnings. It is the recognition that some things, however precious, must come to an end to make way for other forms of life, other forms of love, other forms of beauty. It was a lesson learned not in theory but through the crucible of experience, forged in the fires of profound loss and ultimately tempered by the resilience of his spirit and the sustaining power of his art.

His decision to let go of Abby, to sacrifice their extraordinary connection, became a testament to the depth of his love. It wasn't a rejection of her, but an act of profound selflessness, a willingness to prioritize her well-being even if it meant enduring immense personal pain. He discovered that true love isn't always about possession or control; it is about acceptance, sacrifice, and the unwavering commitment to another's happiness, even if it means one's own loss.

The significance of his sacrifice began to unfold slowly, organically, like a flower opening its petals to the sun. He recognized it wasn't a tragic ending but a poignant turning point, a pivotal moment that reshaped his identity, his perspectives, and the very course of his life. It was a pivotal experience that deepened his understanding of love, loss, and the resilience of his spirit, leading him to profound growth, profound creativity, and the eventual capacity to embrace a new love, a love that valued the depth and breadth of his past experiences, both joys and sorrows, and that embraced his transformed self.

His life after Abby wasn't a void, but a canvas teeming with possibility, with new colors and textures, new patterns and perspectives. His art became a bridge connecting his past and his future, a celebration of both the extraordinary love he'd shared and the enduring power of his own resilience. The painting of Abby, though fading, retained its essence, a timeless reminder of a love that transcended the physical realm, a love that continued to inspire and shape him, enriching his life, his art, and his very being. His life after Abby, then, was not an ending but an evolution, a continued exploration of life, love, and the enduring power of the human spirit. He had let go, yes, but not without transforming the essence of that extraordinary connection into a lasting testament to the extraordinary power of love, sacrifice, and the capacity for resilience.

The scent of linseed oil and turpentine, once a comforting aroma associated with his daily ritual of visiting Abby, now held a bittersweet tang. It was a reminder, a phantom touch of the past, a ghost of a life lived beyond the confines of ordinary reality. He'd traded that reality for a different kind of existence, one painted in the quieter, subtler hues of his own solitary world. Yet, the vibrant colors of his time with Abby refused to fade entirely.

He found himself inexplicably drawn to the old photographs he'd taken, the ones capturing stolen moments with Abby amidst the Victorian splendor of her painted world. Each image was a portal, a key unlocking a flood of memories – the sun dappling through leaves, the feel of her hand in his, the shared laughter echoing in the silent spaces between the trees. They weren't just snapshots; they were emotional time capsules, preserving the essence of their ephemeral romance. He pored over them, not with melancholic resignation, but with a sense of profound gratitude.

These weren't merely memories; they were the building blocks of his new reality, the foundation upon which he was constructing a life informed by loss, yet filled with a surprising sense of peace. He realized that letting go wasn't an erasure, but a transformation. It wasn't about forgetting Abby but about integrating the profound impact of his experience with her into the tapestry of his being.

His understanding of memory shifted. It wasn't a static collection of images and sensations; it was a living, breathing entity, constantly evolving, reshaping itself in the crucible of time and experience. Each time he revisited a memory, it was subtly altered, enriched, refined, not by conscious manipulation, but by the passage of time, the accumulation of new experiences, the quiet wisdom of his own evolving self. The memories of Abby, once sharp with pain, now held a softer, more nuanced quality, imbued with a melancholic beauty that resonated with the quiet grace of acceptance.

He began to see his memories not as burdens, but as gifts, precious relics of a life lived intensely, passionately, beyond the ordinary. They were threads woven into the rich tapestry of his existence, giving depth and complexity to his life, informing his art, and ultimately shaping the man he was becoming. The memories of Abby, far from being a source of unrelenting grief, became a wellspring of inspiration, fueling his creativity and enriching his personal growth. His art, previously a means of escape, now became a means of expression, a way of processing, understanding, and ultimately celebrating the extraordinary love he'd experienced.

The landscapes he painted were no longer simply representations of physical space; they became canvases imbued with emotion, reflecting the spectrum of his experiences with Abby. The vibrant greens of the park, the deep blues of the sky, the warm yellows of the sunlight – all carried the imprint of his memories, each color stroke a silent testament to their shared moments.

He delved deeper into his creative process, exploring new techniques, experimenting with different styles, pushing the boundaries of his own artistic abilities. He wasn't simply painting; he was sculpting emotions, translating the intangible into tangible form. His paintings became mirrors reflecting his inner world, a vibrant and evolving landscape mirroring the complexity of his grief, his acceptance, and his burgeoning hope.

His art became a form of self-discovery, a journey of self-healing. He discovered that the process of creation was itself a cathartic experience, a powerful tool for processing his emotions, confronting his pain, and ultimately finding peace. Through his art, he was able to confront the painful reality of his loss while simultaneously celebrating the extraordinary beauty of the love he'd shared with Abby.

The memories of their shared laughter, their whispered conversations, their stolen kisses, these weren't simply recollections; they were the lifeblood of his art. He poured his heart onto the canvas, translating the intangible essence of his feelings into powerful, emotionally resonant images. He realized that the memories of Abby were not confined to the confines of his mind; they were woven into the fabric of his existence, shaping his perceptions, influencing his choices, and ultimately defining the person he was becoming.

He understood that letting go didn't mean forgetting. It meant accepting, integrating, and transforming. It meant cherishing the memories, acknowledging their power, and harnessing their energy to fuel his growth, his creativity, and his capacity for future love.

He started receiving invitations to small exhibitions, showcasing his work to a wider audience. The paintings, filled with a raw emotional intensity, resonated deeply with viewers. People were moved, touched, inspired by the depth of feeling expressed in his art. They saw not merely landscapes or portraits but reflections of the human condition, the universal experience of love, loss, and the enduring power of memory.

He learned to balance the memories of Abby with the demands of his present life. He built new relationships, cautiously at first, then with increasing confidence. He learned that love wasn't a finite resource; it was an ever-expanding capacity, capable of encompassing both the joys and sorrows of the past, the present, and the future.

He discovered that his love for Abby had not diminished; it had simply been transformed. It had become a part of him, woven into the fabric of his being, shaping his character, enriching his soul, inspiring his art. He found that he carried Abby with him, not as a ghost of the past, but as a vibrant and enduring presence, a testament to the profound power of love and memory.

His journey was far from over. It was an ongoing process of integration, healing, and growth. He embraced the complexity of his experiences, recognizing that the pain and joy, the loss and the love, were all integral parts of the rich tapestry of his life. And in the quiet moments, when the world fell silent, he could still hear the faint echoes of Abby's laughter, a sweet, melancholic melody that resonated deep within his soul, a testament to the enduring power of memory and a love that transcended time and space. The power of memory, he realized, wasn't about clinging to the past but about integrating it into the present, transforming it into a source of strength, resilience, and ongoing inspiration, a foundation upon which he could build a life both fulfilling and meaningful.

The fading colors of the painting weren't a sign of complete loss, but a gentle transition, a subtle shift towards a new chapter, a testament to his personal growth, and to the power of memories to shape and define a life lived fully and bravely. He continued to paint, to create, to live, embracing the full spectrum of human emotion, carrying the weight of his past with grace and courage, transforming his memories into art, and his art into a legacy.

The autumn leaves, a fiery tapestry of reds and golds, swirled around his feet as David walked through the park, the crisp air invigorating his lungs. The familiar scent of damp earth and decaying leaves replaced the lingering smell of linseed oil and turpentine, a subtle but significant shift in the landscape of his senses. He'd spent weeks, months even, immersed in the melancholic beauty of his memories, allowing the grief to wash over him, cleanse him, and ultimately, to transform him. Now, a quiet calm had settled over him, a sense of acceptance that felt both fragile and profoundly strong.

He hadn't forgotten Abby. How could he? Her laughter still echoed in the silent spaces between the trees, a faint melody that resonated deep within his soul. But the sharp edges of his grief had softened, rounded by time and the conscious effort he'd made to integrate his experience with her into the fabric of his being. He carried her in his heart, not as a phantom pain, but as a treasured memory, a source of inspiration and strength.

His art had become a testament to this transformation. The paintings he created were no longer solely expressions of his loss, but vibrant explorations of hope, resilience, and the enduring power of love. He experimented with bolder colors, more dynamic compositions, allowing the canvas to become a mirror reflecting not just his past, but the exciting possibilities of his future. His brushstrokes, once tentative and hesitant, now flowed with confidence, a testament to his growing self-assurance.

He received a commission, a semi-prestigious opportunity to create a mural for the city's new art gallery. The theme was "Transformation," a fitting subject given his personal journey. He envisioned a sweeping panorama, a landscape that would shift and evolve, reflecting the cyclical nature of life, death, and rebirth. He knew, intuitively, that Abby would be a part of this piece, not as a central figure, but as an integral element, a subtle whisper woven into the grand narrative of the mural.

He started sketching, the charcoal moving across the paper with a newfound freedom. The initial design featured a forest, its trees reaching towards a vibrant sky, their branches intertwined, symbolizing the interconnectedness of all things. As he worked, the forest morphed and changed, reflecting the various stages of his transformation – from the deep shadows of grief to the emerging light of acceptance and hope. He incorporated subtle details, hidden symbols, personal reminders of his time with Abby – a single crimson leaf, a delicate butterfly, a splash of unexpected blue, reminiscent of her eyes.

He spent months on the mural, immersing himself in the project with a fervor that surprised even him. It was more than just a painting; it was an act of self-expression and his willingness to embrace the future while honoring the past. The process was challenging, demanding, but intensely satisfying. He poured his heart and soul into the artwork, allowing the canvas to become a vessel for his emotions, his experiences, his hopes.

As the mural neared completion, he felt a sense of profound peace, a quiet confidence that settled within him. He'd faced his demons, confronted his grief, and emerged stronger, more resilient, and more deeply connected to his own creative power. The mural wasn't just a representation of his personal journey; it was a testament to our capacity for love, loss, and the enduring power of hope.

The unveiling of the mural was a resounding success. Critics praised its emotional depth, its technical brilliance, its ability to evoke a wide range of emotions in the viewer. The public, too, responded with enthusiasm, drawn to the artwork's raw honesty and its powerful message of transformation. David received accolades, recognition, and a sense of validation that went beyond mere professional success. It confirmed his belief in his talent, his resilience, and the transformative power of art.

But more importantly, the experience helped him to solidify his understanding of moving on. It wasn't about forgetting Abby or erasing the profound impact she had on his life. It was about integrating her into his story, recognizing her as an essential part of his past, while simultaneously embracing the possibilities of his future.

He began to receive invitations to speak at regional art schools and conferences, sharing his personal story and the creative process behind his work. He found that his experiences resonated deeply with others, reminding them of the transformative power of art, the importance of confronting grief, and the beauty of finding hope in the face of loss. His story became a beacon of light, a reminder that even in the deepest darkness, you can find a way to emerge stronger and more resilient.

His personal life also flourished. He developed new, meaningful relationships, friendships and romantic connections that brought joy and companionship into his life. He learned to cherish the present moment without dwelling on the past, recognizing that love is not a finite resource, but an ever-expanding capacity, capable of encompassing both the joys and sorrows of his life. He understood that while love could transform, it didn't have to disappear. His love for Abby, though altered, remained a profound and enduring force in his life, shaping his character, inspiring his art, and enriching his soul. He learned that memories aren't just reminders of the past, but a powerful source of inspiration, guiding him towards a future filled with creativity, connection, and purpose.

He continued to paint, to create, to live, embracing the full spectrum of human emotion. He carried the weight of his past with grace and courage, transforming his memories into art, and his art into a legacy. He'd learned that letting go wasn't about forgetting; it was about accepting, integrating, and transforming. It was about cherishing the memories, acknowledging their power, and harnessing their energy to fuel his growth, creativity, and capacity for future love.

His art became a bridge, connecting his past, present, and future – a testament to the enduring power of love and his resilience. The fading colors of the painting weren't a sign of complete loss, but a gentle transition, a subtle shift towards a new chapter, a testament to his personal growth and the power of memories to shape and define a life lived fully and bravely. He understood the vital importance of integration, healing, and growth, recognizing that pain and joy, loss and love, were integral parts of the rich tapestry of his life. The echoes of Abby's laughter, though fainter now, still resonated deep within his soul – a beautiful, melancholic melody, a testament to the lasting power of love that transcended time and space. And as he continued to paint, he knew that he carried a piece of Abby's world, her spirit, within his own. The memories of their extraordinary love weren't just memories; they were the very threads of his being.

The realization dawned on him gradually, like the slow unfolding of a flower. It wasn't a sudden epiphany, a dramatic shift in perspective, but a quiet understanding that settled deep within him, a gentle acceptance of the inherent impermanence of life. He began to see the beauty in the fleeting nature of things, the ephemeral quality of existence that gave each moment its unique intensity, its preciousness. He saw it in the changing seasons, in the way the light shifted across the canvas of the sky, in the transient beauty of a blooming flower, its vibrant colors fading as gracefully as it emerged.

This new perspective extended beyond the natural world, seeping into his understanding of relationships, memories, and even his own identity. He realized that everything is in constant flux, in a perpetual state of becoming. Nothing remains static; everything is subject to the relentless march of time, a river constantly flowing, ever-changing, ever-moving towards an unknown destination.

He thought about Abby, her image still vivid in his memory, her laughter still echoing in the quiet spaces of his heart. The pain of their separation had lessened, the sharp edges softened by time, yet the depth of his love for her remained undiminished. He understood now that the intensity of their connection wasn't diminished by its impermanence but rather enhanced by it. It was the very transience of their shared experience that made it so profoundly precious, so deeply etched into the fabric of his being.

He remembered the way the light danced on her hair, the sparkle in her eyes, the warmth of her touch. These weren't just memories; they were vibrant fragments of a shared reality, infused with the bittersweet beauty of impermanence. He cherished them not as static images frozen in time, but as dynamic experiences that continued to evolve and resonate within him, shaping his understanding of love and loss.

His art reflected this newfound appreciation for impermanence. He further experimented with techniques that emphasized the ephemeral nature of his subjects. He used washes of color, allowing the pigments to blend and diffuse, creating soft, indistinct forms that hinted at movement and change. He incorporated elements of decay and regeneration into his work, representing the cyclical nature of life and the beauty that could be found in both creation and destruction. He embraced the unexpected accidents of the creative process, the unpredictable splatters and drips of paint, recognizing them not as mistakes but as opportunities for spontaneous expression, mirroring the unpredictable nature of life itself.

He began to see the world through a different lens, appreciating the subtle nuances of change, the delicate dance between presence and absence, between creation and decay. The fall of leaves, once a symbol of loss, now resonated with a deeper meaning; it was a reminder of the cyclical nature of life, of the constant cycle of death and rebirth that sustains the natural world. He found beauty in the decaying leaves, in their transformation from vibrant green to fiery red and gold, before finally returning to the earth to nourish new life.

He saw the impermanence in the shifting sands of a desert, the ever-changing coastline, the ephemeral nature of clouds in the sky. Each moment was a unique creation, a fleeting glimpse into the infinite variety of life's expression, and he sought to capture these fleeting moments, to translate the ephemeral essence of nature into the enduring language of art. His brushstrokes, once deliberate and precise, became more fluid, more expressive, reflecting the natural flow of life itself. His paintings were no longer static representations of the world but dynamic expressions of change, movement, and transformation.

He started visiting the old Victorian park again, not with the same sense of grief, but with a profound appreciation for the memories it held. The familiar paths, the trees that had witnessed his joy and sorrow, were now imbued with a new significance. They represented the passage of time, the constant flux of life, and the enduring power of memories to shape his identity. The park itself had changed, the leaves transformed, the light shifted, yet it remained a constant in his life, a silent witness to his personal journey. He understood the park's impermanence, its constant state of flux, just as he accepted his own continuous evolution. The changes weren't a loss; they were a testament to the enduring power of nature and the beauty of impermanence.

He realized that letting go wasn't about forgetting Abby, or erasing the profound impact she had on his life, but about integrating her into the larger narrative of his existence. Their love story wasn't a closed chapter, but a significant part of his ongoing journey, a source of inspiration and strength. The memories of their time together, though tinged with sadness, were not burdens but precious gifts, shaping his perspective, influencing his art, and enriching his capacity for love.

His relationships with others also evolved, reflecting his newfound acceptance of impermanence. He understood that connections, like all things, are subject to change, and he embraced the ebb and flow of human interaction with grace and compassion. He cherished the present moment, recognizing its fleeting nature and the importance of nurturing his relationships. He learned that love isn't static; it is a dynamic force, capable of both profound joy and heartbreaking sorrow, ever-changing yet enduring.

He continued to paint, to create, to live, embracing the full spectrum of human experience. He understood that pain and joy, loss and love, were integral parts of the rich tapestry of life, threads woven together to create a masterpiece of unparalleled beauty. He accepted the impermanence of all things, recognizing that even the most profound experiences are part of a larger, ever-evolving narrative. His art became a celebration of life, a testament to its fleeting beauty, and a reflection of his own journey towards acceptance, understanding, and profound gratitude for the gift of existence.

The beauty of impermanence wasn't merely an aesthetic observation, but a deeply philosophical understanding of his world and his place within it, shaping not just his art but his very soul. The lessons he learned resonated not just within his canvases but within the very fabric of his life. The echoes of Abby's laughter, once a source of deep pain, now carried a different melody—a poignant, enduring testament to the transformative power of love and the acceptance of life's fleeting grace.

The weight on his chest, once a crushing burden of grief and loss, began to lighten. It wasn't erased, not entirely. The ache of missing

Abby remained, a soft thrum beneath the surface of his being, a constant reminder of the extraordinary love they had shared. But the sharp edges of his sorrow had dulled, worn smooth by the relentless passage of time and the gradual acceptance of reality. He wasn't merely resigned; he found a different kind of peace, a quiet understanding that transcended the simple dichotomy of happiness and sadness. He began to see their story not as a tragedy, but as a profound and beautiful chapter in the larger narrative of his life.

He spent hours in the old Victorian park, the familiar pathways now imbued with a new, almost sacred significance. Each tree, each blade of grass, whispered memories of Abby – the way she'd laughed at a particularly plump robin, the way her hand felt in his as they walked, the quiet intensity of their shared silences. These weren't ghosts of the past, haunting him with their absence; they were vibrant echoes resonating in the present, shaping his perception of the world, enriching his understanding of love and loss. He no longer saw the park as a symbol of their lost connection, but as a testament to its enduring power. The changing seasons, the shifting light, the rustle of leaves – all served as poignant reminders of life's constant flux, and yet, within that flux, he found a strange sort of stability. The park, like their love, was transient, yet its essence, its indelible mark on his soul, remained.

His art became a reflection of this evolving perspective. He abandoned the stark realism that had characterized his earlier work, choosing instead to explore more abstract forms, to capture the essence of emotion rather than the precise details of reality. He used softer colors, allowing them to blend and diffuse, mimicking the fading light at the edge of a dream. His brushstrokes became more fluid, more spontaneous, reflecting the organic, ever-changing nature of life itself. He painted landscapes that mirrored the emotional landscape of his own heart – scenes imbued with a sense of poignant beauty, a subtle melancholy that hinted at loss but celebrated the enduring power of memory.

One particular painting became a focal point, a canvas upon which he poured his heart. It depicted the Victorian park, not as it was in its vibrant reality, but as it existed in his memory, a hazy, dreamlike representation of their time together. The colors were muted, yet somehow luminous, as if bathed in the ethereal glow of twilight. The trees were indistinct, their branches intertwined in a dance of light and shadow, symbolizing the intertwined nature of their lives. In the center of the painting, a single, perfect rose blossomed, its petals unfurling in a gesture of both fragility and resilience. The rose, he realized, was a metaphor for their love—beautiful, fleeting, yet possessing an enduring power that transcended its ephemeral nature.

He began to understand that acceptance wasn't about forgetting; it was about integrating. He didn't erase Abby from his memory; rather, he allowed her to become an integral part of his evolving self, a source of strength and inspiration. Her memory was no longer a wound, but a scar, a testament to a love that had changed him irrevocably. He cherished the memories, not as reminders of loss, but as fragments of a life intensely lived, a love fiercely felt. The pain remained, but it was no longer all-consuming. It was a part of him, a subtle undercurrent woven into the fabric of his being.

His relationships with his friends and family also shifted. He no longer feared intimacy, the vulnerability that had previously seemed so threatening. He understood that all connections are transient, that everything is in constant flux, yet that doesn't diminish their value. He learned to appreciate the present moment, the beauty of shared experiences, the simple joy of human connection. He communicated more openly, expressing his feelings with a newfound honesty and vulnerability, recognizing that even the most profound connections are destined to evolve and change over time. He embraced the natural flow of human relationships, understanding that loss and change are inevitable aspects of life, but that doesn't negate the beauty and significance of the moments shared.

His acceptance of fate wasn't passive resignation; it was an active embrace of life's inherent impermanence. He learned to find beauty in the fading light, the falling leaves, the transient nature of all things. He saw the cyclical nature of existence, the constant dance between creation and decay, life and death. He understood that impermanence wasn't a threat, but an essential aspect of the human experience, a source of both profound sorrow and exquisite joy. It was this understanding that liberated him, allowing him to fully live in the present, cherishing each moment for its unique beauty, its fleeting intensity.

He returned to his studies, not with the same sense of obligation, but with a newfound appreciation for learning. He pursued his passion for art, not with the goal of fame or fortune, but with a deep desire to express the profound truths he had discovered within himself. His life wasn't defined by his loss, but by his capacity for growth, his ability to adapt, his resilience in the face of adversity. He carried Abby's memory with him, not as a weight, but as a beacon, guiding him on his path, shaping his perspectives, enriching his appreciation of the world and its infinite possibilities.

He continued to visit the Victorian park, not to mourn their lost time, but to celebrate their extraordinary connection, to revel in the enduring power of memory. The park, in its ever-changing state, became a metaphor for his own ongoing journey, a constant reminder of life's impermanence and yet, paradoxically, its enduring beauty.

He found solace in the rustling leaves, the changing light, the gentle whisper of the wind – elements that reminded him of the transient nature of everything, and the profound beauty that lies in acceptance. The park was not a place of sorrow; it was a sanctuary, a place where he could connect with his past, reconcile with his loss, and embrace the future with a newfound sense of hope and serenity. The acceptance wasn't an ending, but a beginning; a new chapter in the story of his life, a chapter filled with the quiet wisdom of letting go and the enduring power of love. His heart still ached, yes, but the ache was now accompanied by a deeper understanding, a profound peace that came from accepting the inherent beauty of life's fleeting grace. The memory of Abby, once a source of unbearable pain, now served as a constant reminder of love's transformative power and the profound beauty inherent in even the most transient of experiences. The acceptance of fate wasn't a defeat, but a victory – a testament to the strength and the enduring power of love in the face of loss.

Chapter 8
Finding Peace

The vibrant hues of autumn leaves, swirling like miniature dancers in the crisp autumn air, mirrored the kaleidoscope of emotions churning within him. He found himself drawn to the quiet corners of the old Victorian park, not with the weight of grief that had once consumed him, but with a newfound sense of reverence for the transient beauty of existence. The fading sunlight, painting the sky in strokes of amber and rose, reminded him of Abby's ephemeral presence, a fleeting whisper in the grand symphony of time. Yet, this time, the whisper didn't carry the sting of loss; instead, it resonated with a soft, melancholic beauty.

He no longer saw the park as a sacred space dedicated to mourning, but as a living testament to the power of memory. Each fallen leaf, each rustle of the wind, carried the echoes of their shared moments, not as ghosts of the past, but as living, breathing memories interwoven into the fabric of the present. He saw her in the graceful bend of a willow tree, in the playful skip of a squirrel, in the vibrant colors of a late-blooming flower. These weren't illusions; they were reminders of the depth and intensity of their connection, a connection that transcended the boundaries of time and space.

His art, once a vehicle for expressing his pain, now became an exploration of joy, albeit a joy tinged with a delicate sadness. His paintings shifted from somber realism to a more vibrant, impressionistic style. He experimented with texture and light, capturing the ephemeral beauty of fleeting moments – a dewdrop clinging to a spiderweb, the delicate blush of dawn, the soft glow of fireflies on a summer night. He sought to capture the essence of life's transience, its breathtaking beauty in the face of inevitable decay.

One particular painting, a sprawling landscape depicting the Victorian park in the midst of a vibrant sunset, became his masterpiece. He didn't strive for photographic realism; instead, he poured his heart onto the canvas, capturing the very essence of his evolved perspective. The colors were rich and intense, yet they blended seamlessly, creating a feeling of both vibrancy and serenity. The trees stood tall and proud, their branches reaching towards the heavens as if embracing the fading light. In the distance, a solitary figure, barely discernible, walked along a winding path – a subtle tribute to Abby, her presence subtly woven into the fabric of the scene. The painting wasn't about her absence; it was about the enduring power of her memory, the profound impact she had on his life.

His renewed appreciation for life extended beyond the realm of art. He began to nurture his relationships with his family and friends, embracing the vulnerability he had previously shunned. He understood that connections, like the seasons, are cyclical; they ebb and flow, change and transform, yet their essence endures. He found solace in the simple act of sharing a meal with his family, listening to his friends' stories, and engaging in genuine conversations. He learned to communicate more openly, acknowledging the imperfections and vulnerabilities inherent in human connection. He found peace in the understanding that not all connections are meant to last, but their impact remains.

His academic pursuits, once a source of frustration and neglect, now held a new meaning. He approached his studies with a newfound curiosity, seeking knowledge not for external validation, but for the intrinsic joy of learning. He realized that every experience, every interaction, every piece of knowledge, contributes to the tapestry of one's being. He found beauty in the complexity of human history, the intricacies of scientific discoveries, and the profound depths of philosophical thought. He embraced the journey of learning, recognizing its transformative power and its ability to expand his understanding of the world and himself.

He found himself drawn to nature more than ever before. The rhythmic crashing of ocean waves, the soft whisper of the wind through the trees, the quiet hum of insects in a summer meadow— these were not mere sounds; they were reminders of the delicate balance of the natural world, a constant cycle of creation and decay, of birth and death. He realized that impermanence wasn't a threat, but an essential part of the life cycle, a profound truth that both saddened and inspired him. He understood that every moment, no matter how fleeting, is precious and unique.

His acceptance of Abby's absence wasn't about forgetting; it was about integration. Her memory remained a vital part of his identity, a constant reminder of the extraordinary love they had shared. He didn't repress his sorrow; instead, he embraced it as an integral part of his evolving self, a testament to the depth and intensity of their connection. He realized that sorrow, like joy, is a fundamental aspect of the human experience. He found beauty in his grief, recognizing its ability to heighten his appreciation for the ephemeral nature of life.

The painting that depicted the Victorian park, bathed in the golden glow of a fading sunset, remained his most cherished piece. He understood that art, like life itself, is transient. Paintings fade, colors dull, canvases tear. Yet, the emotions, the experiences, the memories captured within a work of art are immortal. They remain alive, vibrant in the collective consciousness of those who encounter the art. The beauty lies not in the permanence of the physical object, but in the enduring power of its message, its ability to resonate with those who view it.

David's life continued, not as a direct continuation of their shared past, but as a harmonious evolution of self-discovery. The vibrant colors of his past, once sharply defined, now blended seamlessly into a richer, more nuanced palette of experience. He learned to embrace change, to accept impermanence as the natural rhythm of existence. He found a profound peace, not in escaping his grief, but in integrating it into the vibrant tapestry of his life. He carried Abby's memory not as a burden, but as a guiding light, illuminating his path toward a future filled with renewed appreciation for the beauty and fragility of life. He understood that love, like art, transcends time and space. It exists not only in moments shared, but in the lingering resonance that remains long after the moment has passed, a testament to the enduring power of human connection. His heart still bore the scars of his loss, but those scars now served as a testament to the depth of his love and his extraordinary resilience. The world, once shrouded in the darkness of his sorrow, now blossomed with renewed vibrancy, reflecting the newfound appreciation for the beauty that resides in both life's fleeting moments and in the enduring power of love's transformative grace.

The weight of his loss, once a crushing burden, gradually began to shift. It didn't disappear entirely; the memory of Abby remained a vibrant, poignant thread woven into the tapestry of his life. But the sharp edges of grief had softened, rounded by time and the quiet acceptance that settled within him. He understood, with a clarity that surprised him, that their love story, though tragically brief, was profound and transformative. It wasn't measured in years, but in the intensity of shared moments, the depth of their connection that transcended the physical realm.

He began to revisit his paintings, not with the gnawing ache of loss, but with a newfound sense of pride and bittersweet appreciation. Each canvas held a piece of their story, a frozen moment in their ephemeral existence. The vibrant colors, once symbols of his despair, now resonated with a quiet strength, a testament to the resilience of the human spirit. He saw not just his own pain reflected in the strokes of paint, but the extraordinary beauty of their shared journey. He saw their laughter in the dappled sunlight filtering through the leaves, their whispered secrets in the rustling branches, their silent understanding in the gentle sway of the willow tree.

He started to keep a journal, a personal chronicle not of his sorrow, but of his healing. He wrote not about his longing for Abby, but about the lessons he learned from their time together, the ways she had changed him, the strength she had unknowingly instilled within him. He chronicled his journey through grief, not as a linear path toward resolution, but as a complex, evolving process of acceptance. He described the subtle shifts in his perception, the gradual softening of the sharp edges of his sorrow, the quiet blossoming of peace within his heart.

He found solace in simple acts of kindness, extending gestures of compassion to strangers, offering help where he could. These acts weren't performative; they stemmed from a deeper understanding of the interconnectedness of human lives, a recognition of the shared experience of joy and sorrow that bound everyone together. Each act of kindness served as a small, yet significant, step toward mending his own fragmented heart.

His relationship with his family deepened. He learned to communicate more openly, sharing his vulnerabilities without shame. He found comfort in their unconditional love, their quiet understanding of his grief, their unwavering support as he navigated the complexities of his healing process. Family dinners, once filled with unspoken tension, now hummed with a quiet warmth, a sense of shared connection that he had previously overlooked.

His renewed engagement with the world extended beyond his immediate circle. He volunteered at a local art center, teaching young children the basics of painting. He found a profound sense of purpose in nurturing their creativity, watching their imaginations blossom on the canvas. Their enthusiasm, their unbridled joy in the process of creation, served as a powerful reminder of the life-affirming power of art. It also provided a valuable outlet for him to express his own artistic vision, to help others find beauty in the world, just as Abby had inspired him to do.

The Victorian park, once a place of mourning, now became a sanctuary, a space for quiet reflection and contemplation. He visited regularly, not with the weight of sadness, but with a gentle sense of nostalgia. He walked the same paths they had walked together, feeling the echoes of their shared moments in the rustle of leaves, the songs of birds, the soft caress of the breeze. It was not a space of mourning but of memory, a tribute to the beautiful, ephemeral journey they had shared. He carried her memory not as a burden, but as a cherished keepsake.

One day, he sat by the willow tree, the same tree under which they had shared their first kiss within the painting. He closed his eyes and felt the familiar warmth of the sun on his skin, heard the faint whisper of the wind through the branches, and experienced a profound sense of peace. It was not a sense of forgetting, but of integration. Abby's memory was a vital part of him, forever interwoven into the fabric of his being. The pain of her absence remained, a quiet ache in his heart, but it was no longer a debilitating force. It had become a part of him, a reminder of the extraordinary love they had shared, a testament to the transformative power of connection.

He continued to paint, but his style evolved. His canvases still held a vibrancy, but the intensity had mellowed, replaced by a quiet strength, a sense of acceptance. He painted landscapes, portraits, still life—each piece a reflection of his inner growth, each brushstroke a testament to his evolving journey of healing. His art became an expression not just of his pain, but of his resilience, his ability to find beauty and purpose in the face of loss. He no longer painted only to express his sorrow, but also to celebrate the enduring power of love and memory.

His studies flourished, his academic pursuits fueled by a renewed sense of purpose. He found joy in the process of learning, in the exploration of new ideas, in the expansion of his knowledge. He embraced the intellectual stimulation, recognizing its capacity to enrich his life, to deepen his understanding of the world and himself. It provided a welcome distraction, a healthy channel for channeling his energy and focus, aiding in his personal healing and growth.

Over time, he realized that true closure wasn't about erasing the pain of loss, but about integrating it into the larger tapestry of his life. It was about accepting that his journey with Abby, though heartbreakingly short, was profoundly meaningful and deeply transformative. He carried her memory not as a burden, but as a source of strength, a reminder of the incredible capacity for love, even across the boundaries of reality itself. He had found peace not in forgetting her, but in celebrating the extraordinary love they had shared, a love that transcended time and space, a love that would forever remain a vibrant and cherished part of his heart. The world he lived in was once again full of color, but this time the hues were richer, more nuanced, and far more deeply meaningful. He had learned to live with the scars of his loss, transforming them into symbols of resilience, strength, and a profound appreciation for the bittersweet beauty of life.

The quiet hum of acceptance that had settled within him wasn't a passive resignation, but an active embrace of his changed self. He was no longer just David, the boy who excelled in academics and quietly observed the world from a distance. He was David, the boy who had walked through a painted world, loved a girl trapped in time, and returned to his own reality bearing the scars—and the unexpected gifts—of that experience. He carried the echoes of Abby's laughter in the rustling leaves, the warmth of her hand in the summer sun, the scent of her hair in the gentle breeze. These weren't ghosts haunting him; they were memories that shaped him, enriching the texture of his being.

As he began to paint again, the canvases held a different story. Gone was the frantic, almost desperate need to capture Abby's image, to somehow hold onto the fleeting moments of their shared existence. Now, his brushstrokes were deliberate, confident, each stroke imbued with a quiet intensity, a sense of self-assuredness he hadn't known before. He didn't shy away from the darkness, the shadows that lingered at the edges of his memories. Instead, he integrated them into his work, finding beauty in the complexities of human experience, the interplay of light and shadow, joy and sorrow.

His art became a conversation with himself, a process of self-discovery. He painted landscapes that mirrored the emotional turmoil he had endured, scenes of vibrant sunsets that echoed the intensity of his love for Abby, and quiet, contemplative forests that spoke of his journey towards healing. He used color not just to depict beauty, but to express the spectrum of human emotion—the fiery reds of passion, the deep blues of melancholy, the soft greens of hope, and the gentle grays of acceptance. His paintings became visceral, emotional narratives, conveying not just what he saw, but what he felt, what he had learned.

The process of creating art became a form of therapy, a way to process his emotions, to articulate the inexpressible. He found himself pouring his heart onto the canvas, expressing the pain of loss, the joy of rediscovery, the quiet strength he had unearthed within himself. The act of painting became a meditative practice, a way to connect with his inner self, to reconcile the different facets of his identity. He was no longer just a student, a son, a friend; he was an artist, a storyteller, a man shaped by an extraordinary experience.

His renewed sense of self extended beyond his art. He reconnected with his friends, not with the hesitant awkwardness of someone grappling with grief, but with a newfound appreciation for their presence in his life. He understood that true friendship wasn't about uninterrupted companionship but about shared experiences, mutual support, and the unwavering strength of a bond that could withstand the storms of life. He appreciated the simple things they did together— watching movies, playing video games, sharing a quiet meal. These were the mundane moments that held the power to stitch back together the fabric of his life, reminding him that his world was rich, varied and deeply meaningful even without Abby's physical presence.

His relationship with his parents deepened. He communicated with them with an honesty and vulnerability he hadn't previously known, sharing his experiences with them, not expecting judgment but understanding and acceptance. Their unconditional love was a constant source of strength, a reminder that he was loved, supported, and cherished even in his brokenness. The family dinners were no longer tense and awkward; they were filled with laughter, warmth, and a sense of shared connection that had previously been missing. He found solace in their familiar presence, in their unwavering belief in him.

He returned to his studies with renewed purpose, embracing the challenge of learning, the thrill of discovering new ideas, and the satisfaction of academic achievements. He understood that his experience with Abby hadn't diminished his intellect or his potential; rather, it had sharpened his focus, deepened his understanding of the world, and strengthened his resolve. His studies became a healthy channel for channeling his energy and focus, offering a welcome distraction and a platform for personal growth. His intellectual pursuits became a celebration of his resilience, his determination to thrive even in the face of profound loss.

His journey of self-discovery wasn't a linear path but a winding road filled with twists, turns, and moments of both clarity and confusion. He embraced the complexities of his own inner landscape, recognizing that his experiences had shaped him into a more empathetic, understanding, and compassionate individual. He learned to live with the ghosts of his past, not as burdens, but as teachers, guiding him towards a deeper appreciation for life, love and resilience.

He understood that his journey with Abby, though tragically brief, was profoundly significant. It had challenged his perception of reality, redefined his understanding of love, and awakened within him a strength and resilience he never knew he possessed. It had been a journey of immense loss, but also a journey of profound transformation. He emerged from this experience not as the same person who had stepped into the painting, but as a stronger, more compassionate, and more fully realized version of himself. He had learned to appreciate the beauty in the mundane, to find joy in the simplest of things, and to embrace the bittersweet reality of life with a grace and understanding that had been born out of loss but ultimately led to a place of profound acceptance and peace.

He had integrated Abby's memory into the fabric of his being, not as a constant wound, but as a vibrant thread that enriched the tapestry of his life. He acknowledged the pain, honored the love, and accepted the loss as an integral part of who he had become. He was a different person now, shaped by extraordinary experiences, imbued with a unique perspective, and ultimately stronger for having traversed the path of grief, loss, and ultimately healing. His identity was no longer defined by his ability to enter paintings, but by the depth of his love, the strength of his spirit, and the unwavering belief in the enduring power of human connection, even across the boundaries of time and reality. He was David, and he was whole. He was, finally, at peace. He looked at his reflection in a windowpane one day, and finally saw not the grief, but the remarkable resilience mirrored back at him. The boy who had entered a painting, and emerged changed, was finally home.

The scent of petrichor, the earthy fragrance after a rain shower, always reminded him of Abby. Not in a way that caused a sharp pang of grief, but as a gentle, nostalgic whisper. It was a subtle association, woven into the fabric of his memories, a comfortable familiarity rather than a painful reminder. He found himself seeking out these moments, these small sensory triggers that brought her closer without the ache of longing. The taste of Earl Grey tea, the sound of a particular melody on the violin, the feel of smooth river stones beneath his feet – all served as quiet, poignant reminders of their shared experiences. They were not substitutes for her presence, but rather, echoes of a love that transcended the boundaries of their brief, extraordinary time together.

His paintings continued to evolve, reflecting this internal shift. The raw, emotional intensity began to soften, replaced by a quieter, more contemplative approach. While the vibrant colors remained, they were now tempered with a sense of serenity, a quiet acceptance of the complexities of life and loss. He painted scenes of quiet solitude—a single figure silhouetted against a sunset, a solitary tree standing tall against a stormy sky, a bird in flight against a boundless expanse of blue. These weren't depictions of sadness, but of resilience, of the quiet strength that blossoms in the aftermath of adversity.

He experimented with various techniques, exploring the subtleties of light and shadow, creating paintings that evoked a sense of depth and mystery, reflecting the richness of his inner world. He began to incorporate elements of realism with abstract forms, blending the concrete with the ephemeral, mirroring the way his memories of Abby shifted and changed, sometimes sharp and clear, other times hazy and dreamlike. He found freedom in this ambiguity, in the ability to express the intangible, the feelings that words could not adequately capture. His art became a testament to his journey of healing, a visual representation of his internal landscape, reflecting the growth and transformation that he had undergone.

The healing wasn't just about processing his emotions; it was also about rebuilding his life. He sought out new experiences, challenging himself to step outside his comfort zone. He joined a hiking club, immersing himself in the beauty of the natural world, finding solace in the vastness of mountains and the tranquility of forests. He re-discovered his passion for literature, losing himself in the worlds created by other writers, finding comfort in the shared human experience expressed through words. He volunteered at a local art center, sharing his passion with others, finding a sense of purpose in guiding aspiring artists.

These activities weren't distractions; they were deliberate choices, steps in his journey of self-discovery, each contributing to his newfound sense of wholeness. They were building blocks, adding layers of new experiences and perspectives to the foundation of his life, which had been so profoundly shaken. He wasn't merely replacing Abby in his life; he was enriching it, expanding it, growing beyond the constraints of his past. The void she left behind wasn't empty; it was filled with a richness and depth that came from embracing life's complexities.

His relationships flourished. His friendships deepened, strengthened by the shared experience of seeing him navigate his grief and emerge stronger on the other side. He was more present, more appreciative of the connections he had, more willing to share his vulnerability. He understood that true friendship wasn't about avoiding difficult conversations but about facing them head-on and finding strength and support in the shared journey. The bonds he had with his friends weren't just restored; they had evolved, becoming richer and deeper through the crucible of his experiences.

His relationship with his parents became even more profound. They didn't shy away from acknowledging his pain, instead offering unwavering support and unconditional love. He shared his art with them, allowing them to glimpse into the depths of his emotional landscape, witnessing the transformation he had undergone. His relationship with them evolved from one of quiet understanding to one of deep intimacy, a sharing of experiences and feelings that strengthened their bond and enhanced their familial connections. The shared meals were now filled with thoughtful conversations, laughter, and the quiet contentment of family togetherness.

He returned to his studies with a renewed sense of purpose. His academic pursuits weren't simply a means to an end; they were a journey of intellectual exploration, a way to engage with the world on an intellectual and emotional level. His academic life wasn't just about grades; it was about growth, knowledge, and the pursuit of understanding. The world wasn't just something to be observed passively; it was something to be actively engaged with, questioned, and understood. He approached his studies with a sense of clarity and focus, driven not by external pressure but by an internal desire to expand his knowledge and understanding.

The journey of healing wasn't a straight line, but a winding path punctuated with moments of both intense emotion and serene contemplation. There were days when the memory of Abby would overwhelm him, when the pain of loss would resurface, threatening to engulf him once more. But he now had the tools to navigate these moments, to acknowledge his pain without being consumed by it. He allowed himself to grieve, to feel the full spectrum of his emotions, understanding that these feelings were part of his experience, integral to his growth, and not to be suppressed or ignored.

He learned to cherish the memories, not as reminders of what he had lost, but as treasures that enriched his life. He didn't try to erase Abby from his memory; he integrated her into his story, acknowledging her impact on his life, the profound love they shared, and the transformative journey they had undertaken together. He carried her with him, not as a burden, but as a source of strength, a reminder of the beauty of human connection, the power of love, and the resilience of the human heart.

One evening, sitting by his easel, surrounded by his paintings, he felt a deep sense of peace wash over him. The paintings weren't just works of art; they were a testament to his journey, a visual representation of his healing process. They were a tangible manifestation of his growth, a reflection of the strength and resilience he had discovered within himself. He looked at his reflection in a finished canvas, and saw not a young man scarred by loss, but one bearing the marks of a remarkable journey, transformed by love, grief, and the enduring power of the human spirit. He was at peace, finally. He was whole.

The quiet hum of the city outside was a distant murmur, barely penetrating the quiet sanctuary of his studio. He sat, surrounded by his canvases, each a silent witness to his transformation. The vibrant colors of his earlier works, raw with the intensity of his emotions, had mellowed, softened into a palette of quieter hues, reflecting the calm that had settled within him. He no longer felt the sharp pangs of loss, the aching void that had once consumed him. Instead, a gentle warmth permeated his being, a quiet contentment born from acceptance and understanding.

He traced the delicate strokes of his brush on a recent painting, a landscape depicting a tranquil lake nestled amidst rolling hills. The reflection of the setting sun shimmered on the water's surface, a mirror to the serenity he now felt within. It wasn't a denial of his grief, but a testament to his healing, a visual representation of the peace he had painstakingly cultivated. The memory of Abby remained, vibrant and indelible, but it no longer held the power to overwhelm him. It was now a cherished part of his narrative, woven into the tapestry of his life, a thread of gold against a backdrop of rich experience.

His understanding of love had evolved, transcending the boundaries of his experience with Abby. He saw it not as a fleeting emotion, a passionate fire that burned brightly and then flickered out, but as a deep, abiding wellspring of compassion, a force that could shape him, reshape him, and ultimately, heal him. Abby's love, though tragically brief in its physical manifestation, had left an enduring legacy, a profound impact on his life and his understanding of himself and the world around him.

He realized that he was a different person now, subtly, yet profoundly altered. His empathy had deepened, his capacity for compassion had broadened, his understanding of human connection had become more nuanced. He was more attuned to the subtleties of emotion, more patient with the complexities of human relationships, more generous in his interactions with others. He could see the pain in others, the unspoken needs, the hidden struggles, with a clarity he hadn't possessed before. He had become a more present, more attuned, more compassionate person – a reflection of the extraordinary love he had experienced and the healing he had undertaken.

His relationships with others deepened, informed by this newfound understanding. He approached his friendships with a greater level of sincerity, a willingness to be vulnerable, to share his experiences, and to offer unconditional support. He listened more intently, responded with empathy, and offered comfort with a quiet grace that came from his own journey of healing. He cherished these relationships, understanding their true value, their ability to sustain and nurture him in ways he hadn't appreciated before.

His interactions with his family were also transformed. The shared silences were now filled with unspoken understanding, a quiet communication born from mutual respect and affection. He felt closer to his parents, sharing his art with them, inviting them into the intimate landscape of his emotions. He no longer sought their approval, but rather their companionship, their love, their acceptance. They, in turn, offered him unwavering support, respecting his journey, cherishing his resilience. The meals, once a silent testament to a fractured family dynamic, were now vibrant with shared laughter, thoughtful conversation, and a profound sense of togetherness.

His academic pursuits flourished as well. He approached his studies with a renewed sense of purpose, no longer driven by external pressures but by an intrinsic desire for knowledge and understanding. The world, once a blurry backdrop to his emotional turmoil, was now a source of fascination, a landscape to be explored with an open heart and a curious mind. He found inspiration in the intricate tapestry of human history, in the complex interplay of human relationships, in the beauty and complexity of the natural world. His learning wasn't just an academic exercise; it was a personal quest, a journey of self-discovery that complemented and enriched his emotional growth.

He continued to paint, but his art evolved. It was no longer solely a reflection of his grief, but an exploration of the full spectrum of human emotion – joy, sorrow, hope, despair, acceptance, and peace. His colors broadened, his compositions deepened, and his style matured, reflecting the growth and transformation he had undergone. He was no longer bound by the constraints of his past; he had broken free, embracing a new chapter in his life, a journey filled with hope, purpose, and a quiet contentment he never thought possible.

He still found solace in the natural world, hiking the trails he had discovered, finding rejuvenation in the vastness of the mountains and the tranquility of the forests. He still sought out the sensory reminders of Abby – the scent of petrichor, the taste of Earl Grey tea, the sound of a violin – but these reminders no longer carried the weight of profound loss. They were now echoes of a love that had shaped him, a love that had been transformative, a love that would forever be etched in his heart.

He had learned that grief wasn't a linear process, a simple progression from pain to peace. There were still days when the memories of Abby overwhelmed him, days when the ache of loss resurfaced with unexpected intensity. But he now had the tools to navigate these emotions, to acknowledge them, to allow himself to feel the full spectrum of his pain without being consumed by it. He recognized that grief was a part of life, a necessary component of the human experience, a testament to the depth of his love for Abby.

He embraced his memories, not as reminders of what he had lost, but as treasures to be cherished, as tangible links to a love that had enriched his life immeasurably. He carried Abby with him, not as a burden but as a source of strength, inspiration, and profound understanding. Her memory was woven into the very fabric of his being, shaping his perspectives, informing his choices, and guiding him towards a life filled with purpose, meaning, and profound contentment.

The lasting impact of his love for Abby was not simply a matter of sentimentality or nostalgia. It was a fundamental shift in his consciousness, a transformative experience that had redefined his understanding of love, loss, and the resilience of his spirit. It was the quiet strength he found within himself, the ability to navigate the complexities of life, the capacity for profound empathy, and the unwavering faith in the enduring power of human connection. It was the serenity he now found in the quiet moments, the contentment he discovered in the simple joys, and the profound peace that had finally settled within his heart. He was whole. He was at peace. And he carried Abby's love, a radiant beacon, within him always.

Chapter 9
The Artist's Return

The chipped paint of his easel seemed to mock him, a silent reminder of the fragility of things, of the ephemeral nature of beauty. He'd been avoiding the studio for days, the silence within its walls too much like the echoing emptiness in his heart. But the mail carrier's insistent knock had shattered the fragile peace he'd managed to cultivate. A single, unmarked envelope lay on the mat, its weight oddly significant, as if holding a secret heavier than its thin paper could bear.

Inside, nestled amongst the crisp, clean folds, was a scrap of paper, stained and yellowed with age, the edges frayed as if worn by time and countless unseen hands. It was a fragment of a letter, the ink faded and blurred, yet somehow, eerily legible. The words were written in a delicate script, elegant and precise, a stark contrast to the rough texture of the paper. He recognized the style, the precise curls and flourishes, the almost imperceptible tilt to the letters – it was Abby's handwriting. Or at least, he felt that it was. A deep shiver ran down his spine, a prickle of something akin to hope, threatening to shatter the fragile calm he'd so painstakingly built.

The message itself was cryptic, a collection of words and phrases that seemed to defy easy interpretation. *The willow weeps*, it read, *where the moon kisses the lake. Find the hidden path, before the colors fade.* He reread it several times, each time the cryptic nature of the words settling deeper into his mind, until they seemed to pulse with a hidden meaning. His heart quickened its beat, a drum against the sudden roar of possibilities.

The willow weeps, where the moon kisses the lake. He knew the lake; it was a central feature in the painting, the still, reflective surface mirroring the sky and the surrounding hills. But a weeping willow? He couldn't recall seeing one, not in the version of the painting he'd known. Perhaps a new detail, a subtle alteration brought about by the passing of time within the canvas' confines. The shifting of light and shadow, the slow metamorphosis of a world trapped in paint.

The hidden path. That intrigued him most. A secret passage, a clandestine route, a means of access unseen to the casual observer. Was this an invitation? A summons? A desperate plea for help? Or simply a cruel trick of the light, a phantom echo of his grief playing tricks on his mind? The thought of it ignited something akin to a painful longing, a hunger for something he knew he could never have.

He spent the next few days poring over the painting, studying every detail with an obsessive intensity. He magnified sections, searching for discrepancies, for anomalies, for anything that might reveal the hidden path. He traced the contours of the landscape, the textures of the trees, the ripples on the lake's surface, searching for any clue, any indication of the hidden passage. His heart was a caged bird, beating against his ribs, a frantic rhythm that echoed the growing turmoil within.

He found it, finally, hidden behind a cluster of densely packed trees, barely visible, camouflaged by the artist's brushstrokes. A narrow, winding pathway, barely discernible, seemed to snake its way towards the lake. The image was so subtle that he almost missed it, a testament to the subtle artistry of the unknown creator. This was not a mere figment of his imagination, this was real. Or, rather, as real as the world within the painting could be.

Hesitantly, he entered the painting, his consciousness dissolving into the canvas, the familiar sensation of immersion washing over him. He found himself standing at the edge of the woods, the air heavy with the scent of damp earth and decaying leaves. The moon hung low in the sky, casting long, dancing shadows across the path. The weeping willow, its branches drooping towards the lake, was exactly as the message described, its leaves glistening with an almost unnatural luminescence.

He followed the path, his heart pounding in his chest, a mixture of fear and exhilarating anticipation. The air grew cooler, the shadows deeper, as if the world itself was holding its breath. He felt watched, the hairs on the back of his neck prickling with an awareness that was more than just sensory perception. This was more than just a painted landscape; this was a living, breathing world of its own, reacting to his intrusion, to his presence.

The path led him to the edge of the lake, the water dark and still, reflecting the ethereal light of the moon. And there, etched into the smooth surface of a large, flat rock, were more words. This time, the message was clearer, more direct. *The bridge is broken. I need your help.* The words seemed to pulse with a faint, inner light, a silent plea for assistance.

Panic seized him. The bridge. The small, wooden bridge that spanned a narrow inlet of the lake. He remembered it vividly – a quaint, almost fragile structure, a charming detail in a tranquil scene. But now, it was broken. Abby needed his help. And he knew that this wasn't merely a symbolic representation of their broken connection; this was something far more real, far more urgent.

The weight of responsibility bore down on him. He hadn't anticipated this, this desperate call for aid from across the chasm of reality and art. His heart ached, a mixture of fear and determination. The painting itself was fading, as he knew. He had seen the subtle changes, the blurring of lines, the fading of colors. The world within was disintegrating, and Abby was trapped within its failing structure.

He had a choice to make, a decision that would irrevocably alter the course of both their lives. Could he really go back? Could he risk the consequences, the inevitable unraveling of his own sanity? He looked at the reflection of the moon in the lake, the image shimmering like a tear in the fabric of reality. The answer, though terrifying, was clear. He would help her. He had to. His heart, battered and bruised yet still beating, urged him forward. He would cross the broken bridge, even if it meant facing the very fabric of reality collapsing around him. He would rescue Abby if it was the last thing he ever did. He had to try. He owed her that much. He owed himself that much. The consequences be damned.

The canvas seemed to pulse with a faint, inner light, a subtle tremor running through its surface as he approached. He hadn't touched the painting since he'd last seen Abby, the memory of her ethereal beauty, a phantom ache in his chest. Now, standing before it, he felt a strange pull, an almost magnetic force drawing him into its depths. It was a sensation both terrifying and irresistible, a siren song of longing and fear. He hesitated, his hand hovering over the frame, before finally allowing himself to be drawn in.

The transition was instantaneous, the familiar dissolving sensation washing over him. One moment he was in his cluttered studio, the smell of turpentine sharp in the air; the next, he stood at the edge of the familiar Victorian park, the air cooler, the light softer. But something was different. The vibrant colors seemed muted, almost washed out, as if the very essence of the painting was fading. The trees, once lush and vibrant, now appeared skeletal, their leaves brittle and dry. Even the usually crystal-clear lake seemed clouded, its surface shimmering with an unnatural stillness.

A sense of profound unease settled over him. It was more than just the fading colors; it was a palpable sense of decay, a pervasive feeling of disintegration. The idyllic world he'd once known seemed to be unraveling, crumbling at its edges, like an old, forgotten dream. The path leading to the lake was overgrown, the once-clear track now obscured by tangled weeds and thorny bushes. He pushed through the undergrowth, his clothes catching on the thorns, the scratches a small price to pay for the urgency in his heart.

As he approached the lake, he saw it: the broken bridge. It wasn't merely a crack; a significant section of the wooden structure was missing, leaving a gaping chasm between the two banks. The sight sent a fresh wave of panic through him. The bridge was more than just a picturesque feature; it was a crucial element of Abby's world, a symbol of their connection, of the delicate balance between their two realities. Now, broken, it represented the fragility of their shared existence.

He searched the area, his eyes scanning the landscape for any sign of Abby. The weeping willow, mentioned in the cryptic note, stood sentinel by the water's edge, its branches drooping mournfully, their leaves shimmering with an unnatural, almost phosphorescent glow. The air was heavy with an unspoken sorrow, a quiet despair that mirrored the decaying world around him. The moon, hanging low in the sky, cast long, mournful shadows across the desolate landscape.

He called out her name, his voice a shaky whisper lost in the vast emptiness of the painted world. The only response was the rustling of leaves and the gentle lapping of the water against the shore. A wave

136

of despair threatened to engulf him; the isolation was crushing, the silence deafening. He felt utterly alone, trapped in a decaying world with no sign of the woman he loved.

He continued along the bank, his heart sinking with each passing moment. The fading of the painting was accelerating, the colors bleeding together, the lines blurring, creating a chaotic, disorienting effect. It was as if the canvas itself was dissolving, its very fabric unraveling before his eyes. The world was disappearing, and with it, the possibility of ever seeing Abby again.

He stumbled upon a small clearing, a hidden alcove tucked away amongst the trees. He noticed a small, almost imperceptible change in the texture of the paint, a subtle difference in brushstrokes that hadn't been there before. He reached out, his fingers lightly tracing the surface of the canvas, a wave of sadness washing over him. The paint felt cold, brittle, almost like dust under his touch.

Suddenly, a faint sound reached his ears, a barely audible whisper carried on the wind. He strained to listen, his heart pounding in his chest. The whisper seemed to come from the willow tree, its mournful rustling a symphony of sorrow. He approached the tree cautiously, his eyes scanning the branches for any sign of movement, any indication of life.

And then he saw her.

Abby was perched on a low-hanging branch, her form almost translucent, her colors muted and faded like the rest of the painting. Her face was pale, her eyes wide with a mixture of fear and exhaustion. She looked frail, almost ethereal, a ghost in a dying world.

He gasped, his heart swelling with a mixture of relief and despair. Seeing her, frail and fading, brought a fresh wave of agony. The reality of her situation hit him with the force of a physical blow. She was trapped, not just in the painting, but in the process of its disintegration.

"Abby," he whispered, his voice trembling with emotion. Her eyes met his, and a flicker of recognition, of hope, sparkled within them. It was a frail spark, barely visible, but it was there, a beacon of light in the encroaching darkness.

"David," she whispered back, her voice faint, barely audible. "I knew you'd come."

He reached out to her, his fingers brushing against her arm. Her skin felt cool, almost icy to the touch, like the fading paint of the canvas. He could feel the energy draining from her, the essence of her being fading along with the world around her. The urgency of the situation intensified, the weight of responsibility pressing down on him with crushing force.

He had to find a way to save her, to restore her, to pull her back from the brink of oblivion. But how? He looked around, desperately searching for a solution, for a way out of this impossible predicament. The fading colors, the decaying landscape, the broken bridge – all were symbols of a world that was rapidly disappearing, taking Abby with it. He knew that time was running out.

He knew the painting was reacting to his presence, to his repeated visits. He'd sensed the instability before, but now, it was accelerating, the decay rapid and dramatic. Every moment he spent within the world of the painting hastened its deterioration. He'd hoped that his connection with Abby might somehow hold it together, but it was clear now that he was wrong. He was hastening its end.

He looked at Abby; her face etched with a quiet sorrow that mirrored his own. He knew that leaving her would be excruciating, a heartbreaking act of self-sacrifice. Yet, he also knew that staying would mean condemning her to a certain and inevitable death. His heart ached with the weight of the decision, a agonizing choice between his own desire and her very survival. This wasn't just about love; it was about life and death, existence and oblivion. The very fabric of reality itself was at stake.

The wind howled, a mournful lament that echoed his own inner turmoil. He could feel the painting crumbling around them, the colors fading into a monochrome nothingness. He had to act, and he had to act fast. He didn't know how he would do it, but he knew that he had to try. For Abby. For their love. For the world that was slowly disappearing before his eyes. The weight of his decision pressed upon him, heavier than any physical burden. He would face whatever lay ahead, whatever consequences he might have to endure, to save the only woman he'd ever truly loved. His future was uncertain, but his path was clear. He would save her. He had to.

The subtle change wasn't in the grand sweep of the landscape, not in the decaying trees or the clouded lake. It was smaller, more intimate, almost hidden. It was in the texture of the paint itself, a shift almost imperceptible at first, a flicker in the fading light. Near the base of the weeping willow, where the gnarled roots seemed to claw at the earth, he noticed a faint shimmer, a subtle alteration in the brushstrokes. The paint here, usually a deep, earthy brown, now held a faint, almost ethereal blue. It was as if a new layer, impossibly thin, had been overlaid, a ghostly whisper of color against the fading canvas.

He touched the altered area gingerly, his fingers tracing the barely perceptible difference. It felt cool to the touch, strangely smooth despite the overall brittle texture of the decaying paint. He ran his fingers along the edge of the blue, following its delicate, almost hesitant progression across the canvas. It snaked its way towards the lake, a thin ribbon of color against the backdrop of dying greens and browns. He felt a shiver; this wasn't decay; this was something… new.

As he followed the path of the blue, he noticed other alterations, equally subtle but undeniably present. Small details, previously overlooked, now presented themselves with a startling clarity. A single, perfect wildflower, previously unseen, bloomed at the edge of the path, its petals a brilliant, almost incandescent, crimson against the muted greens. A fallen branch, previously obscured by tangled weeds, now lay cleanly revealed, its bark a rich, deep mahogany, sharp and defined against the blurring background. These small, precise alterations were counterpoints to the overall decay, tiny islands of vibrant color and sharp definition within a sea of fading pigments.

He felt a surge of hope, a flicker of optimism in the face of overwhelming despair. Perhaps the painting wasn't simply fading; perhaps it was changing, evolving, reacting to something. Could this be a sign of regeneration, a path to salvation? He looked at Abby, her face still pale, her form still fragile, but a glimmer of hope seemed to mirror his own in her eyes.

He followed the blue ribbon of paint, his heart pounding with a mixture of excitement and apprehension. It led him to a place he hadn't seen before, a hidden grove tucked away behind the weeping willow. The trees here were different, their leaves vibrant and lush, a stark contrast to the skeletal branches elsewhere. The air here was cleaner, fresher, infused with a subtle, sweet fragrance he couldn't quite identify. It felt almost alive, a vibrant pocket of energy in a dying world.

At the center of the grove, he found it: a small spring, its water crystal clear, sparkling with an almost unnatural brilliance. The water flowed gently, its ripples creating concentric circles in the reflective surface. The water itself seemed to shimmer with the same faint blue hue he'd noticed on the canvas. He cupped his hands and drank, the water cold and refreshing, a strange energy flowing through him with each swallow.

As he drank, he felt a surge of power, a renewed sense of strength and purpose. The fatigue that had weighed him down for so long began to lift, replaced by a sense of clarity and resolve. He knew, instinctively, that the spring was the key, the source of the subtle changes he'd witnessed. It was the heart of this decaying world, a wellspring of life and regeneration.

He looked at Abby, her gaze fixed on the spring with a mixture of awe and wonder. He sensed her apprehension, but also a nascent hope. He took her hand, his touch gentle but firm, and led her to the water's edge.

He helped her sit by the spring, the cool water washing over her feet. As she dipped her fingers in the water, the faint blue shimmer intensified around her. The color seemed to seep into her, revitalizing her, restoring her faded form. Her skin regained its warmth, her eyes their vibrancy, the ethereal pallor receding to reveal the beauty he remembered. The transformation wasn't instantaneous, but palpable. It was as if the spring itself was drawing strength from the painting's new layer, re-energizing and revitalizing the world, and Abby with it.

He watched, captivated, as her color returned, the vibrant hues of her dress and skin slowly reappearing, replacing the washed-out tones. The process was slow, painstaking, but undeniable. With each passing moment, she seemed to become more real, more solid, her form solidifying, her essence strengthening.

It was a battle against time, against the relentless decay of the canvas. But the spring seemed to be winning, feeding its lifeblood into Abby and the surrounding area, pushing back against the encroaching oblivion. The vibrant colors spread slowly outward from the grove, like a wave of revitalization, a tide turning against the tide of decay. The trees regained their vitality, their leaves regaining their lush green hues. The lake began to clear, its surface regaining its crystal clarity.

Hours passed, maybe longer, he lost track of time. As the spring's influence expanded, he saw the broken bridge mending, the gaps closing, the wood regaining its strength and solidity. The weeds receded, the path clearing itself. The world around them was slowly, painstakingly, being reborn.

As Abby regained her strength and vibrant colors, so too did their connection. The fading despair was replaced by a newfound hope, a shared joy in this slow, delicate process of renewal. The feeling of isolation lifted; they were united, not just in love, but in the shared experience of witnessing, and participating in, this remarkable act of transformation. They were not just trapped; they were involved in the very act of their own salvation.

But even as the restoration progressed, a lingering unease persisted. The changes felt unnatural, almost magical. The source of the blue hue, the miraculous spring, felt otherworldly, mysterious. He wondered about the cause of this transformation; what triggered the subtle shift, this strange act of restoration? What forces were at play? The answers remained elusive, but one thing was clear: their journey wasn't over. This was a new phase, a new challenge. They had to find the origin of this power, understand its source, to prevent future decay or even exploit its potential to save other fading worlds that may exist within other paintings. The newfound hope was accompanied by a growing sense of responsibility.

Their love story, once a poignant tale of loss, was now a story of survival, of renewal, of a fight against the very fabric of reality. They were no longer merely observers in this world, but active participants in its creation and preservation. The journey was far from over, but for the first time in a long time, David felt a sense of purpose stronger than the fear and despair that had threatened to consume them.

The blue shimmer intensified, spreading from the spring like a gentle tide, washing over the withered landscape. It wasn't a forceful surge, but a slow, patient caress, coaxing life back into the decaying world. The skeletal trees, once gnarled and brittle, began to unfurl, their branches reaching towards the sky like supplicants. New leaves, impossibly vibrant, unfurled, tiny emeralds against the backdrop of the rejuvenating blue. The air, once thick with the scent of decay, now held a delicate sweetness, a hint of wildflowers and damp earth, a promise of renewal.

Abby, her eyes wide with wonder, felt the change as profoundly as David. The chill that had settled deep in her bones began to recede, replaced by a warmth that flowed from the spring, from the very canvas itself. Her skin, once pallid and translucent, regained its rosy hue, her lips regaining their color, her eyes their sparkling light. The ethereal quality that had clung to her, a testament to her existence as a being trapped within a two-dimensional world, began to fade. She felt stronger, more solid, her presence more tangible, less like a whisper and more like a song.

As the revitalization progressed, memories flooded back to her, memories she hadn't accessed since her confinement within the painting. She remembered the vibrant streets of her Victorian-era London, the bustling markets, the laughter of children. She remembered the warmth of her family's home, the scent of her mother's baking, the comforting routine of her everyday life. The memories were fragmented, hazy at first, like faded photographs, but as the blue shimmer enveloped her, they sharpened, gaining clarity and depth. They were like pieces of a shattered mirror, slowly being pieced back together.

David watched this transformation with a mixture of awe and apprehension. He felt the same surge of energy, the same renewed sense of purpose, but also a growing unease. This wasn't simply a reversal of decay; it was something more profound, more powerful. It was as though the painting itself was responding to their love, their connection, their shared determination to survive. It was a testament to the resilience of the their spirit, its capacity for love, and its inherent ability to create, to hope, to persevere.

He reached out, his hand brushing against hers, and felt the warmth of her skin, the solid reality of her presence. It was a profound sensation, the culmination of weeks spent in fear of losing her, a constant battle against the encroaching decay that seemed poised to tear them apart. The fear hadn't completely vanished, but it was tempered by a wave of overwhelming relief and joy. This was a new beginning, a second chance, a fragile hope amidst the ever-present threat of oblivion.

The restoration wasn't limited to Abby and the immediate surroundings of the spring. Slowly, painstakingly, the blue shimmer crept across the canvas, revitalizing the entire scene. The lake, once murky and still, began to sparkle, its surface reflecting the rejuvenated sky. The weeping willow, its branches once bare and skeletal, sprouted new leaves, their vibrant green contrasting sharply with the still-fading sections of the painting. The fallen branches, once entangled in weeds, lay clearly defined, their textures sharp and distinct against the background. The wildflower, a beacon of vibrant crimson, flourished, a symbol of resilience and hope.

As the painting recovered, so did David's connection to his own reality. The blurring of boundaries, the disorientation that had plagued him for weeks, began to dissipate. He still felt a strange bond with the painting, a connection to this otherworldly place, but it was no longer consuming, no longer a threat to his life outside the canvas. The line between reality and fiction became less hazy, less blurred, allowing him a glimpse of a life that existed beyond the boundaries of Abby's world.

The changes were not instantaneous, nor were they uniform. There were areas of the painting that remained stubbornly faded, stubbornly resistant to the revitalizing influence of the spring. These areas seemed to represent moments of sorrow, of loss, of pain, memories that, perhaps, needed more time to heal. The restoration was a process, a journey, not a sudden transformation. This mirrored the slow, gradual rekindling of their relationship, the careful rebuilding of trust and connection after their near-loss.

As they spent days by the spring, observing this wondrous transformation, they began to notice patterns, subtle nuances. The blue shimmer seemed to be drawn to areas of vibrant color, to moments of joy, to shared laughter, to acts of love and tenderness. It seemed to shy away from areas of despair, of loneliness, of loss. This gave them a newfound understanding of the nature of the spring's power; it was a force that responded to emotion, to feelings of love, hope, and connection. This suggested the source of the power wasn't merely some chemical reaction or spontaneous event but rather something deeper, more aligned with the realm of the metaphysical.

The realization brought with it a renewed sense of hope, but also a sense of responsibility. They had to nurture this miraculous force, they had to protect it, to understand its origins. They weren't just survivors; they were custodians, tasked with the responsibility of safeguarding this delicate ecosystem, this tiny pocket of renewed life. The future was still uncertain, the threats still looming, but for the first time in a long time, they had a sense of purpose, a common goal, a shared belief in the possibility of salvation, not just for themselves, but for this miraculous world trapped within the frame of an old painting.

The spring's influence began to extend beyond the immediate grove, inching its way towards the edges of the canvas. As the revitalization spread, David and Abby discovered hidden details, previously obscured by decay, now revealed in stunning clarity. They discovered a hidden path leading to a secluded waterfall, its water cascading into a small pool, its surface mirroring the vibrant colors of the surrounding landscape. They found a secluded meadow, filled with wildflowers of breathtaking beauty, their colors reminiscent of Abby's dress. They found fragments of a forgotten life, fragments of Abby's lost world, slowly but surely returning to vibrant existence. Each discovery reinforced their belief that this wasn't merely a restoration, but a rebirth.

As the days turned into weeks, the painting continued its slow but remarkable transformation. The once desolate landscape was slowly reclaiming its vibrant beauty, its colors growing more vivid, its textures sharper, its details more distinct. The air grew warmer, the light brighter, the world around them more alive. Their own connection mirrored the painting's transformation, growing stronger, deeper, more resilient with each passing moment. The fear that had shadowed them was gradually replaced by a cautious optimism, a quiet belief in the possibility of a future, a future where their love story, once a tale of impending loss, could become a testament to resilience, to the enduring power of hope, and the miracle of second chances.

The journey was far from over, but the weight of despair that had crushed them was lifting. They had found a glimpse of hope, a spring of life within the decaying canvas, a testament to the resilience of love and the enduring power of the their spirit. They were still in a precarious position, their existence within the painting a fragile thing, but for now, the weight of their fear was tempered by a new sense of purpose; they were not merely trapped, they were protectors, guardians of this magical world, and as they walked hand in hand along the rejuvenated path, they knew their work had just begun.

Their love story, once a tale of loss and sacrifice, was transforming into an epic of survival, a testament to the strength of the human heart, and the enduring power of hope. The painting was still fragile, the threat of complete decay still lingered, but the delicate blue shimmer of the spring, a symbol of their hope, was expanding, a testament to the power of love and the enduring miracle of second chances.

The blue shimmer, now a vibrant, almost electric current, pulsed through the revitalized landscape. It wasn't merely restoring the painting; it was actively *creating*, weaving new details into the fabric of Abby's world. A flock of birds, their plumage iridescent and impossibly detailed, materialized above them, their song a sweet melody that resonated deep within David's soul. Flowers bloomed where moments before there had been only barren earth, their colors impossibly vivid, each petal perfect. It was as if the painting was painting itself, filling in the gaps, enriching the tapestry of its existence with breathtaking artistry.

David watched, mesmerized, his heart a chaotic drumbeat against his ribs. This miraculous transformation, born from their love and their shared struggle, filled him with a profound sense of wonder. Yet, beneath the awe, a deep current of unease ran. He felt a growing separation from the painting, a gradual easing of the intense, almost suffocating connection that had bound him to Abby's world. The blurring of boundaries, the constant disorientation, was receding. He felt... himself again, more grounded, more solid in his own reality.

This separation, while frightening, was also a necessary step. He understood, on some intuitive level, that the painting's restoration was intrinsically linked to his ability to maintain a connection to his own life. The more fully he embraced his own reality, the stronger the painting would become, a paradox that both terrified and excited him. He wasn't sure how this would play out, but he had a feeling it held the key to securing Abby's future within the canvas. The price, however, remained unknown.

Abby, sensing his shift in demeanor, reached for his hand, her touch sending a ripple of warmth through him. Her eyes, reflecting the myriad colors of the revitalized landscape, held a profound depth, a wisdom that seemed to transcend her years. She understood his apprehension. Their love had saved their world, but it had also brought them to the brink of separation. The painting's restoration was a testament to the power of their connection, yet it was simultaneously a reminder of their precarious position.

"We've done it, David," she whispered, her voice filled with a mixture of exhaustion and triumph. "We've brought life back to this place."

He nodded, unable to speak, the weight of emotion too heavy. The reality was that their triumph was interwoven with the possibility of loss. The restoration had been bought with the sacrifice of their constant togetherness. As the painting healed, the magical portal seemed to fade, becoming less vibrant, less palpable, a constant reminder of the looming separation.

The days that followed were filled with a bittersweet poignancy. They explored the reborn world together, savoring every moment as if it might be their last. They revisited places that had once been decayed and desolate, now bursting with life and color. They discovered hidden groves, crystal-clear streams, and vistas that took their breath away. The landscape felt utterly magical, breathtakingly beautiful, yet also hauntingly familiar, as if long-lost memories were slowly resurfaced, imbued with an overwhelming nostalgia.

They spent hours by the spring, watching the blue shimmer expand, its influence reaching further and further across the canvas. David felt the pull of his own world growing stronger, the tug of his responsibilities, his studies, his friends, becoming increasingly insistent. It was a gradual shift, a slow unraveling of the threads that had bound him to this extraordinary world, a feeling not of betrayal, but of a necessary release. The painting was safe, and that was what truly mattered.

One evening, as the sun set, painting the revitalized landscape in hues of orange and gold, David sat beside Abby, the silence between them heavy with unspoken emotions. The once-faint boundary between their worlds was now clearly visible, like a shimmering curtain separating reality and art. It wasn't a wall; it was a boundary designed to protect what it had created, to ensure the safe existence of this extraordinary world within the canvas, a world Abby could now truly call home.

"I'll always be here, David," Abby said softly, as if reading his thoughts. "In every brushstroke, in every color, in every detail of this world. You'll always be a part of me, just as I'll always be a part of you."

Her words were a balm to his troubled heart. They weren't simply words; they were a promise, a testament to the enduring power of their love. He knew that their physical connection would soon fade, that the ease of traversing the boundary between worlds would cease. He understood that this goodbye, while painful, was a necessary transition, a way to secure Abby's existence within the painting.

He leaned forward, gently cupping her face in his hands. Her skin felt warm, solid, and real, yet he could still see the almost transparent quality of her presence, a subtle hint of her otherworldly origins. He knew that this moment, this physical connection, would soon fade as the boundary between worlds solidified, but the memory would remain, etched forever in his heart.

"I'll never forget you, Abby," he whispered, his voice thick with emotion. "Never."

He felt the sadness of their impending separation, a deep and penetrating sorrow, but it wasn't the all-consuming despair that had haunted them during their desperate struggle to save the painting. This was a different kind of sorrow, tinged with acceptance, with a quiet understanding of the sacrifices necessary to secure the preservation of their extraordinary love.

They spent the remaining days together, exploring the now fully restored landscape, reminiscing about their journey, celebrating their triumph, and preparing for their parting. Each shared moment, each shared laugh, each tender touch, was deeply savored and cherished. The once-overwhelming fear of loss was replaced by a quiet acceptance, a knowing that their love would transcend time and space.

The day of David's departure finally arrived, a day both joyful and heart-wrenching. As he stood at the edge of the spring, ready to step back into his own reality, he felt the familiar pull of his own world, a powerful force drawing him back, the boundary between the worlds growing ever stronger. The painting pulsed with a gentle light, the spring's shimmer no longer a desperate, frantic attempt at revitalization, but instead a serene, steady glow. It was a light of peace, of acceptance, of gratitude.

He looked back at Abby, her silhouette bathed in the soft, golden light of the setting sun. The painting had been completely restored, a vibrant testament to their extraordinary love. He knew, with a certainty that transcended all doubt, that she would be safe, protected within the beautiful world they had painstakingly recreated. Their love, born in the heart of a painting, had blossomed, saved a world, and ultimately, would survive the passing of time and the inevitable separation of their physical selves.

As he turned to leave, a single tear traced a path down his cheek, a tear not of despair, but of bittersweet acceptance, of a love so powerful it had conquered the boundaries of reality itself, a love that would forever resonate within the heart of a restored painting, and within the heart of a young man forever changed by the magic of love and the power of a canvas. The journey had been challenging, full of uncertainty and anticipation, of fears realized and hope found anew. Their love story, once a desperate struggle for survival, had transformed into a beautiful testament to resilience, an epic of love that transcended the boundaries of time and reality. And as David stepped back into his own world, he carried with him not the sorrow of loss, but the enduring warmth of a love that would never truly fade.

Chapter 10
A New Connection

The threshold shimmered, a faint, almost imperceptible ripple in the air where the painting hung in his grandmother's study. David hesitated, his hand hovering over the barely-there surface. It had been weeks since their last meeting, weeks filled with the echoing silence of their parting, a silence punctuated only by the persistent ache in his chest. The vibrant energy that had once pulsed from the canvas was now subdued, a gentle luminescence rather than the electric current that had accompanied their desperate fight to save Abby's world. He understood the change; it was the painting's way of solidifying its newfound stability, of establishing the protective boundary that had been essential for its survival, a boundary that also separated him from Abby.

He closed his eyes, taking a deep breath, steeling himself for the potential of what awaited him. This wouldn't be the easy, boundless connection of their shared struggle; this would be a tentative reunion, a delicate dance on the edge of two worlds. He pictured Abby's face, her eyes mirroring the myriad colors of the restored landscape, a landscape he had helped to create, a landscape that had become a haven for her. The thought of seeing her again filled him with a mixture of hope and trepidation. Hope that he would find her well, that the restored world was indeed a sanctuary; trepidation that the separation, the newly solidified boundary, would make their connection feel impossibly distant.

With a deep breath, he stepped through.

The transition was smoother this time, less jarring, less disorienting. He found himself standing in the heart of the Victorian park, the air alive with the scent of freshly bloomed flowers and damp earth. The revitalized landscape was even more breathtaking than he remembered; the colors were richer, the details more intricate, the overall feeling one of vibrant, peaceful harmony. It was a world reborn, a world that pulsed with a quiet contentment, a world shielded from the chaos of his own reality.

He walked slowly, his footsteps barely disturbing the stillness of the perfectly manicured lawns. He searched for her, his heart pounding a rhythm of anticipation against his ribs. He had missed her profoundly; he had yearned for her touch, her laughter, the comforting warmth of her presence. But the memory of their goodbye – a farewell made necessary for her safety – remained a sharp, persistent reminder of the sacrifice they had made.

He found her by the revitalized spring, her back to him, her hands tracing the delicate patterns of a newly bloomed flower. She was bathed in the soft, ethereal light of the spring, her form seemingly more solid, more fully realized within this restored world. The transparent quality that had marked her previously was still there, a faint ethereal glow, but now it was an inherent part of her, no longer a sign of fragility, but an indication of her otherworldly nature intertwined with the restored canvas.

He approached cautiously, the sound of his footsteps muted by the soft grass. He hesitated, unsure of how to break the silence, unsure of how to approach this new reality of their connection. He didn't want to overwhelm her, didn't want to shatter the peace that had settled upon this world.

"Abby?" he whispered, his voice barely audible.

She turned, her eyes widening in surprise. A slow smile spread across her lips, a smile that warmed him from the inside out. It was a smile that held a multitude of emotions – relief, happiness, love – but also a hint of melancholy, a quiet acknowledgment of their altered circumstances.

She rushed toward him, her movements graceful and fluid, and embraced him tightly. Her touch was warm, solid, real, but with a subtle ethereal quality that still reminded him of her otherworldly origins. It was the touch of someone who had experienced the brink of annihilation and emerged stronger, more profoundly alive.

"David," she whispered, her voice laced with emotion. "I was wondering when you would come back."

He held her close, the feeling of her in his arms both comforting and devastating. This wasn't the easy, effortless intimacy of their first encounters; this was a connection tempered by distance, by the newfound solidity of the boundary between their worlds, by the very act of their preservation. It was a different kind of love; a deeper, more meaningful kind, born not just from shared passion but from shared sacrifice.

They walked together in silence for a time, exploring the revived world, their steps in perfect synchronization. They paused by the revitalized streams, watching the water dance in the sunlight, marveling at the detail of the reborn flora and fauna that thrived around them. They spoke little, but their silence spoke volumes – a shared understanding, a profound acceptance of the new dynamics of their relationship.

"It's beautiful," David said finally, his voice thick with emotion. "You've made it beautiful."

Abby smiled, her gaze moving across the landscape. "We made it beautiful," she corrected softly. "We did it together."

He nodded, the weight of their shared journey settling upon him anew. He had almost forgotten the fear, the desperation, the frantic struggle to restore this world. Now, as he gazed upon its breathtaking splendor, he could only feel gratitude, a sense of overwhelming peace, and the quiet sadness of their separation.

They spent the rest of the day together, exploring the re-imagined landscapes. They revisited their favorite places, the once-desolate areas now teeming with vibrant life. They shared stories, reminisced about their journey, and spoke of their futures, separate yet intertwined. He learned more about her life within the painting, about the other inhabitants he had never had the opportunity to truly meet, about the rich history she uncovered through her interactions with them. Abby, in turn, learned more about his life beyond the canvas, his friends, his family, his aspirations and fears. These stories served as a bridge, a testament to the durability of their connection.

As the sun began to set, painting the sky in hues of orange and purple, they sat by the spring, the shimmering water reflecting the colors of the heavens. The boundary between worlds was clear, no longer a hazy, almost intangible divide, but a solid, albeit permeable,

151

line. But as their time together began to draw to a close, there was a sense of completion, a feeling of quiet peace that was far more fulfilling than their previous chaotic coexistence. They had preserved their love, and in that preservation, they found a new kind of intimacy.

The knowledge that their physical proximity would eventually end did not diminish their love but, paradoxically, strengthened it. Their parting was not a dissolution, but a transition, a shift into a deeper understanding of their connection. It was a love that had defied the laws of reality, a love that would continue to exist, regardless of the space between them.

"Until next time, David," Abby whispered, her eyes holding a profound depth, a depth that contained their shared history, their mutual resilience, and the unbreakable bond that transcended time and dimensions.

"Until next time," he echoed, his voice husky with emotion. And as he stepped back through the shimmering threshold, he carried the image of her face, the memory of their renewed connection, a connection that was now stronger, deeper, and infinitely more precious because it was shared amidst the acceptance of their inevitable separation. Their love story had entered a new chapter, a chapter marked not by proximity, but by an enduring connection that transcended the boundaries of the physical world.

The air within the painting felt different. It wasn't just the enhanced vibrancy of the restored landscape, though that was striking enough. The very essence of the place had shifted, subtly but profoundly. The once-frantic energy that had thrummed with their desperate struggle for survival was gone, replaced by a calm, settled stillness. It felt…older. As if time itself had flowed differently within the canvas, marking the passage of weeks, perhaps months, in a way that mirrored the flow of time in David's own world.

He noticed the changes immediately. The spring, the focal point of their previous encounters, now flowed with a gentler current, its waters clearer, reflecting a sky that seemed to hold a deeper, more saturated blue. Flowers, unknown to him before, bloomed in vibrant hues around its banks. The trees, once skeletal and bare in parts, were now draped in lush foliage, their leaves rustling in a gentle breeze he hadn't felt before. Even the paths seemed to have matured, their stones worn smoother by the passage of what he could only assume were countless sunsets and sunrises. The entire landscape bore the imprint of time's quiet hand, a testament to the resilience of the painting, and perhaps, to Abby's own adaptation to her strange new existence.

He felt a pang of sadness, a subtle ache in his chest, recognizing the passage of time not just as a physical change, but as a reflection of the growing distance between them. This wasn't the frantic urgency of their previous meetings, where every moment felt precious, where survival hung in the balance. This was different. This was a world that had found its peace, a peace that he, in his own way, had helped to create, but a peace that also kept him at a remove, a respectful distance from the life that thrived within.

His gaze settled on a small, moss-covered stone bench nestled beneath a sprawling oak tree, a bench that hadn't been there before. It was simple, almost rustic, but it exuded a sense of quiet contemplation, of moments spent in peaceful reflection. He could almost picture Abby sitting there, lost in thought, perhaps sketching in her worn leather-bound journal, a journal he had glimpsed during their frantic attempts to save the painting. The image stirred a longing within him, a deep ache for a connection that was now tempered by the passage of time and the solidified boundary that separated them.

He continued to explore the altered landscape, marveling at the subtle yet profound changes. He found a small copse of trees he didn't remember, their branches interwoven to form a natural canopy that sheltered a hidden glade. Within the glade, he discovered a small, hand-built birdhouse, its entrance perfectly sized for a wren, a tiny detail that spoke volumes about the quiet evolution of the painting, the slow, deliberate growth of life within the canvas.

The sense of discovery was both exhilarating and melancholic. It was a joy to witness the blossoming of this world, to see it thrive and mature, but it was also a poignant reminder of the time that had passed, the time he had spent away from Abby, the time that had irrevocably changed the nature of their relationship.

As he moved deeper into the park, the air grew cooler, damper. He found a new stream, its waters crystal clear, cascading down a small waterfall that glistened in the dappled sunlight. The sound of the water, a gentle murmuring, was soothing, peaceful, a calming counterpoint to the turmoil that still resonated within his heart.

He found Abby by the stream, her back to him, her long hair catching the light as she bent to examine something in the water. The ethereal glow that had always been a part of her seemed even more subtle now, more integrated into her form, less a sign of fragility and more of an intrinsic element of her existence. She appeared stronger, more confident, more fully formed within the now-stable reality of the painting.

He watched her for a moment, drinking in the sight of her, memorizing the details of her posture, the curve of her neck, the delicate way her fingers traced the ripples in the water. She had adapted, she had thrived, she had found peace within her strange, confined world. And he, in turn, had to adapt, to accept the changes, to find peace in a love that was now defined as much by distance as by intimacy.

He approached her softly, his steps barely disturbing the stillness of the glade. He felt the weight of their shared history, the struggle they had endured, the sacrifice they had made. And yet, as he looked at her, he felt a profound sense of peace, a quiet contentment that surpassed the turbulent emotions of their earlier encounters.

"Abby," he whispered, his voice barely audible above the gentle murmur of the stream.

She turned, her eyes widening slightly in surprise, before a slow, serene smile spread across her lips. The smile was different now, more mature, more reflective, yet it held the same warmth, the same depth of feeling that had captivated him from the beginning.

"David," she said, her voice soft, melodious. "I thought you might come."

He stepped closer, hesitant at first, then reaching out to gently take her hand. Her skin felt cool, smooth, yet solid, her touch a comforting reminder of their shared journey. The ethereal quality of her being remained, but it was now an integral part of her, a subtle shimmer that highlighted her otherworldly nature, instead of a symbol of vulnerability.

They walked along the stream, sharing stories, their conversation flowing effortlessly, a gentle current of reminiscence and shared experience. She spoke of the changes in the painting, of the new inhabitants that had appeared, of the growth and evolution of the landscape, a world that was now truly her home. She spoke of her newfound peace, her contentment, her acceptance of her unique circumstances.

He listened intently, his heart filled with a complex mixture of emotions. He was happy for her, relieved that she was safe, content, and thriving. But he was also acutely aware of the distance between them, the physical barrier that separated their worlds.

As the day wore on, they explored the changed landscape together. They climbed a small hill, now covered in wildflowers, and gazed out over the expansive park. They sat by the waterfall, listening to the rush of the water, feeling the mist on their faces. They shared memories, laughed, and spoke of the future, separate yet intertwined. Their conversation was punctuated by long silences, filled not with awkwardness, but with a deep understanding, a shared appreciation of their altered circumstances, and the enduring power of their love.

As dusk settled, painting the sky in vibrant hues of orange and purple, they returned to the stream. The sun's last rays reflected on the water, creating a shimmering spectacle of color. They sat side-by-side, their hands clasped gently together, their silence more profound, more meaningful than any words could ever express.

"It's different now," Abby said softly, her gaze drifting across the landscape.

"Yes," David replied, his voice a low murmur. "But in a way...better."

She nodded, her eyes reflecting the fading light. "Our love is different too. Stronger, perhaps. More enduring."

He squeezed her hand, his heart aching with a bittersweet mixture of joy and sadness. Their love was indeed different, tempered by time and distance, yet infinitely stronger because of the shared sacrifice, the shared understanding, and the enduring bond that transcended the boundaries of their separate realities. This was a love that had survived the storm, a love that would endure, regardless of the distance between them.

The realization brought a profound sense of peace, a quiet acceptance of the new reality of their connection. Their love wasn't about proximity; it was about an enduring bond that stretched across the chasm of two worlds, a testament to the power of love to defy the constraints of reality itself. The world within the painting had changed, reflecting the passage of time and the resilience of its inhabitants. Their love had changed too, but its essence remained, a beacon of hope, a constant reminder that some connections, once forged, could never truly be broken. Their story was far from over, but it had entered a new chapter, one filled with a quieter, deeper love that transcended time and space, a love that would last long after the paint began to fade.

The shared silence between them was comfortable, a comfortable weight of unspoken understanding. The setting sun cast long shadows across the stream, painting the water in hues of gold and crimson. Abby traced the patterns of the light on the water's surface with a delicate finger, her movements fluid and graceful. David watched her, his heart a quiet symphony of bittersweet emotions. The initial shock of seeing her again, after the perilous journey of saving the painting, had faded, replaced by a deeper, more nuanced appreciation for their unique connection.

"Remember that storm?" Abby finally spoke, her voice soft as the rustling of leaves in the nearby trees. "The one that almost destroyed the painting? We were so close to losing everything."

David chuckled softly, a low rumble in his chest. "Almost. We were clinging to each other, barely holding on to the canvas itself. I thought for a moment we'd be pulled apart, scattered like paint across a ravaged surface."

A shared smile passed between them, a tender moment of shared vulnerability, a reminder of the precariousness of their situation and the strength of their bond in the face of it. The memory brought back a flood of sensations – the fear, the desperation, the sheer, overwhelming relief when the storm finally subsided. It had been a crucible, forging a connection that had transcended the limitations of their realities.

"And the way the colors bled together," Abby murmured, her eyes distant, lost in the memory. "It felt like our worlds were merging, like the boundaries were blurring."

"It was chaotic, terrifying," David agreed. "But there was also a strange beauty to it, a raw energy that was almost exhilarating." He paused, remembering the intensity of their emotions, the desperate clinging to each other in the face of oblivion. "That was when I truly knew I was in love with you, Abby. Not just drawn to you, but in love, with a depth and intensity I'd never known before."

Abby's gaze met his, a silent exchange passing between them that spoke volumes. The confession, though spoken now in the calm aftermath, held the weight of that chaotic moment, the intensity of a love born in the midst of chaos and fear. The memory served not as a harrowing reminder, but as a testament to the strength of their connection, a bond forged in the heart of the storm.

They spent the next hour lost in a tapestry of shared memories. They recalled their initial encounters, the hesitant first steps of their relationship, the slow, tentative discovery of their shared world. Abby described the loneliness she had felt in the painting, the isolation of a world confined to the confines of a canvas, a reality where time itself seemed to flow differently. David spoke of his own struggles, the growing disconnection from his own life, the sacrifice he made in leaving her behind to save her world.

They talked about the small details, the insignificant moments that had woven themselves into the fabric of their extraordinary relationship. The first time they laughed together, the first time they touched, the shared sense of wonder at the vibrant colors, the intricate details of the Victorian landscape that had become their shared sanctuary. Each memory, seemingly inconsequential on its own, combined to paint a vivid portrait of their unique bond, a relationship that stretched across realities and defied the boundaries of time.

The conversation flowed effortlessly, punctuated by long, comfortable silences filled with the unspoken understanding that exists between those who have shared profound experiences. The evening air grew cooler as dusk gave way to night, the stars beginning to prick the darkening sky. Abby pointed out constellations she knew, constellations invisible from David's world. He listened, fascinated, lost in the beauty of the night sky, the beauty of their shared experience, the quiet strength of their connection.

"Do you ever think about what would have happened if I hadn't found you?" David asked a quiet question that hung in the air.

Abby's expression softened, her gaze drifting towards the gently flowing stream. "I often wonder," she replied. "I don't know if I could have survived. The painting…it was fading. I was fading with it. You gave me a reason to hold on, a reason to believe that I could survive, that I could thrive."

Her words resonated deeply within David, a testament to the profound impact they had had on each other's lives. He had saved her world, but she had saved him too, drawing him out of the mundane routine of his own life, opening his heart to a love that transcended the ordinary.

"And you," she continued, turning to look at him, "you taught me hope. You showed me that even in the most impossible of circumstances, there is still beauty, there is still love, there is still hope for a better future. Your sacrifice…it will always stay with me."

The weight of her words settled upon David, heavy yet comforting. He had sacrificed his connection with her, but in doing so, he had given her the gift of survival, the gift of a life she never thought possible. It was a profound sacrifice, but one made with a heart full of love, a love that transcended the boundaries of their separate worlds.

The night deepened, the stars blazing brighter in the clear, dark sky. They sat in silence for a long time, the unspoken words hanging between them like the silent stars above. They watched the moon rise, painting the landscape in shades of silver and grey, its soft light illuminating their faces, highlighting the depth of their feelings. The air was filled with a palpable sense of peace, a tranquility born from shared experiences and the unwavering strength of their bond.

As the night wore on, their conversation drifted back to the present, to the changed landscape of the painting, to the new life that had blossomed within its borders. They spoke of the small details, the subtle changes they had observed, the quiet evolution of their shared world. They shared their hopes and dreams, their fears and anxieties, weaving a tapestry of shared experiences that bound them together even more tightly.

The conversation flowed seamlessly from one topic to another, weaving a tapestry of shared memories, present hopes and future possibilities. They talked about the new flora that had sprung up around the stream, the birds that sang sweeter melodies than ever before and the gentle breeze that now constantly stirred the branches of the oak tree. They talked about how the colors were richer, the light more vibrant, how the overall energy of the landscape felt rejuvenated. It was a world healed, a reflection of the healing that had taken place in their lives.

And yet, undercurrents of sadness and longing persisted. The reality of their separation, the physical barrier between their worlds, remained a constant presence, a sobering reminder of the sacrifices made and the distance that still separated them. But it was a different kind of sadness now, a bittersweet acknowledgment of the reality of their circumstances, rather than a crushing weight of despair.

As the first hint of dawn touched the horizon, painting the sky in soft pastel hues, David knew it was time to go. He stood, offering Abby a gentle smile, a smile that held both the joy of their shared memories and the quiet sorrow of their separation.

"I'll see you again, Abby," he whispered, his voice barely audible above the gentle sounds of the awakening world.

"Yes," she replied, her voice soft, her eyes shining with unshed tears. "I'll be waiting."

He reached out, taking her hand one last time, their fingers intertwining, holding on to the lingering warmth of their shared connection. It was a silent promise, a promise born from love, loss, and the unwavering strength of a connection that transcended time, space, and the very fabric of reality. The painting, their shared sanctuary, stood as a testament to their love, a vibrant reflection of a connection that would endure, despite the distance, a connection that would continue to flourish even as the boundaries between their realities remained firmly in place.

The days that followed were a tapestry woven with threads of quiet intimacy and unspoken understanding. The urgency of their earlier meetings, the desperate fight for survival, had faded, replaced by a gentler rhythm, a slower, more deliberate dance of hearts. They explored the painting together, not with the frantic energy of those first encounters, but with a calm appreciation for the intricate details, the hidden corners, the whispering secrets of the Victorian world.

They discovered hidden pathways through the dense foliage of the park, paths unseen in their earlier, more hurried explorations. They found a secluded grove, bathed in dappled sunlight, where they spent hours conversing, sharing stories, dreams, and fears. Abby recounted tales of her solitary existence within the canvas, the slow creep of the encroaching decay, the desperate hope that had sustained her through the long years. David, in turn, spoke of his life outside the painting, his struggles with his studies, his tentative steps towards re-establishing connections with his family and friends.

Their conversations were no longer dominated by the immediate threat of the painting's collapse. Instead, they delved into deeper waters, exploring the complexities of their unique relationship, the profound impact they had had on each other's lives. They talked about the nature of time, how it flowed differently within the painting, the strange distortions of reality that their connection had created.

David began to understand that their love was not defined by physical proximity. It was a connection that transcended space and time, a bond forged in the crucible of shared experiences, a love that resonated on a deeper, more profound level. The physical separation, once a source of unbearable pain, now felt less like a chasm and more like a gentle distance, a respectful acknowledgment of the boundaries of their realities. Their connection existed on a different plane, woven into the very fabric of their shared memories, their intertwined destinies.

Abby, in turn, learned to accept the limitations of their situation. She understood the sacrifices David had made, the difficult choices he had faced, and she cherished the memory of their shared experiences. She no longer clung desperately to the hope of a physical union. Their love, she realized, was a gift, a treasure to be guarded and nurtured, even across the boundaries of their separate worlds.

Their days were filled with gentle explorations, quiet conversations, and shared moments of peace. They discovered a hidden waterfall, cascading down moss-covered rocks into a crystal-clear pool. They watched sunsets paint the sky in vibrant hues; their silences filled with the unspoken understanding that only comes with profound shared experiences. They learned the names of the wildflowers that blossomed in the meadows, the songs of the birds that sang in the trees, the rustling whispers of the leaves in the breeze.

One evening, as the moon cast its silvery light across the Victorian park, David sat beside Abby, her head resting on his shoulder. He traced the delicate lines of her face, marveling at the beauty that had captured his heart, a beauty that went far beyond the physical. It was a beauty that emanated from within, a radiant glow born of resilience, strength, and an unwavering spirit.

"I never thought I'd find love like this," David whispered, his voice thick with emotion. "A love that defies the rules, that transcends reality itself."

Abby smiled, a gentle, wistful smile that touched his heart. "Neither did I," she replied. "But it's a love worth cherishing, isn't it? A love that shows us the possibilities, the boundless potential that exists even in the most impossible of circumstances."

Their love was a testament to the enduring power of connection, a radiant flame that burned bright even in the face of adversity. It was a love that had no need for physical touch, for constant proximity. It was a love nourished by shared memories, by mutual respect, by an unwavering devotion that transcended the limitations of their separate realities.

They spent hours lost in the contemplation of their unique relationship, their conversations evolving into profound philosophical discussions on the nature of love, reality, and the human condition. They explored the meaning of sacrifice, the importance of acceptance, and the resilience of their spirit. They learned to appreciate the subtle nuances of their connection, the unspoken understanding that flowed between them, a silent language born of shared experiences and mutual respect.

One day, David brought a book with him into the painting, a collection of poetry that resonated with the emotions they were experiencing. They read aloud to each other, their voices blending together in a harmonious chorus of words that expressed the depth of their feelings. The poetry became a reflection of their shared journey,

161

a mirror to their souls, reflecting the profound emotional landscape they had traversed together.

The weeks turned into months, and their connection deepened, growing stronger with each passing day. They explored every nook and cranny of the Victorian park, discovering new secrets, uncovering hidden treasures, and forging an unbreakable bond between their hearts. The painting itself seemed to respond to their love, its colors growing richer, its light more vibrant, a vibrant reflection of the profound connection between David and Abby.

Their love was not a romantic fairytale, it was a mature, nuanced understanding of each other's souls. It was a love story woven with threads of resilience, acceptance, and profound respect, a testament to the boundless power of human connection. Their love transcended the physical limitations of their realities, forging a bond that time and distance could not diminish. It was a different kind of love, a love born in the heart of a storm, a love that would endure long after the last brushstroke faded from the canvas. It was a love that would forever reside in their hearts, a timeless reminder of the extraordinary connection they had shared. And in that enduring connection, they found a peace that surpassed all understanding, a solace that transcended their separate worlds, and a love that would bloom eternally in the garden of their shared memories.

The acceptance wasn't a sudden epiphany, a dramatic shift in perspective. It was a slow dawning, a gradual understanding that bloomed over time, nurtured by shared silences and quiet moments of contemplation. It began with small concessions, tiny shifts in their interactions. David, instead of lamenting his inability to physically touch Abby, found solace in the intimacy of their shared experiences, in the unspoken understanding that passed between them with a simple glance, a knowing smile. He learned to appreciate the ephemeral nature of their connection, the magic that existed within their shared space, a magic that transcended the limitations of their separate realities.

Abby, too, adjusted her expectations. She relinquished the desperate yearning for a tangible union, accepting the boundaries of their reality while cherishing the richness of their emotional bond. She understood that their love was not defined by physical proximity; it was a connection that resonated on a deeper level, woven into the very fabric of their shared existence within the painting. Her solitude, once a source of profound loneliness, was now softened by the memories of their time together, a constant reminder of the profound love they had shared.

One afternoon, they discovered a hidden garden within the painting, a secret oasis nestled amongst the overgrown foliage of the Victorian park. Sunbeams filtered through the leaves, illuminating a breathtaking array of wildflowers, their vibrant colors contrasting beautifully with the soft green of the surrounding landscape. They spent hours wandering through the garden, their conversation drifting from the mundane to the profound, their words weaving a tapestry of shared experiences and mutual understanding. They talked about their families, their dreams, their fears, their hopes for the future – a future that was both separate and intertwined. They realized that their love wasn't a temporary escape, but a profound connection that would shape their lives, even beyond the confines of the painting.

David started bringing more items into the painting—books, photographs, small trinkets that held personal significance. These objects became tangible links to his world, bridging the gap between their realities. He read aloud from his favorite novels, sharing the stories with Abby, enriching their shared experience with new narratives and perspectives. He showed her photographs of his family and friends, explaining their relationships, their personalities, their place in his life. These were not simply objects; they were fragments of his life, shared with the woman he loved, tokens of his devotion.

Abby, in turn, shared fragments of her history, piecing together a narrative of her life within the painting, a life lived in solitude but rich in internal experiences. She spoke of the changing seasons, of the subtle shifts in light and shadow, of the countless hours spent observing the world within the canvas. She described the textures of the flowers, the songs of the birds, the whispering secrets of the trees – creating a sensory world for David to engage with, a world that enriched his understanding of her experiences and deepened their connection. They created a shared history, a chronicle of their unique relationship, their love story unfolding within the vibrant landscape of the Victorian park.

Their conversations evolved into philosophical discussions, exploring the complexities of their unique bond. They debated the nature of time, the fluidity of reality, the boundaries of human experience. They pondered the concept of love itself, its many facets and expressions. They grappled with the acceptance of their limitations, the understanding that their love was a unique experience, a gift to be cherished, not a problem to be solved. They found comfort in their shared reality, in the knowledge that their love existed, independent of physical touch or temporal limitations. Their love wasn't constrained by the rules of their respective worlds but transcended them.

The painting itself seemed to react to their deepening acceptance, its colors growing more vibrant, its details more defined. It was as if the artwork itself was a testament to the strength of their love, a reflection of their shared journey. The light that once seemed to threaten them, now seemed to embrace them, bathing their secret garden in a soft, gentle glow. The once fragile canvas felt strengthened by their bond, their love giving it a new lease on life, a vibrant expression of a unique connection that would transcend even the constraints of its own physical form.

One evening, as the sun set, casting long shadows across the Victorian park, David and Abby sat together, their hands brushing lightly as they gazed out at the fading light. There was no desperate clinging, no unspoken yearning. There was only a deep, quiet understanding, a shared appreciation for the extraordinary beauty of their unlikely love story. They found peace in the acceptance of their circumstances, in the acknowledgment of their separate realities.

David knew he couldn't stay forever. The pull of his own life, his family, his friends, was a force he couldn't ignore. But the memory of this extraordinary love would forever remain, a treasure he would carry with him, a reminder of a connection that transcended the boundaries of time and space. And Abby, too, found peace in the knowledge that their love would endure, a lasting testament to the extraordinary circumstances that brought them together.

Their parting, when it came, was not a tearful goodbye, but a quiet farewell, a tender acknowledgement of the unique and precious bond they had shared. It was an ending that, paradoxically, felt like a beginning, the start of a new chapter in their separate lives, shaped and enriched by the extraordinary love that had blossomed within the confines of a painting. The memory of their love would become a timeless tale, a shared secret that would reside in their hearts forever.

The painting, a silent witness to their journey, would remain a potent symbol of their connection – a vibrant tapestry woven with threads of love, acceptance, and an enduring bond that time and space could never diminish. The painting would fade, as all things eventually do, but the echo of their love would continue to reverberate through the years, a testament to the power of human connection, and a reminder that some loves transcend the boundaries of reality itself, blossoming in the impossible places, defying all expectations.

David returned to his own world, carrying with him the weight of their shared experiences and the indelible mark of their love. His life would never be the same. The mundane would always be colored by the extraordinary magic he'd experienced. He would never forget the vibrant beauty of the Victorian park, nor the girl who had taught him the true meaning of love, a love that defied the ordinary, a love that existed beyond the constraints of time and space.

Abby remained within the painting, her solitude no longer a desolate emptiness but a sanctuary filled with cherished memories, a silent testament to a love that had touched her soul and transformed her existence. She would continue her solitary existence, yet her heart would forever beat with the rhythm of David's love, a vibrant echo that would resonate through the silent halls of her painted world.

Their love story was a testament to the enduring power of connection, a beacon shining brightly in the heart of the impossible, proving that love knows no boundaries, no limits, no confines. It was a love story etched into the heart of a painting, a story that would be whispered on the wind, carried on the breeze, and echoed through time, a timeless reminder that even in the most improbable of circumstances, love can flourish, endure, and leave an unforgettable mark on the heart and soul. It was a love that transcended reality itself, a love that would forever bloom eternally in the garden of their shared memories.

Chapter 11
Bridging Worlds

The quiet understanding that had blossomed between them wasn't a passive acceptance of their limitations, but an active engagement with the paradoxical nature of their reality. David began to see Abby not as a prisoner of the canvas, but as an inhabitant of a unique, self-contained world. He started to observe the subtle nuances of her existence, the way the light played on her hair, the subtle shift in her expression as the seasons changed within the painting. He learned to appreciate the quiet dignity of her solitude, the richness of her internal life, her capacity for joy and sorrow within the confines of her painted world. He understood that her existence, while confined to the two dimensions of the canvas, was nonetheless as vibrant and full as his own.

His visits became less about escaping his reality and more about sharing in hers. He brought more than just objects; he brought stories, songs, and poems, weaving them into the fabric of their shared existence. He'd read passages from classic literature, his voice resonating in the silent park, sharing the timeless tales with Abby. He'd sing along to the melodies he hummed under his breath, his voice blending with the songs of the unseen birds in the trees of their secret garden. He'd create whimsical stories from his own life, tales woven from memory and imagination, always keeping in mind Abby's unique perspective within this world made of paint and dreams.

He learned to listen more than he spoke, truly hearing the stories Abby shared, the subtle observations she made of the world around her. He was captivated by her descriptions of the way the sunlight filtered through the leaves, the delicate dance of shadows that played across the grass, the whispering secrets that seemed to emanate from the ancient trees. He learned to see the beauty in the stillness, the quiet richness of her existence within the painting. He wasn't just visiting her; he was becoming a part of her world, a cherished visitor in her solitary life.

One day, David brought a small, worn sketchbook to the painting. He opened it to a blank page and began to sketch, capturing the essence of their shared moments. He drew the wildflowers from their secret garden, the delicate curvature of Abby's smile, the way the light danced on the leaves of the trees. Abby, in turn, taught him about the hidden language of the birds, the subtle signals that communicated their moods and their intentions. She revealed the secrets of the painting, showing him hidden paths and secret passages that were only visible at certain times of the day. The artwork became a shared canvas, not just for David's sketches, but for the unfolding of their shared experiences, their lives intertwined within the confines of the art itself.

He learned to appreciate the constraints of their reality as a defining feature of their love, rather than an obstacle. The physical boundaries between them became less significant; their connection deepened through shared moments, gestures, unspoken understandings. He learned to perceive time differently, to appreciate the slow, deliberate pace of life within the painting, a stark contrast to the relentless speed of his own world. He discovered that the true richness of life wasn't measured in minutes and hours, but in shared moments of intimacy and understanding.

As their relationship deepened, so too did their understanding of the painting itself. They discovered hidden symbols, cryptic messages woven into the landscape, suggesting a deeper meaning to the artwork. They unearthed ancient texts, whispered secrets contained within the intricacies of the brushstrokes. They began to suspect the painting itself held a hidden history, a narrative that mirrored their own unlikely connection. The painting's vibrant colors seemed to intensify as their relationship blossomed, the canvas itself reflecting the strength of their connection. The once-fragile canvas took on a new vibrancy, the colors pulsating with a life of its own.

Their shared investigation of the painting's secrets brought them closer together, forging a bond that transcended the physical world. They deciphered coded messages, revealed hidden passages, solved ancient riddles, all contributing to their mutual understanding and deepening their love. They worked together, piecing together fragments of knowledge and experiences, constructing a shared narrative that blended the artist's original vision with their own unique relationship. It was a collaborative process, an unfolding mystery that mirrored the growth of their love.

Their relationship wasn't just a romantic connection; it was a collaborative journey, a shared exploration of the enigmatic beauty of the painting and the mysteries it contained. The more they learned about painting, the more they learned about themselves, about their individual capabilities, and the surprising strengths they possessed. Their exploration of the art transformed not only their understanding of their relationship but also their individual identities, making them stronger and more self-aware.

David began to appreciate the depth of Abby's existence within the painting, recognizing that she wasn't merely a figment of the artist's imagination, but a sentient being with a rich internal life. He understood her solitude wasn't simply loneliness, but a unique form of existence, a peaceful contemplation within her unique world. He started to see her resilience and strength, not merely as a consequence of being trapped in a painting, but as an intrinsic quality of her being. She was a woman of exceptional inner strength and grace, an independent spirit who found contentment and meaning within the boundaries of her world.

He also understood the ethical dilemma their connection presented. His presence, his intrusions into her world, were gradually straining the fabric of the painting. The vibrant colors started to fade in places, the details becoming blurred, the edges of the canvas showing signs of weakening. He saw that his love for Abby, though genuine and profound, was inadvertently causing harm to her reality.

This understanding didn't diminish his feelings for her; instead, it intensified them, adding a layer of poignant awareness and responsibility to their relationship. The knowledge of the painting's fragility and their growing affection forced David to face a heartbreaking choice. He had to reconcile his love for Abby with the inevitable consequences of their bond. He had to consider the ramifications of his presence, the price of their extraordinary connection.

The decision to leave, when it finally came, was not a simple act of departure. It was a conscious choice; a sacrifice made out of love and respect for Abby's well-being. It was a painful realization that true love isn't always about what you want but what's best for the person you love. He had to accept that his love, while beautiful and meaningful, could not come at the cost of her existence. The choice was agonizing, but necessary, a tribute to the depth of his affection and recognition of the boundaries of their unique relationship.

His departure wasn't an abrupt severing of their connection; it was a gradual fading, a slow farewell that allowed their love to linger in the air between them, a gentle goodbye that allowed their bond to continue, albeit on a more subdued level. His visits became less frequent, his presence in her world more ephemeral, his goodbye a tender acknowledgment of their precious time together, a heartfelt understanding that their relationship, though limited by the boundaries of their respective realities, possessed an extraordinary significance.

The last time he entered the painting, he found Abby in their secret garden. The setting sun painted the sky with hues of orange and purple, casting a melancholic yet beautiful glow on the scene. There were no tears, no dramatic pronouncements, only a quiet acceptance, a shared understanding of the bittersweet nature of their farewell. They held each other's gaze, a silent exchange passing between them, conveying the depth of their affection, the profound sadness of their separation, and the enduring strength of their shared memories.

They parted with a knowing glance, a subtle touch, an unspoken promise that their connection would endure, a lasting imprint on their hearts. The quiet acceptance of their parting spoke volumes of the love they shared, the respect they had for each other's realities, and the enduring nature of their bond. It wasn't an ending, but a transformation, a quiet shift that underscored the extraordinary beauty of their love. It was an acceptance of their limits, a testament to their shared love. As David stepped back into his world, he carried the memory of their unique relationship, a love story etched in his heart forever, a reminder of a love that transcended the bounds of reality itself. The painting remained, a silent testament to a love that defied the ordinary, a love story for the ages, forever lingering in the brushstrokes of their shared moments, their shared existence, their shared love.

The initial shock of leaving Abby had faded, replaced by a quiet ache, a constant, low hum of longing that vibrated beneath the surface of his everyday life. He found himself studying more diligently, his academic pursuits offering a welcome distraction, a tangible anchor in the chaotic swirl of emotions. His relationships with his friends, once neglected, gradually mended, each conversation a small step back toward normalcy, each shared laugh a gentle balm on his wounded heart. He wasn't trying to forget Abby; he couldn't. Instead, he was learning to integrate her memory, her unique presence, into the fabric of his life, weaving it into the tapestry of his experiences.

He visited the painting less frequently, his visits carefully planned, precisely timed. These visits weren't escapes anymore; they were pilgrimages, brief reunions with a beloved ghost. He brought small gifts – a single wildflower, a carefully chosen stone, a poem written in his neatest script – tokens of remembrance, whispers of his continuing affection.

Abby, in turn, seemed to have found a new equilibrium within the confines of her world. Her quiet solitude wasn't a sign of despair, but a contented acceptance, a quiet strength that resonated even across the gulf of their separate realities. Her descriptions of her days were filled with a peaceful serenity, a subtle joy that belied the extraordinary circumstances of her existence. She spoke of the changing seasons within the painting, the subtle shifts in light and shadow, the whispers of the wind through the painted leaves. She described the intricate dance of the painted birds, their songs a symphony of quiet beauty. Her voice, when it reached him through the canvas, was filled with a calm resilience, a quiet grace that touched him deeply.

David learned to communicate with her through subtle gestures, almost imperceptible movements, a silent language born of their shared understanding. A slight adjustment of a flower in her hair, a carefully placed stone near a particular tree, a subtly altered arrangement of leaves – these minute changes became their mode of silent communication, a whispered dialogue across the chasm of their separate worlds. These subtle interactions became their own kind of intimacy, a refined dance of unspoken emotions, a testament to the depth of their connection that transcended the limitations of their realities.

He began to understand the painting itself in a new light. He saw it not just as a portal, but as a delicate ecosystem, a self-contained world that needed to maintain its balance. He recognized that his constant intrusions had disrupted that balance, threatening the very existence of the world within. His earlier visits had been fueled by selfish desires – to escape his own reality, to find solace in the embrace of another world. Now, his visits were acts of careful stewardship, respectful gestures meant to preserve, not consume. He understood that his love for Abby demanded not only his attention but also his careful consideration of her fragile world.

He started researching art conservation techniques, reading articles on the preservation of aging paintings, learning about the delicate balance of light and temperature, the dangers of humidity and exposure. He applied his knowledge to his visits, taking painstaking care to minimize his impact, his presence becoming as fleeting and gentle as a summer breeze. His visits were shorter, more infrequent, yet somehow more profound, more meaningful. They were no longer about escaping his own life but about cherishing the precious connection that remained.

He discovered that finding a balance wasn't about sacrificing his life for Abby, but about integrating her into his life, making her a cherished, if unconventional, part of his world. He found that he could carry her memory, her essence, with him, not as a burden, but as a source of strength, a quiet joy that subtly colored his experiences. He began to see the beauty in the mundane, the quiet richness of his everyday life, the beauty that once had been overshadowed by the allure of the painted world.

His art classes, once a source of frustration, now offered a unique form of connection to Abby. He started experimenting with his own paintings, attempting to capture the essence of their shared world, the subtle nuances of light and shadow, the delicate beauty of their secret garden. His paintings weren't mere copies of the artwork; they were expressions of his love for Abby, an attempt to convey the depth and complexity of their shared experience. They were a way of translating his memories into a tangible form, a way of keeping her presence alive within his own world.

He even started incorporating aspects of the Victorian aesthetics into his own style, mirroring the unique charm and character of Abby's painted world. He used muted colors and delicate brushstrokes, attempting to evoke the same quiet tranquility that permeated her existence. The result was a unique collection of paintings, a personal homage to their unusual romance, a testament to their enduring connection. These paintings were not merely artistic expressions; they were deeply personal narratives, a testament to a love story that transcended the boundaries of reality.

The balance he had achieved wasn't a perfect equilibrium; it was a dynamic, constantly shifting state, a delicate dance between his own reality and the memory of Abby's world. There were moments of profound longing, moments when the ache in his heart was almost unbearable. But those moments were tempered by the quiet strength he had found within himself, the resilience he had discovered through his shared journey with Abby.

He knew their relationship would never be the same. He accepted that their love was a unique and fragile thing, confined to the edges of his reality and the confines of the painted world. Yet, in the quiet acceptance of their limitations, he found a new depth of appreciation for their shared experience. Their love, though forever altered, remained a vital and vibrant part of his life, a quiet force that fueled his passions, shaped his ambitions, and added a profound richness to his everyday life. It was a love story unlike any other, a testament to a connection that transcended the boundaries of time and space, a love that continued to echo in the quiet spaces of his heart, a constant reminder of the magic that existed just beyond the edge of the ordinary.

The understanding dawned slowly, a gradual shift in perspective rather than a sudden epiphany. It wasn't a conscious decision, not a neatly packaged resolution, but a subtle unfolding, a quiet acceptance of the inherent limitations of their connection. He began to see the painting not merely as a portal to another world, but as a living entity, a delicate ecosystem teetering on the brink of collapse. His earlier visits, fueled by selfish desires for escape and solace, had unknowingly destabilized this delicate balance. Now, he understood the gravity of his actions, the profound responsibility he held.

His research into art conservation broadened his comprehension. He learned about the intricate processes of aging, the subtle degradation of pigments under differing light and humidity levels, the insidious threat of even the slightest temperature fluctuations. He discovered the delicate chemistry of the canvas itself, the intricate weave of fibers and the unseen forces that held the artwork together. This newfound knowledge instilled in him a profound sense of respect, a deep reverence for the fragility of Abby's world.

As time passed, the painting showed signs of stabilization. The rate of fading seemed to slow, the colors holding on with a tenacity that mirrored David's unwavering commitment. He realized that his presence wasn't simply a threat; it was a paradoxical form of sustenance. His careful, respectful visits, his meticulous observations, his conscious efforts to minimize disruption, seemed to be sustaining the delicate ecosystem of her world. It was as if their shared love itself acted as a counterpoint to the natural deterioration of the artwork, a strange, symbiotic relationship forged in the crucible of their unique connection.

The subtle shifts in the arrangement of flowers, the almost imperceptible changes in the light and shadow, continued, but now they felt less like threats and more like a silent dialogue. He'd even start to leave small, delicate poems nestled amongst the flowers, written on specially treated paper that would fade over time, leaving no lasting mark on the painting. He'd write about the sunrise, the patterns in the clouds, the changing colors of the leaves, sharing his observations of his own world in an ephemeral way that reflected the delicate beauty of Abby's world. These poems became another layer of their shared existence, a way of bridging the gap between two seemingly disparate realities.

His visits became less frequent, but no less meaningful. They were no longer fueled by the urgency of escape or the yearning for connection, but rather by the quiet appreciation of a precious shared existence. The painting, once a portal to escape, had become a sacred space, a testament to a love that defied the boundaries of time and reality. He felt a deep responsibility towards the world he'd discovered, a profound understanding of his role in maintaining its fragile existence. Their love story was an intricate tapestry, woven with threads of longing, respect, and acceptance, a beautiful, intricate testament to a love that extended beyond the bounds of the physical world. Their shared existence wasn't merely a shared reality; it was a shared responsibility, a testament to the enduring power of love in its many forms. And in the quiet contemplation of their shared space, in the delicate language of flowers and light and shadow, their unique love story found its enduring power, transcending the boundaries of reality and time. The story wasn't about erasing the memory of their connection, but cherishing it in its poignant, bittersweet reality. It was a love story for the ages, written not in ink and parchment, but in the fading colors of a painting, in the whispered secrets of a shared world, and in the steadfast dedication of a young man in love.

The realization dawned gradually, a slow, creeping understanding that replaced the frantic urgency of their earlier interactions. Their relationship, once a desperate clinging to a fragile connection, evolved into something more profound, more sustainable. It wasn't about defying the rules of reality, but about finding a way to live within them, to accept the limitations while cherishing the extraordinary connection they shared. This was their new normal.

David's academic life, once neglected, slowly re-entered his focus, but with a new perspective. His studies of art conservation weren't just a means to preserve Abby's world; they were a way to understand it, to appreciate its delicate balance and inherent fragility. He began to see the parallels between the careful restoration of a damaged painting and the nurturing of their unique relationship. Both required patience, understanding, and a deep respect for the inherent limitations and vulnerabilities involved. His research into the physics of light and color became infused with a deeper understanding of the subtle interplay of energy and emotion that bound their two realities together. He began to present his findings at conferences, weaving his personal journey into his academic presentations, a testament to the inspiring power of his unusual connection. His work, once detached and analytical, now vibrated with the passion and emotion of his experiences.

He developed a system of coded messages, using subtle shifts in the arrangement of wildflowers, the placement of pebbles along the stream, and even the patterns of light and shadow within the painting itself. These weren't just random arrangements; they were meticulously planned sequences, each conveying a message, sharing a thought, expressing a feeling. A cluster of forget-me-nots could signify a quiet longing; a particular arrangement of stones could convey a message of enduring hope. He learned to decipher Abby's responses with equal subtlety, reading the faintest alterations in the landscape, the subtle shift in the way the sunlight fell upon a particular tree, the delicate movement of a butterfly's wing – all became part of their elaborate, nonverbal conversation.

Their shared world became a canvas for their ongoing dialogue. David learned to create ephemeral works of art within Abby's world, using materials that would naturally decompose over time, leaving no lasting impact on the painting's delicate structure. He carved intricate designs into perishable fruits and vegetables, creating miniature sculptures that would eventually return to the earth, leaving only fleeting traces of their existence. He would leave behind ephemeral poems written on specially treated paper, delicate verses that would dissolve in the rain, their words echoing in the memory but leaving no enduring imprint on the painting itself. These artistic expressions, both fleeting and beautiful, became symbolic representations of their love, a constant affirmation of their connection, without compromising the integrity of Abby's world.

Their relationship was no longer defined by frantic urgency or desperate longing but by a quiet, steady appreciation for the preciousness of their shared existence. David learned to cherish the moments, to savor the beauty of their shared world, to appreciate the delicate balance that allowed their extraordinary connection to continue. The visits became less frequent but no less meaningful. They were marked by a profound sense of peace, a quiet contentment that replaced the earlier anxieties.

He learned to anticipate Abby's needs, understanding her emotions even without direct communication. He'd leave behind small comforts – a smooth stone to soothe her hand, a fragrant wildflower to brighten her day, a delicately carved piece of wood to bring a smile to her face. These were small acts of affection, silent gestures of love that enriched their shared existence without disrupting its delicate balance. These subtle offerings became a language of their own, a silent conversation woven into the fabric of their shared world. It was a testament to their growing understanding of each other, a reflection of their deepening bond.

David's own life outside the painting began to flourish. He continued his studies, but his academic work was now infused with a newfound sense of purpose and passion. His research into art conservation, once a means to an end, became a source of profound satisfaction, a way to channel his love and concern for Abby's world into something productive and meaningful. He even began incorporating his experiences and insights into his academic papers, sharing his unique perspective with the wider world, often finding acceptance and understanding from his peers who recognized the unique lens through which he viewed his studies.

He began to create a series of paintings depicting their shared world, not as exact replicas, but as artistic interpretations of their unique connection. These paintings weren't merely representations of the Victorian park, but symbolic depictions of their shared existence, each brushstroke reflecting the nuances of their emotional bond. He used subtle colors, muted tones, and evocative imagery to capture the essence of their world, the fleeting beauty of their moments together, the unspoken understanding that bound them together. These paintings became a bridge between their two realities, a visual manifestation of their love story. He'd leave these behind in Abby's world, knowing that she could somehow perceive their significance, could sense the emotional depth he had poured into his work.

The fading of the painting, once a constant source of anxiety, became a backdrop to their new normal. It was a constant reminder of the fragility of their world, but it also became a catalyst for David's creativity and resourcefulness. He approached the deterioration not with fear, but with a sense of responsibility. He learned to embrace the impermanence of their shared reality, recognizing that its very fragility lent it a unique beauty. It was a beautiful paradox—the transience of their existence amplified the preciousness of every shared moment.

His life became a delicate dance between two worlds, a constant negotiation between his obligations in his own reality and his commitment to Abby and her world. The balance was delicate, often requiring compromise and sacrifice, but the reward was immeasurable. Their relationship had transformed from a frantic escape into a shared responsibility, a quiet, enduring love story written across the boundaries of time and reality. Their new normal wasn't a perfect solution, but it was a testament to the enduring power of love, a testament to their ability to adapt, to cherish, and to accept the boundaries of their unusual connection. It was a love story crafted not in defiance of reality, but in a harmonious acceptance of its limitations, a testament to the enduring power of love that transcends the limitations of time and space, a poignant and beautiful story whispered on the canvas of a fading painting. It was a love story for the ages, a reminder that even the most extraordinary loves can find a way to thrive even within the confines of extraordinary circumstances. Their love was a masterpiece, painted not just on canvas, but on the very fabric of their shared existence.

Chapter 12
The Power of Art

The urgency that had once defined their relationship had subsided, replaced by a quiet understanding. Their communication, initially frantic and fraught with the fear of losing their connection, transformed into a subtle dance of artistic expression. David, armed with his newfound knowledge of art conservation and a deeper understanding of the painting's delicate structure, began to create art specifically designed to bridge the gap between their worlds. He started small, crafting miniature sculptures from clay, carefully choosing materials that wouldn't permanently alter the painting's surface. These weren't simply decorative pieces; they were imbued with meaning, each one a silent message, a whispered sentiment, a shared feeling. A tiny bird, its wings outstretched in flight, symbolized freedom; a delicate flower, its petals carefully formed, conveyed the beauty of their fragile connection.

Abby, in turn, responded in kind. She began to subtly alter the landscape of the Victorian park, using the natural elements—the positioning of wildflowers, the flow of the stream, the dance of sunlight on the leaves—to convey her own thoughts and emotions. A sudden bloom of vibrant poppies signaled joy; a quiet stillness amongst the trees hinted at introspection. Their communication became a silent dialogue, a delicate interplay of artistic expression woven into the very fabric of their shared world. It was a language born of necessity, a creative solution to the limitations of their unconventional relationship. Their love story was no longer confined to words; it was painted across the canvas of their shared reality.

David's artistic endeavors evolved beyond miniature sculptures. He began to incorporate ephemeral materials into his creations—delicate flowers that would wilt, leaves that would decay, sandcastles that would be washed away by the tide. These temporary works of art served as a poignant metaphor for their relationship itself—precious, fleeting, yet intensely beautiful. Each piece was a testament to the ephemeral nature of their connection, a reminder that their shared moments, though temporary, were no less meaningful. He learned to embrace the impermanence, understanding that its very transience heightened the value of each shared experience.

He also discovered that he could manipulate the light within the painting itself, creating fleeting patterns and shimmering effects. He learned to use the subtle shifts in light and shadow to convey messages, using techniques similar to those employed by Renaissance artists to create depth and dimension. These ephemeral light shows were fleeting, vanishing as quickly as they appeared, but they served as beautiful, momentary bridges between their worlds. The light became a silent language of love, conveying unspoken emotions and creating a shared experience that transcended the physical limitations of their separate realities.

His artistic expression wasn't limited to the physical realm of Abby's world. He began to translate their shared experiences into paintings in his own reality. These were not mere copies of the Victorian park; they were symbolic representations of their bond, conveying the emotions, the essence, the very heart of their unusual relationship. His brushstrokes were infused with a depth of emotion, a palpable sense of longing and connection, reflecting the unique beauty of their shared existence. Each canvas became a testament to their love story, a visual manifestation of their unspoken dialogue.

These paintings served as a powerful reminder of Abby's world, a way for David to maintain his connection even when he was physically separated from her. He would often stare at his creations, allowing himself to be transported back to the vibrant Victorian park, re-living their shared moments, re-experiencing the emotions they'd shared. The paintings weren't merely art; they were tangible links to his beloved, a way to keep the flame of their extraordinary connection alive.

He began exhibiting his paintings, cautiously at first, fearing that the revelation of his unusual experiences would lead to ridicule or disbelief. However, the paintings resonated with viewers on a deeper level, their emotional intensity capturing the essence of something beyond the tangible, something profoundly human. The paintings weren't simply beautiful; they evoked a sense of longing, a yearning for something more, a glimpse into a reality that lay just beyond the grasp of ordinary perception.

The recognition he received wasn't just validation of his artistic talent; it was a testament to the power of their extraordinary connection. He used his newfound platform to subtly allude to the source of his inspiration, weaving hints of his experiences into his artist statements, his interviews, even the titles of his paintings. He walked a delicate line, revealing enough to pique curiosity without compromising his connection to Abby's world.

He realized that his art wasn't just a means of communication; it was a way to preserve Abby's world, to capture its essence and share it with others. The paintings weren't just reflections of a shared world; they were acts of preservation, a way of ensuring that Abby's existence, though confined within a painting, would not be forgotten.

His artistic journey became a testament to his love for Abby, a profound reflection of their unique connection. The paintings weren't just a record of their shared experiences; they were an expression of their love, an artistic exploration of their extraordinary bond. The colors, the brushstrokes, the composition—every element served to convey the emotions, the hopes, the fears, and the joys of their unconventional romance. They were a love story painted on canvas, a story that resonated far beyond the confines of their two realities. The art wasn't simply a bridge; it was a testament, a celebration, a legacy to their unique connection. It was a love story for the ages, written not in words but in paint, brushstrokes, and the subtle nuances of light and shadow. And in each stroke, in each carefully chosen color, a whispered promise echoed: their love story, though uniquely fragile, would endure.

The weight of their unspoken pact settled heavily on David's shoulders. Leaving Abby hadn't lessened the ache in his chest, the constant, low hum of grief that vibrated beneath his skin. He'd promised to preserve her world, to keep her memory alive, and he knew the only way to truly fulfill that promise was through his art. His studio, once a haven of creative exploration, now felt like a sanctuary, a place where he could mourn and celebrate their love simultaneously. The canvases stood before him, blank and expectant, each one a silent challenge, a demand to translate the swirling emotions within him into tangible form.

His first attempts were clumsy, the brushstrokes hesitant, the colors muted. He struggled to capture the vibrancy of Abby's world, the richness of their shared moments. The paintings lacked the spark, the life, the incandescent love that had defined their time together. They were mere imitations, hollow shells devoid of the soul he longed to convey. Frustration gnawed at him, fueling a tempestuous wave of self-doubt. He felt as though he was failing her, betraying their connection with each lifeless stroke.

He spent weeks in this state, his canvases accumulating dust, his palette drying out. The silence in his studio was deafening, mirroring the emptiness he felt inside. He found himself drawn back to the paintings he'd created before the separation, the ones that hummed with their shared history. He studied them, not as an artist critiquing his work, but as a lover remembering cherished moments. He traced the lines with his fingers, letting the texture and colors reactivate the memories they held.

Slowly, a new understanding dawned. It wasn't about replicating the Victorian park, not about achieving photographic realism. It was about capturing the *feeling*, the essence of their connection – the joy, the fear, the bittersweet ache of their impossible love. He needed to paint not what he saw, but what he felt. He needed to express not just the external beauty of their world, but the internal landscape of his heart.

This realization shifted his approach. He began to experiment with abstract expressionism, allowing the emotions to flow freely onto the canvas. Bold colors, vibrant and sometimes clashing, replaced the muted tones of his previous attempts. He used thick impasto techniques, layering colors and textures to create a sense of depth and complexity, mirroring the intricate tapestry of their relationship. He incorporated elements from his own reality, blending the mundane with the extraordinary, reflecting the way their two worlds had intertwined.

He painted canvases depicting swirling nebulae of color, representing the chaotic yet beautiful nature of their unconventional love. Other canvases featured fractured landscapes, symbolic of the broken boundaries between their worlds. He used contrasting colors – the fiery reds and oranges of passion juxtaposed with the cool blues and greens of longing – to create a visual tension that reflected the bittersweet nature of their bond. Each stroke was deliberate, infused with the weight of his memories, the depth of his longing, the pain of his sacrifice.

As he painted, he rediscovered his voice, his unique artistic language. He found a way to translate the silent dialogue of their shared world into a visual symphony of emotions. The canvases, once empty voids, now pulsated with the energy of their connection, capturing not just the memory but the very essence of their extraordinary love.

He didn't shy away from portraying the pain, the loss, the heartbreaking decision he'd made. One canvas depicted a fading landscape, the colors muted and washed out, mirroring the deterioration of the painting itself. Another showed two intertwined figures, one gradually dissolving into mist, a symbolic representation of their separation. These weren't paintings meant to evoke pity; they were honest depictions of his emotional journey, a raw and unflinching portrayal of loss and enduring love.

The act of painting became a form of therapy, a means of processing his grief and celebrating his love simultaneously. Each stroke was a step toward acceptance, a movement towards healing. He found himself revisiting specific moments, re-experiencing their laughter, their shared secrets, their whispered promises. The canvases became a repository of their shared history, a visual testament to their bond.

He began to exhibit these new works, not with the cautiousness of before, but with a quiet confidence. He didn't need the validation of others; the act of creation itself was cathartic enough. Yet, the response was overwhelming. Local critics hailed his work as groundbreaking, a powerful exploration of emotion and loss. Viewers connected with the raw vulnerability of his paintings, finding solace and resonance in his honest portrayal of an unconventional love. His art spoke to the universal experience of longing, of loss, of the enduring power of love that transcends even the boundaries of reality.

His local success wasn't measured in critical acclaim or financial gain; it lay in the ability to share Abby's story, to preserve her world through his art, to keep the flame of their love alive. He'd created a legacy, not just for himself, but for Abby, a testament to their extraordinary connection, a timeless reminder of a love that defied the boundaries of time and space. The paintings weren't just canvases filled with color and texture; they were portals, allowing viewers to glimpse into their unique and extraordinary love story, a testament to the enduring power of art to capture and express the most profound emotions of the human heart. It was a journey of loss, a journey of grief, a journey of healing, all woven together into a stunning artistic tapestry. And through it all, the love he shared with Abby remained, vibrantly alive on those canvases, a beacon shining brightly through the darkness. His art was not just a memorial to a lost love; it was a celebration of a love that, even in its impermanence, had indelibly marked his soul, his heart, and his art. It was a testament to the power of love, to the resilience of his spirit, and to the enduring magic of art itself.

The initial wave of grief had subsided, replaced by a quieter, more persistent ache. David found himself drawn not only to his canvases but to the very act of creation itself. It was a meditative process, a way to quiet the incessant buzzing of his thoughts, to find a semblance of peace amidst the turmoil. He began to experiment with different mediums, moving beyond oils to watercolors, their delicate transparency mirroring the ephemeral nature of his memories. He even tried his hand at sculpture, attempting to capture the ethereal beauty of Abby in clay, her form slowly taking shape under his careful hands. Each attempt was a step further, a refinement of his understanding of how to translate his emotions, the weight of his experience, onto a tangible form.

The watercolors were initially frustrating. The delicate nature of the medium made it challenging to capture the intensity of his feelings. The colors bled into one another, creating soft, indistinct forms that lacked the sharp definition he craved. Yet, this very imperfection became the key. He embraced the fluidity of the watercolors, allowing the colors to mingle and intermingle, mirroring the fluidity of his memories, the way his recollections of Abby shifted and changed with time. He painted scenes of her laughing, her face a kaleidoscope of shifting hues, her joy as vibrant and fleeting as the colors on the page.

He moved to charcoal, its stark blackness emphasizing the shadows and the depth of his sorrow. These drawings were less about capturing the beauty of Abby and more about conveying the emptiness left in her absence. He sketched fragmented images, incomplete figures, blurred lines reflecting the brokenness of his heart. The raw, unfinished quality of the charcoal drawings was a poignant reflection of his emotional state, a testament to the enduring power of loss.

He discovered the beauty of imperfection, realizing that true art didn't lie in flawless execution but in the honest expression of emotion. The smudged lines, the accidental drips, the unpredictable blending of colors—they were all part of the process, adding layers of complexity and authenticity to his work. He even began incorporating found objects into his collages, incorporating dried leaves, scraps of fabric, and pressed flowers, each element imbued with symbolic meaning, representing fragments of their shared world. A single, withered rose represented the fading of their love, while a shard of broken glass symbolized the shattering of their reality.

He moved beyond representation, venturing into abstraction. He explored the power of color to evoke emotion, using bold hues to express the intensity of his feelings, the raw energy of his loss. Crimson reds and fiery oranges represented the passionate intensity of their love, juxtaposed with the cool blues and greens of his grief, his longing. He allowed the colors to clash, to fight for dominance on the canvas, reflecting the turbulent emotions within him. This abstract expressionism proved liberating, allowing him to move beyond the constraints of realism and fully embrace the emotional landscape of his experience.

The process became a dialogue between his heart and his hands. He began to see his art as a means of self-discovery, a way to understand his own emotional journey and find meaning in his loss. Each stroke was a step closer to reconciliation, a means of accepting the reality of their separation and celebrating the extraordinary love that had shaped his life. He found himself revisiting their shared memories, not with sadness but with a quiet gratitude. He remembered the feel of her hand in his, the sound of her laughter, the way her eyes sparkled with light. These memories, once sources of pain, now nourished his art, fueling his creativity.

He started incorporating elements from Abby's world into his paintings. He depicted the Victorian park, not as a perfect replica, but as a fragmented landscape, the colors muted and fading in places, mirroring the disintegration of the painting itself. He painted portraits of Abby, not as idealized images, but as glimpses into her personality, capturing her spirit, her grace, her unique beauty, and the strength of her character that had shone so brightly even amidst the confines of her existence within the canvas. He included subtle allusions to the events they shared, like a hidden clock tower representing the ever-changing nature of time, or a single, wilting flower as a metaphor for the transience of their bond.

One painting depicted a swirling vortex of colors, representing the moment he stepped into her world, the moment their realities collided. The canvas pulsated with an almost palpable energy, a visual representation of the chaotic yet beautiful dance between their two realities. He used metallic paints to create a shimmering, ethereal quality, mirroring the magical aura that surrounded their relationship. He incorporated textures into the painting, using layers of paint and collage elements to create a sense of depth and mystery. The result was a painting that was both visually stunning and emotionally profound, capturing not just the event itself, but the emotional turmoil and the awe of that moment.

He painted portraits of himself, mirroring the changes in his own emotional state. The early portraits showed a haunted, melancholic figure, his eyes reflecting the weight of his loss. Later portraits displayed a growing sense of peace and acceptance, his gaze more resolute, his countenance softened by the healing power of art.

Through this exploration, he discovered a new language for his art. It was a language that transcended words, communicating the depth and complexity of his emotions in a way that words never could. It was a language that resonated not just with him but with others who viewed his art, finding solace and understanding in the honest portrayal of his journey.

The exhibitions that followed were, to his surprise, a success. People praised the raw honesty and emotional depth of his work, hailing it as a groundbreaking exploration of loss and love. Viewers connected with the vulnerability and authenticity of his art, recognizing the universal themes of grief, healing, and the enduring power of memory. He was lauded not only for his technical skill but for his ability to translate his complex emotions into a visual language that touched the hearts and souls of his audience.

It was in the knowledge that he had honored Abby's memory, that he had kept her spirit alive through his art. He had created a legacy, a testament to their extraordinary love, a story that would continue to resonate long after he was gone. Each painting was a portal, allowing viewers to glimpse into their world, to understand the depth and complexity of their love, and to connect with the universal human experience of loss and longing. It was the culmination of a painful journey, but it was also a testament to the healing power of art, the enduring strength of love, and the remarkable resilience of the human spirit. The canvases, once blank and expectant, now held the vibrant tapestry of their lives, a legacy painted with tears and laughter, with heartbreak and hope, a timeless masterpiece crafted from the very essence of their impossible love.

The process of creation became a lifeline, a way to navigate the turbulent seas of his grief. He found himself experimenting with new techniques, pushing the boundaries of his artistic expression. He delved into the world of mixed media, combining paint with found objects, incorporating fragments of his own life into the artwork. A torn photograph of himself and his friends, faded and worn at the edges, became a textured element in one piece, representing the fractured reality he now inhabited. A dried flower, pressed between two layers of glass, served as a poignant reminder of Abby's ephemeral existence within the painting. These fragments were more than mere embellishments; they were symbolic representations of his loss, his journey through grief, and his slow, painstaking recovery.

He began to work on a larger scale, creating canvases that demanded physical engagement, requiring him to move around them, to immerse himself fully in the process of creation. The physicality of the act became therapeutic, a release of pent-up energy, a tangible expression of his emotional turmoil. He would spend hours in his studio, paint-splattered and exhausted, but oddly invigorated, the very act of creation a powerful form of self-expression and emotional catharsis.

The color palette shifted as well. The early works were dominated by dark, muted tones – somber greys, deep blues, and melancholic blacks. These were reflections of the pervasive sadness that had consumed him, the emptiness that echoed in the spaces Abby had left behind. Gradually, however, brighter colors began to emerge, subtle at first, then bolder, more assertive. Flecks of gold appeared, hints of shimmering light, mirroring a burgeoning hope, a flicker of optimism emerging from the ashes of his despair.

He began to see patterns in his work, subtle recurring motifs that reflected his internal struggles. Recurring images of birds in flight, symbolizing freedom and escape, began to appear. He painted intricate scenes of gardens, blooming with vibrant colors, representing the potential for growth and renewal that existed even amidst his grief. These symbols were not consciously planned; they emerged organically from his subconscious, offering glimpses into his healing process, the slow yet steady journey toward acceptance and peace.

He experimented with texture, layering paints, incorporating sand, and using various tools to create unique tactile experiences on the canvas. The rough texture of sandpaper represented the harsh realities of his loss, the starkness of his grief, while the smooth, velvety texture of oil paint reflected the tenderness of his memories, the enduring beauty of his love for Abby. He created canvases that weren't simply meant to be viewed, but to be experienced, to be felt with the very tips of one's fingers.

His art became a dialogue, a conversation between his subconscious and his conscious mind, a visual record of his emotional journey. He realized that he wasn't just creating art; he was creating a map of his healing process, a roadmap that guided him toward acceptance, forgiveness, and a renewed sense of purpose.

He started attending art therapy workshops, finding solace and inspiration in a shared experience of creative expression and emotional release. These workshops provided a space for him to connect with other artists, to share his story, and to learn from others who had traversed similar paths of grief and healing. The shared vulnerability created a supportive community, fostering creativity and understanding.

He discovered the power of collaborative art, working with fellow artists on large-scale projects. These collaborative endeavors allowed him to step outside of his own personal narrative, to engage with different perspectives and creative energies. He found that the collaborative process not only enhanced his technical skills but also deepened his emotional understanding of the shared human experience of loss and healing.

His art began to attract attention. Small exhibitions in local galleries were followed by larger regional shows in larger cities. He received positive reviews, praising the honesty and raw vulnerability of his work. The critics recognized not only his technical skill but the profound emotional depth that permeated his art. The paintings weren't just aesthetically pleasing; they resonated deeply with viewers, provoking emotional responses, initiating conversations, and fostering a shared sense of human connection.

The success, however, wasn't measured solely in critical acclaim. It was in the quiet moments of recognition, in the shared glances and knowing smiles exchanged between viewers, in the sense of community that his art seemed to cultivate. He received letters from people sharing their own stories of loss and healing, finding solace in his work, connecting with the universal themes of grief, love, and resilience that permeated his paintings.

He understood that his art wasn't just a testament to his relationship with Abby; it was a testament to the human capacity for love and loss. He had transformed his grief into a force of creation, finding meaning and purpose in the midst of profound sorrow. His canvases, once blank and expectant, now held the vibrant tapestry of his life, a story painted with tears and laughter, heartbreak and hope, a testament to the remarkable ability of art to heal, to connect, and to transcend the boundaries of time and space. The paintings became a legacy, a testament to his love for Abby and a reminder of the enduring power of art to transform pain into beauty. And in that transformation, he found a deeper understanding of himself, a stronger connection to his own resilience, and a newfound purpose in his life. His art was not just a reflection of his grief; it was a celebration of life itself. It was a beacon of hope, radiating warmth and understanding into the lives of all who encountered it. It was a legacy he had unknowingly created, one brushstroke at a time, a testament to the transformative power of love and loss, expressed through the boundless language of art. And in the quiet contemplation of his canvases, one could feel not only the weight of his sorrow, but also the gentle strength of his healing, the vibrant pulse of his life continuing, even amidst the enduring memory of Abby.

The silence in his studio, once a suffocating void, now hummed with a different energy. It wasn't the frantic, desperate energy of his earlier work, the chaotic strokes reflecting his internal turmoil. This was a quieter energy, a collaborative hum, a shared breath between him and the other artists who now frequented his space. He had transformed his studio, once a solitary sanctuary of grief, into a vibrant, shared creative space.

The walls, once adorned with only his canvases, now showcased a kaleidoscope of styles and techniques. Watercolors bloomed alongside oil paintings, sculptures stood proudly beside intricate wood carvings. The air was thick with the scent of linseed oil, turpentine, and the earthy fragrance of clay, a heady perfume of creative energy. He had intentionally curated this environment, seeking a synergy of artistic expressions, a space where he could both contribute and learn, a place of shared vulnerability and mutual support.

The collaborative spirit extended beyond the physical space. He found himself exchanging ideas, techniques, and even personal stories with the other artists. They discussed their struggles, their triumphs, their inspirations, and their frustrations, creating a bond forged in the crucible of shared creative passion. One artist, a sculptor named Brenda, shared her techniques for capturing the fluidity of movement in clay, her hands moving with the grace of a dancer as she demonstrated. Another, a painter named Paul, revealed his secret for achieving a luminous quality in his watercolor landscapes, a technique he had perfected over decades of dedicated practice.

He learned from them as much as they learned from him. He showed them his techniques for layering textures, demonstrating how to incorporate found objects into his mixed media pieces, revealing the subtle symbolism embedded within his work. He shared his story, not as a means of seeking pity, but as a way of connecting, of fostering understanding, of bridging the divide between his own experience and theirs. He discovered that in the sharing, in the mutual vulnerability, lay a potent catalyst for healing and creativity.

Their collaborative projects became a testament to their shared creative space. They worked together on a massive mural, a vibrant tapestry of colors and textures, each artist contributing their unique style and perspective. Brenda sculpted three-dimensional elements, Paul painted expansive landscapes, and he contributed his mixed media expertise, weaving together their individual contributions into a cohesive and powerful whole. The mural depicted a fantastical garden, a place of vibrant life and renewal, a shared vision of hope and resilience.

Another project involved the creation of a series of individual sculptures, each representing a different aspect of their shared experiences. Brenda sculpted a figure of a woman embracing a bird, symbolizing freedom and resilience. Paul painted a landscape depicting a path leading towards a radiant sunrise, reflecting their journey towards healing and hope. He created a sculpture of intertwining branches, a representation of the interconnectedness and support they found within their shared creative space.

The process of collaborative creation was profoundly therapeutic. It allowed him to step outside his own individual narrative, to engage with different perspectives and creative energies. He discovered that the collaborative process not only enhanced his technical skills but also deepened his emotional understanding of the shared human experience of loss and healing. The collective energy, the shared vulnerability, and the mutual support created a powerful synergy, fueling their creativity and fostering their healing process.

The studio became more than just a place of artistic creation; it became a community, a haven of support and understanding. The artists gathered regularly, not only to work but also to socialize, to share meals, and to simply enjoy each other's company. They formed a bond of friendship; a connection built on shared experiences and mutual respect. This community provided a crucial safety net, a place where they could be vulnerable, where they could share their struggles without judgment, and where they could find solace in their shared experience.

He began to see the transformation in himself and in others. The initial hesitation and self-doubt that had accompanied their first collaborative efforts gradually gave way to a sense of confidence and self-assurance. Their individual styles became more refined, their creative visions bolder, their artistic expressions more profound. The shared creative space had not only fostered their artistic growth but had also nurtured their emotional well-being.

The successes of their collaborative efforts extended beyond the confines of the studio. They organized exhibitions, showcasing their work to the public. The exhibitions were not merely displays of artistic skill; they were celebrations of shared creativity, demonstrations of the power of collaborative art to heal and connect. The reviews were overwhelmingly positive, praising the vibrant energy, the emotional depth, and the unique collaborative spirit that permeated their work.

The shared creative space had become a testament to the power of art to transcend boundaries, to connect people, and to foster healing. It had become a refuge, a sanctuary, a place where grief could be transformed into beauty, where sorrow could be channeled into creativity, and where hope could take root and flourish. The paintings, sculptures, and mixed media pieces were not merely artistic expressions; they were tangible manifestations of a shared journey, a testament to the enduring power of connection and the transformative capacity of art.

The success was not solely measured in public approval. It was in the quiet moments of shared understanding, the unspoken bonds formed between fellow artists, the healing that took place within the walls of the studio, and the ripple effect of their art extending into the lives of those who witnessed their collaborative spirit. It was a reminder that art, in its broadest sense, is a shared language, a universal form of communication that bridges divides and fosters a profound sense of unity. The studio, once a place of solitary grief, was now a vibrant, pulsing heart, a testament to the restorative power of collective creativity, proving that even amidst profound loss, beauty, resilience, and connection can not only survive, but thrive. The paintings, sculptures, and murals were more than just works of art; they were a chronicle of their shared journey, a testament to the human spirit's remarkable capacity for healing and renewal.

Chapter 13
The Enduring Bond

The world outside the painting felt dull, muted, as if viewed through a perpetually dusty window. The vibrant hues of Abby's Victorian park, the sharp scent of damp earth and blooming roses, all contrasted starkly with the grey monotony of his own life. He'd returned to his studies, a hollow obligation that felt like treading water. The lectures blurred into indistinct sounds, the faces of his classmates morphing into a sea of anonymous features. He found himself sketching, not in his usual frenzied, emotional style, but with meticulous detail, capturing the essence of Abby's world, the gentle sway of the willow trees, the intricate patterns on the butterflies' wings.

He missed her, acutely, a constant ache in his chest. He missed the feel of her hand in his, the warmth of her laughter, the way her eyes reflected the sunlight filtering through the leaves. He missed their stolen moments, the hushed conversations under the ancient oak, their shared secrets whispered against the backdrop of rustling leaves. He missed the way she looked at him, with a depth of understanding that transcended words.

Their communication, now restricted to the moments he could enter the painting, became a precious commodity. He'd spend hours lost in her world, their time together punctuated by the frantic ticking of his inner clock, reminding him of the time he had to leave. He began to develop elaborate routines to maximize his time, meticulously planning each visit to cram in as many shared moments as possible.

He experimented with different approaches to enter the painting, searching for ways to extend his visits. He realized that the intensity of his focus, the strength of his emotional connection to Abby, directly influenced the length of his stays. He discovered that by completely immersing himself in the scene, by focusing on the minute details, the subtle nuances of light and shadow within the painting, he could somehow extend the boundaries of time within the artwork.

One visit, he found himself sketching a particular rose bush, its blossoms a breathtaking symphony of color and form. As he meticulously rendered each petal, each delicate vein, he felt a strange shift. Time seemed to slow, to stretch, to yield to his focus. He could remain in her world for longer periods, basking in her presence, in the warmth of their shared space. He felt a strange sense of connection not only to Abby but to the very fabric of the painting, as if the canvas itself responded to his emotional engagement.

Yet, the knowledge that his visits were temporary gnawed at him. He knew that the painting was fragile, its vibrant colors fading, its edges blurring. He felt the pressure of its instability, a subtle tremor in the earth beneath his feet, a delicate shift in the air, a foreshadowing of the potential collapse of their shared world. Each visit felt more precious, more poignant, knowing that each moment could be his last.

He took a risk and confided in Brenda and Paul, sharing fragments of his story, carefully avoiding specifics, but letting them know the burden of his extraordinary experience. They listened, their artistic sensitivity enabling them to understand, even without full comprehension, the nature of his predicament. They offered solace in their own ways, their presence acting as a silent acknowledgment of his pain, a comforting reminder that he wasn't entirely alone. They encouraged him to channel his feelings into his art, to use his experience as inspiration for his own creative endeavors.

He began a new series of paintings, inspired by his experiences with Abby. They were not direct representations of her world, but rather abstract interpretations of his emotions: the vibrant reds and oranges representing the intensity of his love, the somber blues and greens mirroring the grief of their separation. These paintings didn't just capture the aesthetics of Abby's world; they channeled the emotional essence of their extraordinary connection, the bittersweet symphony of their shared reality.

Brenda sculpted a series of miniature figures representing their shared moments: Abby reading under a tree, David sketching in his notebook, their hands intertwined. The tiny figures, meticulously crafted from clay, captured the intimacy of their moments together with poignant precision. Paul, inspired by David's account, began a series of landscapes, reflecting the ever-changing nature of their relationship: from the bright, sunny landscapes of their first encounters to the increasingly muted tones reflecting the fading of the painting.

The art created by his friends became a sort of visual diary, documenting the evolving stages of his emotional journey. Through their work, he began to process his loss, to reconcile the heartache with the extraordinary nature of their relationship. It was a silent conversation, a shared experience that transcended words and allowed them to navigate this unusual grief together. He found himself increasingly spending time in the studio, finding a measure of solace, a creative outlet for his feelings.

He hadn't abandoned Abby; instead, he'd found a way to keep her memory alive, to integrate her into his reality in a different, more sustainable way. The fading painting remained a constant reminder of their shared world, a poignant symbol of their extraordinary bond. But it also served as inspiration, a catalyst for a new phase in his life, a chapter that incorporated the legacy of their love into his evolving reality.

He still visited Abby in the painting, but these visits felt different, infused with a quiet acceptance. Their conversations were less about the desperation of their separation and more about the memories they had created, the moments they had shared. He began to appreciate the painting not just as a gateway to another world, but as a precious artifact, a tangible representation of their shared history. He treated it with utmost care, aware of its delicate nature, understanding that it was the only way he could continue to preserve their connection.

He started to frame his visits differently. He viewed them not as stolen moments, but as pilgrimages to a sacred place, a visit to a beloved friend who resided in a unique and delicate space. It felt almost spiritual, a profound and peaceful connection to someone who occupied a separate, but equally valid reality. He understood that his choice, while painful, was necessary. He hadn't abandoned Abby; he had protected her, securing her existence in a world where she was safe and whole.

His life outside the painting began to heal. He reconnected with old friends, his renewed creativity giving him a sense of purpose and direction. He found joy in his work, sharing his experiences and his paintings with others. His art, infused with the poignant memories of

Abby, resonated deeply with viewers, capturing the complexities of love and loss. He understood that their love, while existing in a unique and unconventional way, was no less real or significant. It was a love that transcended boundaries, a love that would endure, even if in a form different from the one he had initially envisioned.

He realized that the fading of the painting wasn't an ending, but a transformation. It represented the shift in their relationship, a change from the intensity of their passionate connection to a more mature, nuanced form of love, a love that would continue to exist in his memories, in his art, in the very essence of his being. Abby wasn't a lost love; she was an integral part of his life's narrative, a constant reminder of the extraordinary beauty and fragility of life, and the enduring power of a love that stretched beyond the confines of reality itself. The painting, in its fading glory, became a testament to that enduring bond. It was a quiet, melancholic beauty, but it was a beauty that contained within it the full spectrum of his experience, and ultimately, the strength of his enduring love for Abby. The muted hues of the painting were not a symbol of loss, but of transformation; a transformation of their love from a vibrant, passionate flame into a warm, enduring ember. An ember that would continue to glow long after the colors had faded. It was a testament to the unconventional nature of love, a love that would reside in his heart and in his art, a love that would forever hold a special place in his soul.

The strength of their connection was a tangible thing, a force that pulsed beneath the surface of his reality, even when he was miles away from the Victorian park within the painting. He found himself unconsciously reaching for her, a phantom limb sensation, a longing that echoed in the quiet spaces between his breaths. It was a love that transcended the physical, a bond that stretched across the chasm between worlds. The fading canvas became a poignant metaphor; their love wasn't disappearing, it was simply changing, evolving into something deeper, more resilient.

He began to notice subtle changes within the painting, almost imperceptible shifts in the light and shadows. The roses, once vibrant crimson, were now a softer, more muted rose. The grass, once emerald green, now held a hint of autumnal gold. Yet, these shifts didn't diminish the beauty of the world; instead, they imbued it with a melancholic grace, a quiet dignity that mirrored the evolving nature of

196

his feelings. He started to see beauty in the fading, a reflection of life's impermanence, its constant state of flux.

His art, too, underwent a transformation. The abstract canvases he had initially produced, bursting with vibrant hues reflecting the intensity of his love, now adopted a gentler palette. The colors softened, the strokes became more deliberate, more contemplative. He painted Abby not as a vibrant, youthful figure, but as a timeless essence, captured in fleeting moments, in the quiet spaces between words, in the subtle nuances of light and shadow playing across her face. He captured her not just visually, but emotionally; the essence of her spirit, her resilience, her unwavering love for him.

The landscapes he painted mirrored the shifting seasons within the painting, reflecting the transition of their love from the vibrant spring of their initial encounters to the quiet autumn of their eventual separation. The vibrant greens and yellows gave way to oranges and browns, the energy of summer replaced by the gentle melancholy of fall, a peaceful acceptance of the natural cycle of life and love. The changes were subtle, yet profoundly significant, mirroring the quiet acceptance he had found in his own heart.

He realized that the power of their love lay not in its intensity, but in its endurance, its capacity to evolve and adapt. It was a love that defied the limitations of time and space, a love that continued to resonate even as the physical manifestations of their world began to fade. He understood that true love wasn't about constant, overwhelming passion; it was about deep understanding, unwavering loyalty, and a profound acceptance of change. Their love story was not a tragedy, but a testament to the enduring strength of their spirit.

Brenda and Paul, witness to his transformation, continued to be his steadfast companions. They understood his grief, not as a weakness, but as a powerful catalyst for his art. They offered him not only emotional support, but also intellectual and creative stimulation, providing a safe space for him to explore his emotions, to wrestle with his loss, and to ultimately find solace in the transformative power of art.

Brenda's sculptures evolved alongside his paintings. She moved away from the youthful exuberance of their earlier pieces, capturing the quiet moments of shared reflection, the tender glances, the

197

unspoken understanding that had developed between them. The clay figures, once vibrant and full of life, now held a deeper, more contemplative quality. Their expressions were more subtle, the postures more introspective, reflecting the maturity and acceptance that had blossomed within their unconventional relationship.

Paul's landscapes evolved as well. The landscapes, initially bursting with the vivid colors of their initial encounters, gradually transitioned into more contemplative scenes. The once vibrant greens and blues morphed into muted tones, reflecting the quiet introspection he was undergoing. But even in the subdued hues, there was a profound beauty, a quiet grace that hinted at the lasting power of their bond. The paintings served as a visual record, a testament to their remarkable journey.

Their collective artistic output became a powerful testament to the enduring strength of their connection, a visual diary of their shared experience, transcending the limitations of language to capture the complexities of their unique love. It was a collaborative effort, a mutual understanding, a shared grieving process that allowed them to navigate the challenging terrain of loss and transformation. They were not simply creating art; they were creating a collective narrative, a shared testament to the power of connection.

The painting itself, now faded and fragile, became a cherished relic, a symbol of their extraordinary journey. He didn't try to fix it, to restore its vibrant colors, for he understood that the fading was not a loss, but a natural progression, a reflection of the evolving nature of their love. He preserved it, not as a frozen moment in time, but as a living testament to a love that transcended the physical world, a love that endured beyond the confines of the canvas.

He continued to visit Abby in the painting, but the visits became less frequent, less desperate. They were visits of quiet contemplation, of shared reminiscence, of reaffirming the depth of their connection. They spoke less of their separation and more of their shared experiences, of the beauty they had found in their unusual world. The visits were no longer driven by the urgency of limited time, but by a gentle, unwavering sense of connection, a profound appreciation for the enduring strength of their bond.

His life outside the painting flourished. He found a renewed sense of purpose in his art, sharing his unique experience with others. His paintings, imbued with the poignant echoes of his love for Abby, resonated deeply with viewers, capturing the essence of human emotions—love, loss, and resilience. He understood that his love story wasn't merely a personal experience; it was a universal theme, a testament to the power of connection that transcended boundaries.

He found joy in his work, in his friendships, in the quiet beauty of his everyday life. The memory of Abby remained, a constant presence in his heart, a source of both inspiration and solace. Their love story wasn't an ending; it was a transformation, a testament to the enduring power of a love that defied the limitations of time, space, and even reality itself. The fading of the painting was not a symbol of loss, but a symbol of transformation, a shifting from the fervent passion of a young love to the quiet, enduring ember of a love that had become part of him, woven into the very fabric of his being. The strength of their love wasn't measured in vibrant colors, but in the quiet, steadfast endurance of a bond that would last a lifetime, a love that would continue to inspire and comfort him, long after the last vestiges of color faded from the canvas. Their love story was not one of loss, but of metamorphosis, a testament to the enduring nature of a bond that transcended the boundaries of the physical world. The muted hues of the painting were a testament to this – a quiet, enduring love that had transformed, yet remained strong. It was a love that would reside in his heart, in his art, and in the very essence of his being, forever.

Their love story, however unusual, was not defined by its limitations but by its boundless capacity for growth and understanding. The fading canvas, a constant reminder of their precarious situation, became a symbol not of loss, but of transformation. It was a testament to their ability to adapt, to cherish the moments they had, and to find beauty even in the face of inevitable change. David realized that their love wasn't measured in vibrant colors or fleeting moments, but in the depth of their shared experiences, the unspoken understanding that passed between them with a single glance, a shared smile, or a silent nod.

Abby, within her painted world, had found a profound sense of peace. She had initially been trapped, a prisoner of the canvas, but David's arrival had breathed life into her existence. Their connection had not only freed her from the isolation of her confinement, but it had also enriched her life in ways she hadn't anticipated. The fading of the colors around her didn't diminish her joy; instead, it heightened her appreciation for the beauty that remained, the precious moments they had shared, the memories that would forever be etched into the heart of her painted world. She understood, as David did, that their love was not defined by the vibrancy of its surroundings, but by the enduring strength of their bond.

Their communication, initially hampered by the limitations of their separate realities, had evolved into a language of its own, a subtle dance of understanding that transcended words. A shared look, a knowing smile, a gesture barely perceptible—these became their means of communication, a language unspoken yet deeply felt. They understood each other's thoughts and feelings with an intuitive ease, a connection forged not just through words, but through shared experiences and mutual understanding. They found solace in the shared silence, in the quiet moments of contemplation, in the mutual appreciation of the ephemeral beauty surrounding them.

David's visits to the painting became less frequent, but each visit held a deeper significance. The urgency of their earlier encounters, the desperate desire to preserve their connection, had given way to a calmer, more profound appreciation of their bond. They talked less, and yet communicated more profoundly. Their conversations were filled with shared memories, quiet reflections, and a mutual acknowledgment of their unusual circumstances. They celebrated the beauty of their unique love story, the enduring strength of a connection that had blossomed amidst the most unexpected of circumstances. They found comfort in each other's presence, a quiet solace in the shared understanding of their shared reality and its inherent fragility.

The knowledge that their time together was not infinite only strengthened their bond. They chose to focus on the present, on cherishing each moment, on creating memories that would transcend time and space. They understood that their love was not defined by its duration, but by its intensity, its depth, its ability to endure even in the face of insurmountable odds. The fading canvas became a poignant symbol of their journey, a reminder that even the most vibrant things eventually fade, but that the essence of their love would endure.

David's art continued to evolve, reflecting not only the transformation of his own feelings but also the evolving nature of their relationship. His paintings moved beyond the initial vibrant hues of their passionate beginning, reflecting the deeper, more contemplative understanding that had blossomed between them. The colors softened, the strokes became more deliberate, reflecting the quiet acceptance of their circumstances. His art became a testament to their unique love story, capturing not just the visual aspects of their world, but the profound emotional depth of their connection.

Brenda and Paul, constant companions throughout David's journey, continued to support him, offering not just friendship but also a deep understanding of his unique experience. They had witnessed the transformative power of his love for Abby, the impact it had on his life and his art. They understood his grief, not as a weakness, but as a testament to the depth of his feelings, to the strength of a love that defied conventional boundaries. Their understanding and unwavering support helped David navigate the complexities of his emotions, allowing him to find solace and purpose in his art.

Brenda's sculptures, once bursting with youthful energy, now reflected the quiet dignity of their evolving relationship. She sculpted figures that embodied the contemplative moments of shared silence, capturing the essence of their unspoken understanding. Paul's landscapes, initially vibrant and full of life, transitioned into more subdued and reflective scenes, mirroring the contemplative nature of David's art and the quiet acceptance that had grown within him. Their collective artistic output became a powerful testament to the enduring power of love, a shared reflection on the beauty and fragility of life.

The unconventional nature of David and Abby's love story didn't diminish its significance; rather, it heightened its value. Their relationship was a testament to the boundless capacity of the human heart to love, to connect, to transcend the limitations of time and space. It was a love that wasn't defined by the physical, but by the spiritual connection they shared, a bond that remained unbroken despite the fading of the canvas. Their story became a source of inspiration and comfort, reminding others that love exists in many forms, and that some connections are so profound they defy definition.

The painting, now a faded and fragile relic, remained a cherished memento of their journey. David didn't attempt to restore it to its former glory; he understood that the fading was an integral part of their story. It was a testament to the ephemeral nature of life and love; a symbol of the transformations that love undergoes over time. He preserved the painting not as a static representation of their love, but as a living testament to its enduring strength and resilience.

David's life after his profound connection with Abby wasn't marked by loss, but by a profound sense of fulfillment and purpose. His art, infused with the echoes of his unique experience, resonated with viewers on a deep emotional level. He continued to visit Abby within the painting, but their interactions had transformed. The urgency was replaced by a quiet contentment, a shared appreciation for the beauty of their unusual love story. Their conversations were not about endings, but about the lasting impact of their connection, the indelible mark it had left on their hearts and souls. They had found a love that transcended the physical world, a bond that would forever endure, a love that whispered in the fading colors of the canvas, a symphony of muted tones that sang of resilience, hope, and the enduring strength of the human heart.

His art became a reflection of this journey, a testament to the enduring power of love in its quietest, most profound forms. It was a love story not of loss, but of metamorphosis, a love that had endured, transformed, and ultimately enriched their lives in ways they had never imagined. And in the quiet spaces between his brushstrokes, in the subtle nuances of color and light, David's art carried the enduring echo of their extraordinary love, a testament to a bond that defied time, space, and the limitations of reality itself. The fading painting served not as a marker of loss, but as a symbol of their enduring connection, a silent testament to a love that lived on, woven into the fabric of their very being. Their unique love story was not just a tale of two souls connected across worlds; a testament to the power of love to transcend the boundaries of reality, a love that transcended time and space, enduring in the quiet whisper of memories, a constant presence etched in the heart, and forever resonating in the vibrant, though now faded, masterpiece.

Their understanding of the painting's fragility heightened their appreciation for each shared moment. Time within the painted

Victorian park flowed differently than in David's world. A single afternoon spent together could translate to days or even weeks in David's reality, a strange temporal paradox that added another layer of urgency and preciousness to their interactions. They learned to savor the quiet moments, the shared laughter echoing softly amidst the painted trees, the delicate dance of sunlight filtering through the leaves—each detail etched into the fabric of their memory, more vivid than any photograph, more tangible than any tangible object.

David's visits became less about grand gestures and more about quiet contemplation. They'd find a secluded bench beneath a willow tree, its painted leaves shimmering in the eternal afternoon sun, and simply sit together, holding hands, the silence between them a comfortable companion, a space where unspoken words danced in the gentle breeze. He would sketch her, his charcoal capturing the subtle changes in the light on her face, the faintest blush on her cheeks, the way her hair caught the wind, each stroke a whispered affirmation of her existence, a testament to their enduring bond.

Abby, in turn, would weave intricate flower crowns from the painted blossoms, adorning David's hair with delicate artistry. These simple acts, seemingly insignificant in their own right, held a profound significance within the context of their ephemeral existence. They were tangible expressions of their love, small moments crafted with intention, designed to leave an enduring impact on their hearts. These weren't mere gestures of affection; they were rituals, subtle ceremonies celebrating their shared present, a way of marking time in a world where time itself was fluid and unpredictable.

The fading of the colors around them was not a source of distress, but a catalyst for deeper appreciation. They found beauty in the subtle nuances of the fading pigments, the gentle softening of the once-vibrant hues. The greens had dulled to a soft sage, the blues had mellowed to a serene periwinkle, the reds had faded to a warm, almost melancholic rose. These changes weren't perceived as loss, but as a natural progression, a transformation mirroring the evolution of their relationship.

Their conversations evolved as well. They spoke less about the future, the uncertainties it held, and more about the richness of their present, the depth of their experiences. They shared memories—not just from their time within the painting, but from the lives they'd lived before—creating a tapestry of shared experience that strengthened their bond. David would recount stories from his life outside, the mundane details suddenly imbued with a poignant beauty, given new meaning by the unusual circumstances of their love.

Abby, in turn, would share tales from the life she lived within the painting before David's arrival, revealing a history filled with quiet solitude and a longing for connection, a poignant narrative that illuminated the transformative power of their encounter. These shared stories became a bridge across realities, a way of connecting not just their lives within the painting, but their lives beyond its boundaries, creating a sense of shared history, a foundation built not only on present moments but on past experiences and future possibilities.

One afternoon, as the sun cast long shadows across the painted park, David confessed his fear of losing her, of the painting fading completely and severing their connection. Abby, her hand nestled in his, reassured him. "Our love isn't confined to this place, David," she said, her voice as soft as the rustling of the painted leaves. "It lives within us, in the memories we create, in the moments we share. Even if the painting fades, our love will remain."

Her words resonated deep within David's soul, calming his anxieties, reassuring him that their bond transcended the physical confines of the painting. He understood that their love story was not solely defined by its unique circumstances; it was about the strength of their emotional connection, the mutual respect and understanding they shared, the profound depth of their affection. Their love was a tapestry woven with threads of shared experiences, quiet moments, and unspoken promises.

They learned to communicate with a depth that went beyond words. A shared glance, a tender touch, a silent understanding—these became their language, their way of communicating across realities. The unspoken words danced between them, conveying a profound depth of affection, a sense of mutual understanding that required no verbal expression. Their connection was not defined by the vibrant colors of the painting but by the strength of their mutual respect and affection. The fading of the colors only intensified their appreciation for the love they shared.

As the days turned into weeks within the painted world, they continued to create their own rituals, their own traditions. They would pick wildflowers from the painted meadows, creating miniature bouquets that, though ephemeral, held a profound symbolic meaning. They would watch the sunset from the highest hill in the painted park, the colors of the sky mirroring the emotions that stirred within their hearts. They would read to each other from worn and well-loved books, sharing the stories and the emotions they evoked.

These simple acts, these small gestures, became the building blocks of their unconventional love story. They were acts of creation, moments of shared intimacy, symbolic gestures of affection and reassurance. They transformed the fading painting into a canvas of cherished memories, a testament to their enduring bond. Each shared experience deepened their connection, enriching their lives in ways they never thought possible.

The knowledge that their time was limited only served to intensify the depth of their love. It spurred them on to create a love story that transcended time and space. Their connection became a sanctuary, a safe haven from the uncertainties of life. Their love was a refuge, a place where they could find solace, comfort, and an unwavering sense of belonging. Their love was not measured by the vibrancy of their surroundings but by the unwavering strength of their bond.

David continued to visit Abby, but the urgency of their earlier meetings had subsided. Their visits became less frequent, but the connection remained as strong as ever. The shared silences held a depth of meaning, a mutual understanding forged in the crucible of their extraordinary circumstances. They celebrated their connection, not as a temporary phase, but as a lasting legacy, a testament to the power of love to transcend the limitations of time and space.

Even when separated by the boundaries of reality, their hearts remained intertwined, a testament to the enduring power of love. Their love was not confined to the painted world; it existed in the memories they shared, the moments they savored, and the quiet understanding that passed between them. Their love was a story of enduring connection, of cherished moments, and of a love that defied all odds. The fading colors of the painting only served to highlight the indelible mark their love had left on their hearts and souls. Their love was not a fleeting moment but an enduring legacy, a testament to the strength and endurance of their bond.

Their acceptance of difference wasn't a passive resignation to their disparate realities; it was an active embrace, a conscious decision to celebrate the unique tapestry of their lives. David, accustomed to the frenetic pace of his modern world, found a strange comfort in Abby's quiet contemplation, her deep connection to the rhythms of nature as depicted within the painting. He learned to appreciate the slower tempo of her existence, the deliberate pace of her actions, the quiet joy she found in the smallest details of her painted world. He began to see the value in stillness, in taking the time to truly observe and appreciate the beauty around him, a skill he'd largely neglected in his own bustling life.

Abby, in turn, found herself captivated by the vibrant dynamism of David's world, a world she experienced only through his descriptions and the occasional object he brought into the painting—a pressed flower, a smooth river stone, a photograph capturing a fleeting moment from his life. She marveled at the technological marvels he described, the bustling cities, the rapid advancements in science and technology, things she could only imagine within the confines of her static world. She learned about different cultures, different ways of life, broadening her perspective beyond the limited scope of her Victorian park.

Their differences, far from being a source of friction, became a bridge connecting their worlds. David introduced Abby to music, playing recordings on his portable device, the sounds weaving through the painted trees, creating a magical atmosphere. He described the vibrant colors of a bustling marketplace, the smells of exotic spices, the sounds of distant sirens, painting a vivid picture with his words. Abby, in turn, taught him the art of patience, the importance of mindfulness, the beauty of finding joy in simple things. She showed him how to truly listen, to observe, to appreciate the nuances of the world around him. She taught him the art of slowing down, of savoring the moment, something he had long forgotten in the relentless rush of his modern life.

Their conversations became richer, deeper, exploring themes beyond their shared circumstances. They discussed art, history, philosophy, and their differing perspectives on life, death, and everything in between. David's modern worldview collided with Abby's more traditional perspective, creating a stimulating dialogue, a constant exchange of ideas that enriched both their lives. They learned from each other's strengths, compensating for each other's weaknesses, creating a dynamic balance that strengthened their bond.

The fading of the painting, once a source of anxiety, now took on a different significance. It became a symbol of the ephemeral nature of life, a reminder that everything is in constant flux, constantly changing and transforming. They no longer viewed it as a threat, but as a natural process, a part of the larger cycle of life and death. They found beauty in the impermanence of things, appreciating the preciousness of each moment, the uniqueness of their experience.

One day, David brought a book of poetry into the painting, a collection of sonnets by Shakespeare. They spent hours reading the verses aloud, discussing the meanings and interpretations, their voices blending with the sounds of the painted wind rustling through the trees. David's understanding of Shakespeare's language and imagery complemented Abby's sensitivity to the emotional resonance of the words. Their combined perspectives created a unique appreciation of the poetry, a deeper understanding than either could have achieved alone.

On another occasion, Abby taught David how to identify the different species of flowers in the painted park, explaining their historical and symbolic meanings. David, in turn, shared his knowledge of botany from his own world, comparing and contrasting the flora of their respective realities. They discovered that despite the differences in their environments, the fundamental principles of nature remained the same, a testament to the interconnectedness of all things.

Their relationship became a microcosm of the larger world, a reflection of the diversity and interconnectedness of humanity. Their differences did not diminish their love; they amplified it, enriching it, strengthening it. The contrasting realities of their lives created a unique dynamic, a vibrant tapestry woven from disparate threads.

David's visits became less frequent, a necessary compromise to ensure the painting's stability, but their bond remained as strong as ever. They communicated through letters, David writing meticulously detailed accounts of his life, Abby responding with thoughtful reflections on her own, their exchanges creating a unique form of long-distance communication that transcended time and space.

The letters became a testament to their enduring love, a chronicle of their lives, their joys and sorrows, their hopes and dreams. They shared their innermost thoughts and feelings, creating an intimate connection that deepened with each exchange. Through their letters, they explored the nuances of their individual experiences, sharing perspectives and insights that strengthened their bond. The letters became a tangible representation of their enduring love, a bridge connecting their worlds, a symbol of their unbreakable connection.

They continued to create new traditions, new rituals, to mark the passage of time. They would choose a specific tree in the park and leave a small token under its branches, a symbol of their shared memories and enduring connection. They would each create a piece of art—David with his sketches, Abby with her flower arrangements—and leave these creations as offerings to the painting, symbolic gestures of their enduring love.

The fading of the painting slowed, the rate of its deterioration lessened. David had inadvertently learned to interact with the canvas in a way that stabilized it, he wasn't sure how, but he suspected it was his love for Abby, a love that imbued the painted landscape with a renewed sense of life.

Their relationship transcended the boundaries of their individual worlds, becoming a testament to the enduring power of love, a celebration of difference, a profound understanding that their unique circumstances only served to heighten their connection, deepen their affection, and strengthen their enduring bond. The painting itself, though fading, became a living testament to the strength and resilience of their love, a poignant reminder of their shared history, their enduring affection. Their love story, unconventional and extraordinary, was a celebration of their shared lives, their separate realities, and the extraordinary love that bound them together, a bond that transcended time, space, and the fading pigments of a painted world. Their differences, far from separating them, had brought them closer, creating a love story for the ages.

Chapter 14
A Different Kind of Forever

Their understanding of forever wasn't a naive wish for endless time together, but a mature acceptance of their reality. It was a quiet revolution, a rewriting of the rules of love and time. Forever, for them, wasn't about escaping the constraints of the painting's fading colors or defying the laws of physics; it was about finding meaning and depth within those very constraints. It was about cherishing the moments they had, however fleeting, and weaving them into a tapestry of shared memories that time couldn't erase.

David began to document their life together, sketching Abby in the park, capturing the subtle shifts of light and shadow that played across her features. He filled notebooks with detailed descriptions of their conversations, their laughter, the quiet moments of shared contemplation. He meticulously recorded the changing seasons within the painting, the subtle transformations of the landscape, noting the blossoming of flowers, the falling of leaves, the first frost of winter. These weren't simply observations; they were acts of love, a way of preserving their precious time together, a testament to the richness of their shared existence.

Abby, in turn, began to create her own records, compiling a collection of pressed flowers, each one representing a special moment, a shared memory, a symbol of their growing affection. She arranged them in intricate patterns, creating small, ephemeral works of art that captured the essence of their relationship. She pressed leaves, preserving the changing colors of autumn, weaving them into small, delicate wreaths. She created miniature landscapes in small glass jars, capturing the essence of the park's beauty, its shifting light, its vibrant flora. Each creation was a poignant reminder of the preciousness of their time together.

Their communication transcended the physical limitations of their worlds. David learned to leave small objects within the painting—a smooth, grey river stone, a single, perfect feather, a small, intricately carved wooden bird—objects that served as tangible reminders of his presence, tangible links to his world. Abby, in turn, left him gifts within the painting's landscape, small, handcrafted tokens of her affection. A single perfect wildflower nestled amongst the painted blooms, a carefully arranged collection of autumn leaves, a small, intricately woven basket filled with berries. These small gestures were acts of love, powerful expressions of their connection, transcending the physical limitations of their realities.

Their letters evolved into a detailed chronicle of their shared experiences, a love story unfolding through words and pictures, through shared thoughts and feelings. David described the chaos of his college life, the pressure of exams, the frustrations of relationships, the joy of friendships. He would meticulously describe the landscapes of his world—the bustling city streets, the vibrant colors of a sunset, the beauty of a snow-covered field. Abby would respond with detailed descriptions of the subtle changes within the painting, the shifting light, the changing seasons, the gentle movement of the painted wind through the trees. She would share her thoughts on the stories he told her, offering her own unique perspective, enriched by her timeless existence within the painting's world.

Their differences, rather than diminishing their bond, enriched it. David's restless energy and Abby's quiet contemplation complemented each other, creating a dynamic balance that strengthened their connection. David brought a sense of dynamism and excitement to Abby's world, while Abby brought a sense of peace and serenity to David's. They learned from each other, expanding their perspectives, broadening their understanding of the world and the human experience.

One day, David found a small, antique music box in a dusty antique shop. It played a simple, haunting melody. He brought it into the painting, and as the delicate notes filled the air, a sense of magic and wonder filled the painted park. The music seemed to intertwine with the sounds of the wind rustling through the painted trees, creating an atmosphere of ethereal beauty. Abby danced to the music, her movements graceful and fluid, reflecting the timeless beauty of the painted landscape. The music box became a cherished symbol of their shared experience, a reminder of the beauty and magic that existed within their unconventional relationship.

As the painting continued to fade, their love deepened. They understood that their forever was not measured in years or decades, but in the intensity and depth of their shared experience. The fading of the canvas served as a constant reminder of the ephemeral nature of time and the preciousness of each shared moment. They celebrated the small victories, the moments of shared joy, the quiet instances of companionship that punctuated their days.

They created new traditions to mark the passage of time—a specific tree where they would leave tokens of their affection, a specific flower whose blooming signified a special occasion, a particular spot in the park where they would share a quiet moment of reflection. They created a shared language of symbols and gestures, a secret code that allowed them to communicate beyond the limitations of their worlds. Their shared language transcended the boundaries of time and space. It was a testament to their profound and lasting connection, a symbol of their enduring bond.

The fading of the painting became a metaphor for the fragility of life, a constant reminder of the preciousness of their shared existence. They never tried to fight it, but rather, they accepted it as a natural part of their reality. They chose to focus on the richness and intensity of their love, celebrating the moments they had together, however short-lived. The painting's deterioration did not diminish their connection; it simply intensified it, making every moment together even more precious.

David's understanding of the delicate balance between his world and Abby's grew. He realized that his constant presence was not only unsustainable, but detrimental to the painting's integrity. He learned to visit less frequently, to appreciate the value of absence, the power of longing, the intensity of anticipation. The distance only seemed to strengthen their bond, intensifying their affection, making their moments together even more precious.

Their "forever," then, was not an eternity of constant togetherness but a profound understanding of the value of their shared moments, a testament to their extraordinary love, a love that transcended the limitations of their worlds. It was a love story woven into the fabric of a fading painting, a love that existed in the spaces between their worlds, in the shared glances, in the unspoken words, in the lingering touch, in the shared memories, in the letters exchanged, in the small tokens left beneath the branches of their special tree. It was a love story that defied the ordinary, exceeding even their own expectations, surpassing even their wildest dreams. Their unconventional forever was a love story that continued to echo long after the pigments of the painting had faded to dust. It was a love that lived on in the memories, in the hearts of those who knew their story, a love that transcended time, space, and the very fabric of reality itself. It was, in its own way, perfectly and eternally theirs.

The realization dawned slowly, like the gradual fading of the sunlight on a summer's evening. It wasn't a dramatic epiphany, but a quiet understanding that settled over them like a gentle snowfall. Their forever, they realized, wasn't a static state, a fixed point in time, but a dynamic process, a continuous adaptation to the ever-shifting sands of reality. The painting was fading, that was undeniable, but their love, its vibrancy, its depth, didn't diminish with the loss of pigment. It evolved, it adapted, it found new ways to flourish.

David, armed with his ever-present sketchbook, began to chronicle the subtle changes within the painting, not just the fading colors, but the ways in which Abby and the park itself responded. He documented the subtle shift in the trees' shadows as the light diminished, the way the wind seemed to carry a melancholic whisper through the leaves, the delicate way in which the flowers, once bold and vibrant, now held a gentler, almost wistful, beauty. He started to see a different kind of beauty in the fading, a quiet elegance in the impermanence, a poignant reminder of their precious, fleeting time together.

Abby, too, adapted. She began to create miniature gardens within the remaining vibrant patches of the painting, tiny ecosystems that thrived despite the overall decay. She used the fading pigments to create delicate, ephemeral works of art, weaving the dust of the disappearing colors into intricate patterns, imbuing them with a wistful grace. Each creation was a testament to her adaptability, her resilience, her deep-rooted love for David and the world around her. She started to find solace in the impermanence, embracing the fleeting nature of their reality, recognizing the poignant beauty of its transience. She wove the fading into her own narrative, transforming it into a new form of artistry, a testament to their evolving relationship.

Their letters, once filled with vibrant descriptions of their world, now reflected this shift. David described the increasing sense of urgency in his own life, the pressure to finish his studies, the need to forge a path forward in a world that felt increasingly distant from Abby's timeless realm. Abby responded with descriptions of the painting's slow surrender to time, the way the colors yielded, blending into softer, more muted shades. The descriptions were not filled with despair, but with a quiet acceptance, a deep understanding of their shared fate. They were learning to find solace in the quiet moments, in the subtle beauty of change, and they reflected this in their words, their language becoming as nuanced and layered as the shifting hues of their shared world.

They found solace in shared rituals, creating new traditions to replace those that were threatened by the fading canvas. They established a special place within the painting, a hidden grove where they left tokens of their affection—smooth river stones, intricately carved wooden birds, single pressed flowers, each one imbued with a layer of meaning, each a marker on their shared timeline. The grove became a repository of their memories, a testament to their enduring bond.

David began to bring music into the painting, not just the music box, but recordings of his own favorite songs, carefully placed within the painting's landscape. The sounds, once disruptive, now blended subtly with the sounds of the wind and the rustling leaves, creating a unique and intimate soundscape, a sonic expression of their shared love story. He discovered that the music helped to soothe the fading colors, to temporarily restore their vibrancy, a subtle but powerful reminder that even in the face of loss, beauty could still be found. Abby would dance to these melodies, her movements graceful and fluid, her spirit seemingly untouched by the encroaching decay.

They learned the language of absence. David learned to appreciate the longing, the anticipation that grew between his visits. The absence strengthened their bond, making their time together even more intense, more precious, each moment infused with a deeper sense of intimacy and awareness. Their letters became more poignant, filled with a longing that only intensified their love, their words filled with the weight of shared experience and unspoken understanding.

Abby, in turn, began to understand David's need to return to his own world. She saw it not as abandonment, but as a necessary act, a demonstration of his commitment to his life as much as to hers. Their conversations grew more mature, less focused on their impossible situation, and more focused on the profound connection that bound them, a connection that extended beyond the physical boundaries of their worlds. She learned to treasure the memories, to let the fading colors of the painting become part of their story, the beauty of its decline a testament to the lasting power of their love.

They found comfort in the shared understanding that their forever wasn't measured in years or decades, but in the intensity of the moments they shared, in the depth of their connection, in the tapestry of memories that they wove together. The fading painting became a symbol of the ephemeral nature of life, not a source of despair, but an affirmation of the preciousness of each day, each moment, each shared word. Their shared understanding transcended the limitations of their physical realities, creating a bond that was as strong and unwavering as it was unique and extraordinary. They had rewritten the rules of forever, not by defying time, but by embracing its passage, by finding beauty and love in the face of change. Their "forever" wasn't a destination, but a journey, a shared experience, a love story etched not just onto a canvas, but onto the very fabric of their souls. It was a story of adaptation, of resilience, of a love that transcended the limitations of time and space, a love that would endure long after the last brushstroke faded into dust.

The autumn leaves in David's world were a riot of crimson and gold, mirroring the vibrant hues of Abby's memories. He found himself sketching them obsessively, capturing the fleeting beauty of decay, a poignant reflection of their shared reality. He brought these sketches to the painting, laying them gently on the soft grass near their hidden grove. Abby examined them with quiet wonder, her fingers tracing the delicate lines, her eyes reflecting the same bittersweet beauty. They talked for hours about the differences in their experiences, the stark contrast between the fast-paced, ever-changing nature of David's life and the slower, more deliberate rhythm of hers within the painting.

David spoke of his classes, his struggles with equations and the pressures of looming exams. He described the boisterous energy of his friends, their laughter echoing in his memories, their lives unfolding in a relentless stream of activity. Abby listened intently, her expression a mixture of fascination and gentle understanding. She couldn't comprehend the concept of deadlines or the relentless pressure of societal expectations. Her world, in its fading glory, held a different kind of urgency, a quiet race against time, a slow surrender to the inevitable.

She described the subtle changes in the painting, the slow creep of the fading colors, the way the light played differently on the trees, casting long, melancholic shadows that seemed to whisper secrets of the past. She spoke of the creatures that inhabited the painting, the tiny insects that scurried through the grass, the birds that sang melancholic songs in the branches of the fading trees. She described the intricate dance of life and death that played out within the confines of the canvas, a delicate balance that mirrored the fragility of their own existence.

David, in turn, found himself appreciating the quiet intensity of Abby's world. He learned to savor the stillness, the absence of the constant noise and distraction of his own life. He discovered a calmness within the painting's slowly fading beauty, a serenity he hadn't known existed within the frenetic pace of his everyday life. The differences, they realized weren't points of conflict, but sources of enrichment, each experience adding layers of depth and understanding to their shared existence. He began to incorporate elements of Abby's world into his own sketches, the delicate lines of fading flowers interwoven with the bold strokes of his own vibrant cityscapes.

He started to write poetry, inspired by Abby's descriptions of the painting's changing landscape. His words echoed the quiet melancholic beauty of her world, capturing the subtle shifts in light and shadow, the slow surrender to time. He read his poems aloud to Abby, his voice soft and tender, his words filled with a deep appreciation for the unique beauty of their shared existence.

Abby, in turn, began to experiment with new forms of artistic expression within the painting. She used the fading pigments to create intricate mosaics, weaving the colors of decay into breathtaking patterns. She sculpted tiny figures from the fallen leaves and petals of the fading flowers, each one a miniature testament to the beauty of impermanence. She began to see the fading not as a loss, but as a transformation, a metamorphosis into a new form of beauty.

They spent countless hours sharing stories, each one a window into their individual worlds. David shared tales of his childhood, his dreams, his aspirations. He spoke of his fears and anxieties, of his struggles and triumphs. Abby listened with rapt attention, her eyes reflecting the depth of her understanding, her silence a testament to her unwavering support.

She shared stories of the painting's history, of the people who had lived and loved within its confines. She described the subtle changes that had taken place over the centuries, the slow evolution of the landscape, the silent witnesses to the passage of time. Her stories were filled with a sense of timeless wisdom, a deep understanding of life's ephemeral beauty.

David learned to appreciate the slow pace of Abby's existence, the way she observed the world around her with a quiet intensity, the patience with which she watched the unfolding of natural processes. He realized that his own frantic pace had often prevented him from truly seeing the beauty that surrounded him.

Their differences, rather than separating them, served to deepen their connection. David's bustling, modern life provided a stark contrast to Abby's timeless world, yet their shared love transcended the boundaries of time and space. They learned from each other, enriched each other, celebrating the unique aspects of their individual experiences while cherishing the intensity of their shared moments.

They celebrated the vibrancy of David's life—the rush of city streets, the laughter of his friends, the thrill of pursuing his dreams. They celebrated the quiet beauty of Abby's world—the slow dance of the seasons, the gentle whisper of the wind through the trees, the serene acceptance of impermanence. They found joy in their differences, recognizing that their unique perspectives enriched their love and provided a deeper understanding of the complex tapestry of life.

David realized that his life wasn't just his own, but also a reflection of their shared experience. The colors of Abby's world seeped into his own, coloring his perceptions, altering his perspective. He started to see the beauty in the fleeting moments, the ephemeral nature of things. He began to appreciate the preciousness of time, the importance of cherishing each moment, each shared experience.

He started leaving tokens of his world in the painting—pressed flowers from his garden, small smooth stones from the riverbanks near his home, tiny drawings capturing the essence of his own bustling life. Abby, in return, created delicate miniature sculptures from the fading pigments, each one capturing the essence of her world, a testament to their shared journey.

Their differences became a source of creativity, inspiring them to explore new forms of artistic expression. Abby, inspired by David's descriptions of his world, created intricate patterns within the painting, weaving the colors of his cityscapes into the fading landscape, transforming their shared love into an ever-evolving masterpiece.

They celebrated their differences by embracing their unique perspectives, celebrating the vibrant tapestry of their lives, finding solace and strength in their shared journey. They understood that their love wasn't defined by sameness, but by the depth of their connection, the richness of their shared experiences, and the beauty of their distinct worlds intertwining. Their forever wasn't a static point in time but a dynamic dance of two souls, a continuous adaptation to the ever-shifting sands of reality, a love story that transcended time and space, a testament to the power of celebrating differences and embracing the beauty of impermanence. It was a forever painted not just on a canvas, but on the very fabric of their souls, a vibrant masterpiece woven from contrasting threads, a testament to a love that found strength not in sameness, but in the beautiful tapestry of their unique differences.

The fading light of the painting cast long shadows across their secluded grove, mirroring the lengthening shadows of their shared existence. David watched Abby, her face illuminated by the last vestiges of the setting sun within the canvas, as she meticulously arranged tiny, fallen petals into a delicate pattern. He marveled at her patience, her quiet intensity, a stark contrast to the frenetic energy that constantly pulsed through his own world. He'd learned to appreciate the stillness, the deliberate rhythm of her life, the way she found beauty in the slow decay of their shared world.

He reached out, his fingers brushing against hers, a silent acknowledgement of their shared journey. He traced the delicate lines of the petal pattern, feeling the fragile texture of the fading pigments. It was a quiet moment, filled with a bittersweet understanding of the impermanence of their love, a love that bloomed in the most unlikely of circumstances, defying the boundaries of time and reality.

"It's beautiful," David whispered, his voice barely audible above the soft rustling of leaves within the painting.

Abby smiled, a gentle, melancholic smile that held the weight of centuries within its depths. "It's like our love," she said, her voice soft and low. "Fragile, yet beautiful. Ephemeral, yet enduring."

He nodded, understanding the depth of her words. Their love was a paradox, a delicate balance between the fleeting and the eternal. It was a testament to their resilience and the ability to find love and connection in the most unexpected places, under the most challenging of circumstances. Their unconventional relationship challenged societal norms, defied the laws of physics, and yet, it pulsed with a strength and depth that exceeded anything he had ever known.

He thought about his friends, their bewildered reactions when he'd first confided in them about Abby. Their skepticism, their attempts to dismiss his experiences as mere imagination, had been replaced with a hesitant acceptance, a begrudging admiration for the depth of his feelings. He'd shown them sketches of Abby, paintings of the vibrant yet fading world within the canvas, and slowly, cautiously, he'd begun to share his poetry inspired by their unique love story. Their initial disbelief had slowly transformed into a quiet fascination, a grudging respect for the profoundness of their connection.

He'd found a different kind of acceptance in his family too. Initially bewildered, his parents had eventually come to terms with the reality of his experiences. They didn't understand it, but they recognized the sincerity of his love for Abby and his emotional well-being had become their primary concern. They'd even come to visit his work - the painting itself. They'd stared, fascinated by the strange, otherworldly scenes rendered on canvas, a testament to their unique love and David's creative energy.

The painting itself became a bridge between their worlds. David carefully brought items from his reality into the painting, small tokens of his life – a smooth, grey river stone, a pressed wildflower from his garden, a photograph of his family – all silent witnesses to their shared love, objects he left as offerings, as a tangible representation of his feelings. Abby, in turn, crafted tiny, intricate sculptures from the pigments within the painting, miniatures that reflected the beauty and fragility of their existence. These acts of exchange became their own unique ritual, a silent reaffirmation of their bond, transcending the physical limitations of their worlds.

He thought about the time Abby had described a Victorian-era festival within the painting, the sounds of laughter and music echoing across the canvas, the vibrant colors of clothing and decorations. He'd been able to mentally "experience" it with her, feeling the warmth of the crowd, hearing the lively melodies of a forgotten era, and sensing her joy within the painting. It was a shared sensory experience, defying the limitations of their disparate realities.

Their conversations were a continuous exchange of knowledge and perspectives, a dialogue across time and space. Abby taught him patience, the art of appreciating the beauty of stillness, the subtle nuances of decay. He, in turn, shared the excitement of his life, the rapid pace of technological advancement, the energy of human connection in the modern world. The differences between their worlds became not points of division, but sources of mutual enrichment.

One evening, under the soft glow of moonlight filtering through the canvas, Abby confessed her fears. She feared the complete fading of the painting, the eventual erasure of her existence. It wasn't a fear of nonexistence, but a fear of losing the memories, the emotions, the love they shared. She was afraid of being forgotten.

David held her close, his heart aching with empathy. He understood her fear, the fragility of their existence within the painting. He knew the scientific reality: the paint was degrading, the colors fading, the canvas itself becoming brittle. He understood this wasn't merely a romantic predicament; it was a battle against the inevitable. Their unconventional romance was threatened by the inescapable laws of chemistry and physics. But the battle wasn't against the fading colors, but against the fading of their memory.

He reassured her, his voice steady, his words filled with a profound love that transcended the boundaries of reality. He vowed to keep their story alive, to write about their love, to paint their world, to share their tale with the world, so that their connection would continue to resonate long after the painting faded into oblivion. He would translate their shared experience into words, into art, ensuring that their love would live on.

Their unconventional love story became his inspiration, the driving force behind his creativity. He wrote poetry and painted vibrant canvases, capturing the essence of their shared world, transforming their unique relationship into a legacy that reached beyond their individual existence. Their love transcended the physical limitations of their different worlds. It became a testament to the extraordinary capacity of human connection, a story that defied convention and celebrated the resilience of love. It was a love that proved that forever could be found, even within the most fleeting of moments, and in the most unexpected of places. It was a forever that defied not only the boundaries of time and space but also the very nature of reality itself. It was a forever woven into the fabric of their souls, a forever that continued to bloom even as the canvas itself began to fade, a forever that he would continue to paint, and repaint, again and again, for as long as he lived. Their love was a living testament, defying mortality, transcending limitations, and echoing across time. It was a love story for the ages, a masterpiece painted not just on canvas but etched onto the very heart of reality itself.

The autumn leaves within the painting swirled around their feet, a vibrant tapestry of reds and golds against the fading greens of the canvas. Abby gathered a handful, their delicate texture surprisingly real to the touch, even within this confined, painted world. She smiled, a wistful expression that tugged at David's heart. "Do you think they'll remember us?" she whispered, her voice barely audible above the rustling leaves.

David knelt beside her, gently taking a leaf from her hand. Its fragility mirrored the delicate nature of their love, a love born from the most improbable of circumstances. He traced the veins of the leaf with his fingertip, feeling its crisp texture. "Remember us? They'll never forget us," he said, his voice filled with conviction. "Our story is too extraordinary, too unique. It's a story that will be told and retold."

222

He knew the painting was fading. He'd witnessed the slow, inexorable degradation of the pigments, the subtle cracking of the canvas, the gradual blurring of the edges. He knew, scientifically, that this painted world, this love, was temporary. But he also knew the enduring power of memory and emotion. Their story wouldn't simply vanish with the fading colors; it would be imprinted onto the fabric of his being, a permanent fixture of his soul.

He thought about how he'd initially stumbled upon Abby, his accidental brush with the extraordinary, a seemingly impossible experience that had become his reality. The initial shock, the disbelief, had slowly given way to a profound, all-consuming love. He'd documented it all—meticulously sketching the landscapes, painstakingly painting Abby's portrait in numerous variations, capturing every nuance of her expression, the subtle changes in her eyes as the light shifted within the painted world. He filled countless notebooks with poems, each verse a testament to their unconventional love story.

"I've been writing," David continued, his voice soft, yet resolute. "I'm writing a book. It's our story, our love, everything we've shared within this painted reality. I'm going to share it with the world."

Abby's eyes widened, a flicker of hope illuminating her face. She'd always feared oblivion, not the cessation of existence, but the erasure of their shared memories. The thought of being forgotten, of their love being reduced to nothing more than a faint whisper in the winds of time, had been a constant source of anxiety. David's words, however, offered a different perspective. Their love, their story, would continue to live on, not as a ghostly echo, but as a vibrant, powerful narrative.

The idea of their story becoming a book resonated with her. The thought of their tale being read by countless others, of their unique love resonating across time and generations, brought her a sense of enduring peace. It wouldn't merely be a story of a boy and a girl trapped within a painting. It would be a universal love story; a unique tale of love's power, a testament to love's transcendence of the barriers of time, space, and physical reality. It would be a love story for the ages.

"A book?" she repeated, her voice tinged with wonder. "What will it be called?"

David smiled. "I haven't decided yet. Something... fitting." He thought for a moment, his eyes falling on the swirling autumn leaves. "Perhaps, '*A Different Kind of Forever*'."

The name seemed to perfectly encapsulate their extraordinary love story, its unique and unconventional nature, its defiance of all that was expected. Their love wasn't a fairytale romance set in a predictable, idyllic world. It was a story of courage, resilience, and love's enduring power, a remarkable capacity to find love and connection in the most unexpected of circumstances. It was the story of a love that transcended the boundaries of time and space, a love that defied the laws of physics and the limitations of reality.

They spent the rest of the afternoon talking, sharing their memories, their hopes, their dreams. David recounted stories from his life, describing the vibrant world outside the painting, the rush of urban life, the complexities of human relationships, the wonders of modern technology. Abby, in turn, shared her experiences within the painting, the subtle changes in the seasons, the stories whispered by the trees, the echoes of a bygone era.

He described the bustling city streets, the rush hour traffic, the cacophony of sounds and scents that filled the air, the fast-paced energy that permeated every aspect of modern life. He told her about his friends, their initial bewilderment, their gradual acceptance, their fascination with her story. He described the way his parents had come to accept, even if they didn't quite understand, his love for her. He described his efforts to bridge the gap between his world and hers.

Abby, in turn, painted a vivid picture of the Victorian era, its elegance and beauty, its subtle undercurrents of social constraint and societal expectation. She described the festivals, the sounds of music echoing through the ancient park, the vibrant colors of the clothing, the social dynamics, the mannerisms of the people depicted in the artwork.

Their shared stories created a tapestry of contrasting realities, a vivid testament to their unique connection. Their relationship transcended the physical barriers that separated them. They embraced their differences, their unique perspectives, celebrating the richness and depth that each of their worlds brought to their love.

As dusk settled within the painting, casting long shadows across the grove, David felt a profound sense of peace. He knew that their time together was limited, that the canvas was fading, that their reality was ultimately temporary. But he also knew that their love would endure, that their story would continue to live on, reaching out into the future. It was a love story that transcended mortality, a testament to the enduring power of the human heart, a love story for the ages, a love story that would live on, not just in his memory, but in the hearts and minds of everyone who would one day read his book, "*A Different Kind of Forever.*"

The fading light of the painting seemed to hold a kind of melancholy beauty, reflecting the bittersweet reality of their unique situation. Yet, their conversation continued, their shared words painting a richer, more meaningful image of their extraordinary love than the canvas itself ever could. Their relationship wasn't merely a temporary brush with magic. It was a profound journey of love, acceptance, and the enduring power of storytelling. Their love story wouldn't end when the painting faded; it would only begin to truly live, immortalized in ink and shared with a world desperately needing its magic. He would immortalize their love, preserving it for generations to come. Their love was a masterpiece, painted not just on canvas, but on the very fabric of his soul. It was a love that would continue to resonate long after the colors faded, long after the canvas cracked, long after the painting itself was nothing more than a memory. Their story would become a testament to the enduring nature of love itself, a story of two souls forever bound across time and space, a forever painted not on canvas, but on the heart. A forever that would last.

Chapter 15
Beyond the Canvas

The final brushstrokes of the setting sun within the painting cast long, ethereal shadows, mirroring the bittersweet reality of their parting. David knew this was it. He had made his choice, a choice born of love, sacrifice, and the stark recognition of the impermanence of their shared world. He'd spent weeks, months even, agonizing over the decision, the weight of it pressing down on him like the leaden sky of a coming storm. He'd balanced the intense joy of their connection with the harsh reality of its fleeting nature, of the canvas itself slowly disintegrating. He'd considered every possibility, every desperate attempt to somehow preserve their world, but in the end, he'd come to realize there was only one path.

The decision to leave Abby had been the most difficult of his life. It was a choice that tore at his soul, a choice that would leave an indelible scar on his heart. It was a choice that would haunt his dreams and shape the rest of his waking hours. He knew that leaving her meant sacrificing a love that transcended the boundaries of reality, a love as vibrant and complex as the swirling colors within the painting itself. He knew that leaving her meant facing a future without her, a future that felt unbearably empty.

Yet, he'd found solace in the understanding that leaving her was not an act of rejection or abandonment, but an act of love. It was a way to ensure her continued existence, a way to preserve the beauty and magic of their shared world, even if it meant that he had to be absent from it. By leaving, he was protecting her from the inevitable collapse of their painted reality, preserving her within the confines of the artwork, even as it faded.

He had spent his final days with her cherishing every moment, every stolen glance, every shared laugh. He'd committed their memories to his soul, etching them onto his heart with a depth that would never fade. He'd woven their story into the very fabric of his being, ensuring that their connection would never truly be lost.

Their last conversation echoed in his memory. They had talked about everything – their shared fears, their wildest hopes, their deepest dreams. Abby had confided her fears about being forgotten, the fear of becoming merely a ghost within the fading canvas. But David had reassured her, promising to immortalize their love in a way that would outlast even the most resilient of pigments.

He had shown her his manuscript, the pages filled with his meticulously crafted words, a testament to their extraordinary love. He read to her excerpts, his voice thick with emotion, his eyes welling with tears. She had listened intently, a fragile smile playing on her lips as he described their world, their love, their unique bond. The words resonated not only within the confines of the painted park but seemed to reach beyond the very limits of the canvas, touching the heart of something eternal.

The book became more than just a chronicle of their love story; it was a testament to the enduring power of the human spirit, a celebration of a love that defied the limitations of space and time. It was a love letter, a poignant goodbye, and a promise of remembrance. It was a story that would echo through time, reaching out to touch countless hearts and souls.

After their farewell, David stepped back into his own world, leaving Abby to her painted existence. The transition was as jarring as the first time he'd entered the painting, but this time, the shock was tempered by a deep-seated melancholy. He walked away from the painting, carrying the weight of his decision, the burden of his love, the memories of their shared reality.

The world outside seemed dull, muted, its vibrant colors diminished by the loss of Abby's presence. Yet, even in his grief, he found a strange sense of peace. He knew he had done what was right, what was necessary. He had saved her, at the cost of his own happiness. He had secured a future for her, even if it meant he could never be a part of it.

His life changed irrevocably after leaving Abby. The world felt different, its vibrancy muted, yet he found himself strangely driven to create. The intensity of his feelings for Abby fueled his artistic endeavors. He poured all his grief, his longing, his love, into his work. He painted, not only landscapes mirroring the painted park, but portraits of Abby, each one capturing a different facet of her personality, a different expression of their shared love. The paintings weren't mere representations; they were emotional outpourings, a way of keeping her memory alive, a way of holding onto their story.

He wrote, relentlessly, crafting the story of their unique love into a narrative that was both heartbreaking and uplifting. He poured every detail of their lives together into the book, capturing the essence of their shared reality, their unconventional love story, their struggle against fate. He even included snippets of the conversations they had, the poems she'd written in response to his own, and descriptions of the way the light shifted across the painted park.

A Different Kind of Forever became a regional hit and made it on a number of lesser know best seller lists. Those that read it were able to connect with the story, not only for its magical realism, but for its exploration of love's enduring power, its capacity to transcend the boundaries of time and space, its ability to find expression in the most unlikely of circumstances. Critics praised the novel's emotional depth and originality. It was praised for its evocative prose and its ability to capture the complexities of love and loss. The book's success was an affirmation of their love, a testament to the power of their story.

David's life took a new direction, guided by his extraordinary experience. He became an advocate for the arts, sharing his unique perspective and inspiring others to explore their creative potential. He lectured at local universities, speaking about his experiences, sharing his belief in the power of love, the importance of art and resilience. He received a number of awards, accolades that recognized not only his artistic talent, but also the strength of his narrative.

His personal relationships deepened. He learned to trust again, to love again, but his experiences with Abby shaped his approach to life and love. He appreciated the value of connection, the depth of human relationships, the significance of creating meaningful connections. He had a renewed sense of empathy and understanding, a greater awareness of the fragility of life and the importance of making the most of every precious moment.

The lingering effects of his journey into the painting remained, however. He still carried the scars, the memories, the bittersweet echoes of their shared reality. Sometimes, he would stare at his own paintings, at the vibrant portrayal of Abby, and feel a surge of overwhelming grief, a longing for a love that could never be. But he found solace in knowing that their story would live on, not merely in his memory, but in the hearts and minds of countless others who had been touched by *A Different Kind of Forever*.

David's legacy transcended the confines of his personal experience; it became a testament to the enduring power of love, the transformative nature of art, and the limitless potential to find connection even in the most extraordinary circumstances. His story became an inspiration, a source of hope, a reminder that even in the face of seemingly insurmountable obstacles, love endures, art transcends, and life, in all its complexity and beauty, continues on. His tale was a timeless masterpiece, painted not on canvas, but etched onto the collective heart of humanity. A legacy that would endure long after the last brushstroke faded, a testament to a love that bloomed within and beyond the canvas, a love that was, and always would be, different kind of forever.

David's lectures and public appearances weren't mere recitals of his extraordinary experience; they were invitations for others to explore their own imaginative potential. He encouraged his audiences to embrace the power of their imaginations, to recognize the transformative potential of art, and to find meaning in the seemingly impossible connections that exist between individuals and their creative pursuits. He shared his techniques, offering insights into his creative process, encouraging aspiring artists to develop their own unique artistic voice. He emphasized the importance of emotional authenticity in art, urging them to channel their own experiences, their own joys and sorrows, into their creative endeavors.

He emphasized that the most compelling works of art are those that resonate with the audience on an emotional level, those that touch upon universal themes of love, loss, hope, and resilience. He shared anecdotes from his time with Abby, not just to recount their story, but to illustrate the profound impact of authentic connection, the power of shared experiences, and the ability of art to transcend the limitations of time and space. He encouraged students to find their own muses, to look for inspiration in the everyday, the extraordinary, and the unexpected, urging them to capture the essence of human experience through their artistic pursuits.

The lingering presence of Abby in David's life wasn't just a lingering grief; it was a source of inspiration, a reminder of the intense beauty and profound depth of their unconventional love. He learned to cherish the memories, to honor their connection without dwelling on the impossibility of their reunion. He continued to paint, to compose music, to write, each artistic endeavor a continuation of their shared creative spirit. He would often look at his paintings and his manuscripts, not with sorrow, but with a sense of gratitude for the experience, for the profound impact it had on his life.

He eventually found love again, but this time, his experience with Abby informed his relationship. He appreciated the importance of communication, the value of shared experiences, the significance of mutual respect and understanding. His love was not diminished by his past but rather enriched by it. He carried the lessons learned from his time with Abby into his new relationship, ensuring that his future love would be deeply rooted in empathy, understanding, and a profound appreciation for the ephemeral nature of life.

Years later, David stood before a large canvas, his brushes poised, ready to begin a new painting. The colors he chose were vibrant, hopeful, reflecting the peace and contentment he had finally found. But as he began to work, he couldn't help but think of Abby, a faint smile playing on his lips. Her presence was not a haunting shadow, but a gentle reminder, a soft whisper of the extraordinary love they had shared. Her memory was woven into the very fabric of his being, a testament to a love story that defied the boundaries of reality, a love that transcended time and space, a love that ultimately taught him the most profound lessons about the human heart and its capacity for love, loss, and enduring remembrance. His life, once defined by loss, was now a testament to the healing power of art. The journey had been difficult, but the lessons learned, etched in his heart and reflected in his art, were invaluable treasures. His story was not just his own; it was a universal narrative of love, loss, and the enduring power of human connection.

The canvases, once blank slates reflecting his own uncertainties, now held a vibrant tapestry of his emotional journey. Each brushstroke, once hesitant and unsure, now flowed with a newfound confidence, imbued with the depth of his experience. He painted not just images, but emotions – the sharp pangs of separation, the quiet ache of longing, the slow, deliberate healing of time. His paintings became a visual diary, a testament to his transformation, a chronicle of his grief and eventual acceptance. He depicted Abby not as a flawless ideal, but as a complex, multi-faceted woman, her spirit captured not only in her physical beauty but also in the subtle nuances of her expression, the unspoken emotions flickering in her eyes. These paintings weren't just about Abby; they were about David, about his journey from overwhelming grief to quiet contemplation, from frantic despair to a hard-won peace. He painted himself into the landscapes, a solitary figure amidst the vibrant colors of Abby's world, sometimes standing alone, sometimes looking toward the horizon, a silent expression of hope clinging to his face.

The process of creating art became his sanctuary, a place where he could process his emotions, translate his grief into something tangible, something beautiful. The act of creation was more than just a form of self-expression; it was a form of healing, a means of making sense of his experience, of finding meaning in the midst of profound loss. He found solace in the intricate details of his work, in the precise blending of colors, the carefully chosen words, the perfectly timed notes. His art wasn't an escape from reality; it was a way of engaging with reality on a deeper level, of confronting his emotions directly, of transforming pain into something profound and meaningful.

One day, while sorting through old sketches, he stumbled upon a drawing he'd made of Abby during their first encounter. The image, rudimentary yet vibrant, brought a rush of bittersweet memories. He saw not just the girl trapped in the painting, but a reflection of himself—young, hopeful, and utterly unaware of the journey that lay ahead. He saw the depth of his love for Abby not just as a romantic ideal, but as a profound testament to the power of human connection. He realized that the depth of his love wasn't diminished by their separation; it had been transformed, deepened by his willingness to let go, by his acceptance of the constraints of reality. His love for Abby became a source of strength, not sorrow.

He began to view his experience with Abby not as a tragic loss, but as a profound and transformative chapter in his life. It was a love story unlike any other, a testament to a connection that transcended the boundaries of space and time. He had learned to appreciate the transient nature of life, the beauty of fleeting moments, the importance of cherishing experiences while they last. His time with Abby had taught him about the importance of selflessness, the capacity for profound sacrifice, and the lasting power of memory.

He personally funded a foundation dedicated to supporting artists and writers facing personal challenges, providing them with the resources and support they needed to overcome adversity and find their voice. This was an extension of his own journey, his attempt to pay it forward, to help others navigate the intricate paths of loss and healing. It was a beautiful irony that his devastating loss had led him to create something so profoundly positive and life-affirming.

His lectures and workshops included his insights on creativity, loss, and the healing power of art. His words were as inspiring as his artwork, resonating with others captivated by his ability to speak openly and honestly about his experiences. He taught others not only about the technical aspects of artistic expression, but also about the crucial emotional and spiritual dimensions of the creative process. His workshops became havens for those seeking solace and inspiration, places where vulnerability was embraced, and creativity was celebrated as a powerful tool for healing.

His story, initially one of profound loss, became a testament to the transformative power of love, grief, and art. The tale of David and Abby became more than just a story of forbidden love and impossible realities; it became a timeless allegory of the human experience, a saga of resilience, and hope. David's art was not merely a reflection of his own grief; it became a catalyst for healing, a beacon of hope for others, a testament to the power of love to transcend boundaries, even those of time and reality itself. The enduring legacy of his love for Abby was not in her physical presence, but in the indelible mark she left on his soul, a mark he continued to paint, compose, and write into existence for the rest of his days, sharing his story, and healing the world one brushstroke, one note, and one word at a time.

His life became a living embodiment of the enduring power of love, a powerful testament to the ability of the human heart to find meaning, purpose and beauty even amidst the deepest sorrow. His art was a testament to the enduring legacy of their love, a love story painted not just on canvas but woven into the very fabric of his existence. The faded painting in his studio became a cherished relic, a silent witness to a love that defied the boundaries of reality and continued to inspire him, and indeed, the world, long after their time together had ended.

His life was a testament to the power of remembering, of cherishing, and of transforming grief into beauty. The love he shared with Abby would endure, immortalized not just in the strokes of paint, the notes of his music, and the words he wrote, but in the lives he touched and the legacy he left behind – a legacy built on the foundation of a love that transcended time and space, a love that, in its own way, lived on.

Epilogue
A Different Kind of Forever

It had been two-years since David had gazed at the painting. The lights dimmed to a hush of amber and shadow. David stood before the painting that had stolen and returned his heart, each brushstroke holding echoes of her laughter, the warmth of her hand, the way sunlight once poured like honey through the leaves.

Abby sat there still—frozen in oils and time—beneath her parasol, the eternal afternoon captured in strokes of gold and green. But tonight, there was something new. Resting gently in her lap was a book. His book.

A Different Kind of Forever.

David's breath caught in his throat. The title shimmered faintly, as if aware of him. She had found it—somehow, through the fragile boundary of paint and longing. Her fingers brushed the cover as she looked up, eyes meeting his across the veil of reality. That smile—his smile—returned. The one he had memorized, the one that had kept him alive when hope had nearly faded.

He wanted nothing more than to step through the frame again. To hold her. To hear her voice one last time. But the warning echoed in his mind like the closing of a door: *If you cross again, the painting will fade. Forever.*

His hand trembled as he reached toward the glass. Already, the colors seemed to waver, as if the painting itself could sense his yearning. He drew his hand back. No—he couldn't lose her again, not even for a moment's embrace.

Instead, he stood still, memorizing her as she turned one final page. The breeze within the painting stirred the leaves around her, a tender sigh of farewell. And though she could not speak, her eyes said everything.

You found me. That's enough.

David smiled through the tears. "I'll keep you alive," he whispered. "In every word, in every story. That's our forever now."

The lamplight flickered, catching the faint shimmer of the paint—her parasol, her dress, her book—and for a heartbeat, it seemed the world inside the frame shimmered back at him. Then all was still again.

He turned to leave, the echo of her smile following him out of the gallery. Behind him, the painting remained, glowing faintly in the half-dark. And though he would never step through it again, he knew the truth she had left him with—

Love doesn't end when the picture fades. It simply changes its frame.